Dave Hill is a freelance journalist who has written for many national newspapers, in particular the *Guardian*, and also contributes to the *Evening Standard*. He has written non-fiction works on football, pop music, politics and gender issues. He lives in east London with his wife and his six children.

First published in 2003
by REVIEW

An imprint of Headline Book Publishing

10 9 8 7 6 5 4 3 2

ISBN 0 7553 0189 7

Typeset in Baskerville by Avon DataSet Ltd,
Bidford-on-Avon, Warwickshire

Printed and bound in Great Britain by
Clays Ltd, St Ives plc

HEADLINE BOOK PUBLISHING
A division of Hodder Headline
338 Euston Road
London NW1 3BH

www.reviewbooks.co.uk
www.hodderheadline.com

dad's life

DAVE HILL

review

For the *bean an ti*

(And for Smokey, RIP)

ACKNOWLEDGEMENTS

The narrator of this novel and its other central characters were originally created for a series of columns I wrote for the Parents' Page of the *Guardian*. These appeared roughly fortnightly for one year from October 1999 under the heading *Home and Away*, and were commissioned by Becky Gardiner who edited the Parents section at that time. My friend and agent Sara Fisher believed that my rudimentary attempts at developing the columns into a novel were worth showing to a publisher, and my editor Martin Fletcher took the project on and guided it to completion with great insight and skill. All others at Headline who've dealt with *Dad's Life* since have done so with gratifying commitment, among them Amy Philip who has been both efficient and kind. Sincere thanks to all above and to Louise down the road, who found time to read the penultimate draft.

DEFINITION

Pillock – a stupid person; a fool [16th c = penis]

Concise Oxford Dictionary

part i: living it

chapter 1

She used to think I was perfect. These days, she's not so sure.

'You swear a lot,' she says.

'No, I bloody don't.'

'And you watch football all the time.'

'But what if I stopped watching? Somebody might score!'

'And you think you're so funny.'

I've got no answer to that. Off she stalks.

Do I think I'm so funny? Can't say I'm feeling like a big barrel of laughs, though I suppose I have my comical side, that's true. As for watching too much football, well, that was a cheap shot: yes, she's caught me getting square-eyed with the sporty guys on Sky, but it's more of a distraction than a passion. These days my emotions go elsewhere.

Anyway, the 'she' who spins so sharply on her heel and leaves the room is my daughter Gloria, aged eleven and three-quarters – or 22 in spitfire years:

already a punchy attitude; already a bosom with big ideas. You've no idea how much I love her and I'm not sure she has either, although it's absolutely plain she doesn't love me like she did when she was the friend I most leaned on after my uneven kind of life took an exacting and – forgive the melodrama – almost ruinous turn.

Gloria: a limited edition, special order sort of girl. I shouldn't let it rile me when today's nail varnish-spilling, bath towel-appropriating, brashly menstruating version gives me a hard time just because she's found me loafing on this November afternoon. You see, I so often delighted in her precocious self-possession, her free-and-forthright style when she was eight or nine and I was the object of her constant adoration rather than her intermittent ire. It came in useful during the months after her mother Dilys, my partner of eleven years, took the stereo, the kitchen table and the ancestral Babygros and moved in with a twentysomething lone male named Chris, a new model sort of fellow whose many distinctive features I'll elaborate on later.

Gloria has two younger brothers, Jed and Billy. Jed had not long been five when their mother took her leave and Billy had just turned three. Cajoling them through breakfast-time and tea-time, bath-time and bed-time would have been even more exhausting if Gloria hadn't already become a self-dressing, table-clearing tweenage sophisticate able to sustain long conversations about *Pet Rescue* and Pop Tarts and how funny it was that Barbie was no longer a skinny bimbo but had become an independent woman of the world.

She would earnestly insist that Jed and Billy were far too young and silly to be allowed to stay up late and snuggle on the sofa with grown-up TV shows like *Changing Rooms* or *Ready Steady Cook*. She'd stridently take issue with Laurence's soft furnishings or Ainsley's melba sauce until, reluctantly, her eyelids would descend and I'd blankly channel hop as she breathed and dribbled softly on my ribs before I too drifted off. I would wake later in fugged dismay to the closing credits of a *Seinfeld* repeat, or *Naked Norwegian Ten Pin Bowling*, or some Jeremy or other holding up the following day's front pages, before shuffling off to the kitchen to deal with the dishes still piled in the sink.

Then I'd carry her up to her room, plant a kiss upon her brow, tuck her pet lion Brian (viscose, stuffed) under her arm then plod on up the stairs to collapse on my own bed. Every night within minutes of 3 a.m., I'd hear Jed and Billy's footfalls heading in my direction from their room. They would appear at my elbow, hugging up the slack of their oversized pyjamas, tousle-haired and peering, full of groggy hope.

'Come on in then, one each side.'

I'd cup my balls inside my hand to save them from the painful prods of tiny knees and heels. 'Crushed nuts are all right on ice cream,' I would mumble, disentangling their bony legs from mine. Who knows what

5

they were thinking? What is Daddy on about? Has he lost his mind?

Maybe he has. Maybe he is looking for it still.

My name is Joseph Stone. I am thirty-six years old and beginning to notice how time flies. I live in a two-storey flat in an uncelebrated part of not-quite-suburban south London where I have earned part of my living in the space beneath my feet that I refer to as 'my studio'. The self-mockery pains me, but forms a handy defence for an artist – darlings, that's me – who hasn't always sold as many of his paintings as he'd like. In theory the studio doubles as a tiny gallery in which the privileged consumers of South Norwood High Street are free to browse. In practice on the very few occasions when it's open they view my work in silence and politely sneak away.

This dynamic creative unit is called A Poor Man's Wealth, a name bestowed by my parents at the back end of the Sixties when they lived over the shop and I was a scabby little boy. Down there, they ran a non-stop restoration operation, salvaging old furniture of substance and distinction. My labours there have been more intermittent. That's because so often I've put my talents with a brush to work at other people's homes.

I'm versatile. Sometimes I've painted their outsides, catwalking on scaffolding or squatting in their front doorways, making sure delinquent gloss doesn't slop on to their brass letter-box. More often I've painted their insides, rollering on the white-with-a-hint-of-something-boring, and picking out the detail in their mouldings. And every so often I've painted domestic interiors of a different kind, the lives that go on inside a home; the lives, in the main, of those vain or foolish enough to pay me to invade their little castles, arrange them among their belongings and capture them in living colours on canvas. They think I'm South Norwood's answer to Hopper and Hockney – which, by the way, I am.

This is the work I enjoy most, though it has yet to make me filthy rich and famous. I haven't stopped dreaming, though. One day, before I'm doolally or dead, there'll be an exhibition at the Guggenheim, the Louvre or Tate Britain titled *The Unacknowledged Genius of Joe Stone*. The star exhibit will be a painting that presently hangs on my own living-room wall. I am looking at it now as I recline on the reupholstered 1950s settee that Mum and Dad saved from oblivion and gave to Dilys and me along with two matching armchairs when we became co-habitees.

The painting shows a man in his thirties sitting on a reupholstered 1950s settee flanked by two matching armchairs. It also shows three small children, two boys and an older girl. The smallest boy is squatting on the carpet, surrounded by toys. His wavy, wiry hair is so shockingly blond that if you saw it on a woman you might suspect it came out of a bottle. The man's left arm is wrapped around a dark-haired, pretty girl, whose back is propped against him, her knees pulled up to her chin. The older boy seems distracted. He sits on the armchair in the corner of the room, turned away from the man whose right hand may or may not be stretching out towards him. The second armchair is occupied by three soft toys: a lion, a seal and a giraffe. Their mood is hard to gauge precisely, as are those of the three children, though most would say the man looks rather serious and tired. He is, needless to say, a great deal more handsome than me.

Are you getting the picture? Let me sketch in some detail.

Jed is eight years old now, and a boy who loves to run, just as I loved to run when I was that age and at the start of the best years of my life. When I was eight years old I could run faster than all the other kids. And I could judge when it was safe enough to run across a road in front of an advancing car; at least, I thought I could.

A few mornings ago I stood watching Jed thinking the same thing. I watched as if in slow motion as he hared across the street that passes in front of his school, my hands flying to my face when the car driver hit the brakes. He stopped with a yard to spare and raised a hand in my direction. I returned it, gratefully: *thank you*. Jed skipped up the farther kerb, turned and stole a glance. I yelled, 'Are you all right? Are you OK?' He nodded, unconcerned, and disappeared through the gate.

Twenty minutes later I was back home alone, muttering to myself, imagining Dilys taking my call.

'Dilys? It's about Jed. He's dead.'

Could it be said any better? Yes, but what would be the point? Jed's life would be over. A small coffin would be required. An awkward gathering would take place at the graveside. My life would be ruined. It would go on anyway.

I think about these things; terrible things. I think about them happening to Gloria, too – and, of course, to Billy, although it's harder to imagine him as anything other than the most alive six year old in the world.

'Daddy?'

'Yes, Billy?'

'Daddy?'

'Yes, Billy?'

'You know what?'

'What?'

'You know S Club 7?'

'Oh yeah. They came to tea the other day.'

'Well,' Billy said, 'do you know what?'

'What?' We were walking to the sweet shop. He pulled me to a halt.

'They got done for *smokin' weed*!' His eyes were reservoirs of wonder.

'Say that again, please, slowly.'

'They got done for *smokin' weed*!'

I adjusted to the scale of his delight. I said, 'Billy?'

'Yeah?'

'Do you know what weed is?'

'No,' he shrugged. 'No idea.'

9

'Have you gone mad, or is it me?'
'It's you, Daddy! It's you!'

What am I like? Search me.

I later came to see the way Dilys departed as deeply revealing. At the time, though, it didn't seem profound at all. The truth is, I didn't mind her leaving. Actually, I danced. I danced in the space where the kitchen table used to be, even though I had no stereo to turn up loud, loud, loud.

Oh yes, I danced. I also sang. I sang to Gloria at bathtime and I sang to Jed and Billy as they lay drowsy in their beds.

> *Go to sleep my babies,*
> *Close your pretty eyes . . .*

> *Golden slumbers kiss your eyes,*
> *Smiles await you when you rise . . .*

A lot of 'eyes' in those lullabies. I looked to see what might be written in the eyes of Jed and Billy. I read trust. What could I do but take advantage? Tenderly, I lied, 'If we do lots of bedtime singing, Mummy will come back sooner from her voyage.'

Her voyage of discovery to Chris's cave of mystic wonders – but I'm racing ahead of myself here.

Gloria said, 'I like your singing, Daddy.'

The boys said, 'Daddy, sing the lullabies again.'

On and on I sang. On and on I danced.

Until I got round to replacing the kitchen table – a weird thing to take, I know – I'd sometimes sit in the bare space where it used to be and inspect myself for signs of misery. It was a thankless task. I thought of Dilys settling in at Chris's place, maybe sanding down his floorboards and bringing her woman's touch to his bijou bachelor pile: an arty *objet* on every ledge, a *pot pourri* in every orifice, all the fluff and flotsam I could never stand. I speculated without rancour on the erotic renaissance of which I guessed she was in the throes. I imagined choice new flimsies falling away in a haze of hot patchouli vapours. I envisaged her new beau's busy buttocks pumping. I heard Eric Clapton droning 'Wonderful Tonight'. I offered thanks to Venus, Aphrodite and the Reverend Al Green for my sweet release.

What kind of bastard did that make me? What kind of cow did it make her? Depends on your perspective, I suppose. There are those – yes, I can name them all – who've always thought of me as being honest, loyal and true. Please bear that in mind during those parts of this story when my feelings towards Dilys are not altogether kind. And believe me when I say I'm not like those angry guys who get on phone-in shows to yell that divorce is much too easy, women are taking all the jobs and the feminists have shrivelled up the penis. For one thing I wasn't married, for another I have a job, and for a third my penis was no more shrivelled up than usual when I caught sight of it this morning. For a fourth I am not here to make a political point. There's been nothing political about the fear and fury I have sometimes felt: it's all been purely personal.

And as for Dilys? Well . . . if I'd known back then what I've found out about her now, this might have been a very different story. If I'd been Dilys *I* would have left me. Oh, I was never a boozer, a beater, a skirt-chaser or a slob. And right from the beginning – well, almost – I was an eager little breeder, then a nappy-changer, school-runner and bed-time reader, a fellow who could strip a puke-encrusted infant in the middle of the night without losing his temper or even opening both eyes. The only trouble was that the ardour and forbearance I brought to being a father I somehow stopped extending to my children's mother – just as she had stopped extending the same qualities to me. And who was to blame for that unhappy situation? You'll have to work that one out for yourself.

chapter 2

Let me ask you this: how does a man react to being dumped on a Monday lunch-time with no kitchen table and three small children to pick up at half past three? Naturally, he goes and gets his hair done; in my case by Clip-Joint Len, the nosiest barber in South Norwood – if not the world.

Len nodded as I walked in. It was the nod of a man who'd seen Brylcreem go in and out of fashion too often in his time to be surprised by anything. As I climbed into his chair he asked me, 'How's the family . . . ?'

Everything Len said had an ellipsis of innuendo trailing in its wake.

'How do you think it is, Len?'

'Well, those boys of yours are smashin' . . .'

'True, Len, very true. Some of your youngest customers.'

'And that little girl isn't so little any more . . .'

'Too big to have her hair done in a *boys'* place nowadays.'

'And your Dilys . . . ?' *dot . . . dot . . . dot . . .*

'What have you been hearing, Len?' I watched him in the mirror.

'Pickford's situation . . .' *dot . . . dot . . . dot . . .*

I said, 'Your spies are everywhere.'

'Permanent Pickford's, by the looks . . .'

'By the looks of it, Len, yeah.'

Len pumped the chair up a few notches as if reflating the male ego. 'I'm sorry to hear that, Joseph,' he said. With Len, barbering was of secondary importance to the gathering of gossip. He unfurled a nylon gown across my chest, tucking it under my collar with the purposeful contentment of a man who had already done the real work of the day. Then he squinted critically at my ragged mop. 'Been a while since your last visit . . .'

Looking glumly into the mirror I addressed Len's reflection. 'Better do something drastic, I suppose.'

'Plenty on the floor then . . . ?'

'Plenty on the floor.'

I left Len's Clip Joint tonsorially shorn and emotionally naked. Perhaps I should have been more careful, but it all happened so fast – just like Dilys's departure. There we'd been in our Home Sweet Home the previous Friday evening: me and Dilys Day making a fair job of pretending to love each other, when suddenly she was announcing that a removal van would pull up at the kerb on Monday morning – a 'Pickford's situation', like Len said.

At first I did what I supposed was the right thing to do. I urged her to think about the effect on the children; I reminded her of the new life up the road in Crystal Palace we'd fantasised about during moments of self-delusion when Billy was newborn. But when these overtures floundered I switched to a strategy that came more easily – I asked her if she needed help packing.

I didn't just roll over, though. Oh no. I might have helped her fill her tea chests, but I still got in some pretty searching questions.

'Er. Where are you moving *to* exactly?' See? I can be tough.

'The edge of Dulwich Village,' she replied.

'Dulwich Village, eh?' Geographically, the Village is one notch north of Crystal Palace. Socially, it tops it by a mile. And it looks down on South Norwood like a baronet on a bin man. 'Got a few bob then, has he?'

'That's not why I'm leaving.'

'Sorry. Low blow. So, uh, how did you meet him then, this, uh, Chris?'

'He just . . . came into my life.'

The Dilys I knew – or thought I knew up to that point – was not the type to flutter a lace hankie. I couldn't help but grin. 'Phew. Tell me all about his mighty charger.'

Dilys emerged from her fluster and gave me a level look. Then she gave me a cute answer. 'Let's just say it's been quite a ride.'

Ouch. Still, I suppose I had that coming. Served me right for playing the wise guy when I was already typecast as the fool. For the most part, though, my conduct was completely calm and neutral: calm as in comatose, neutral as in numb. An 'off' switch tripped somewhere in the hurt feelings department, and I observed myself observing the two of us observing the conventions of an agonising break-up, as if mutually accepting a *fait accompli*. Dilys had her arrangements in place: Pickford's, the day off work, the handover of her keys.

She said that she was sorry.

'No, you're not,' I replied.

'In a way, I am,' she trimmed.

'In what way?'

'I'm sorry for you.'

'Good. It'll save me the trouble of feeling sorry for myself.'

OK, I was a little terse, but there were no histrionics. We told Gloria, Jed and Billy on the Saturday morning: Mummy had decided that she should live somewhere else. Daddy had agreed that she should too. Mummy wouldn't be around after they all came home on Monday but she would be back to see them 'very soon'. Mummy loved them dearly and, oh yes ... Daddy loved them too. Then we all piled into our clapped-out Vauxhall Astra and went for a walk in Crystal Palace Park.

It was the third week in September, and through the first-fallen leaves the children skipped and ran towards their favourite landmark, the famous stone dinosaur sculptures in the ornamental lake – the 'monsters' as the signposts call them. They were still so young. How much of what we'd told them had sunk in? Billy carried on as usual, speaking in bizarre mystic tongues to Neil, his toy seal. Jed, hands deep in pockets, pointed out the imperfections of each stone approximation of a squawking pterodactyl or snarling stegosaurus. He had a soft toy too – Geoff, a daft giraffe.

Gloria alone showed a grasp of her altering situation. She was quiet at the park, and quiet the next day too as I cooked Sunday lunch. In the evening, clutching Brian Lion, she cornered me and enquired, 'Why is Mummy filling up those boxes?'

'We told you. Because she's going.'

'But *where* is she going?'

I improvised. 'She's going on a journey.'

'What sort of journey?'

'Not a very long one. A short voyage on the HMS *Unfaithful*.'

Gloria looked blank for a moment, then pressed on. Eight is a dauntless age. 'Why?'

'She thinks it will be more fun than being here.'

'Why aren't we going as well?'

'Because I'd only get sea-sick and you've got to go to school.'

'But that's not fair.'

I lifted her up, kissed her on both cheeks and said sincerely, 'It might be the fairest thing for everybody in the end.'

* * *

What went wrong, exactly?

I didn't drink too much, sulk too much or break wind too much in bed. I didn't own a Playstation. I didn't get a hard-on at the sight of a Ferrari. I knew where everything was: the clitoris, the toolbox, the Toilet Duck. And I could conjugate the sacred verb 'to care':

I care.
You care.
He cares.
She cares.
We care.
Who cares?
See if I care.
What the hell do you care anyway?

There. Piece of cake.

I speculated idly about Chris. Dilys told me his surname – Pinnock – (nothing funny about that at all). Otherwise, she was cagey.

'Does he really love you, Dilys?'

'Don't push me on this, Joe.'

I recalled the powerful appeal that Dilys once held for me. She was five feet two and fiery. She had straight-up dark brown eyes and straight down dark brown hair (Gloria's eyes, Gloria's hair), a mouth that said, 'I'm friendly,' and a chest that said, 'I'm hot.' We were both twenty-two years old. She was keen and I was flattered. She was brazen. I was too.

I feel foolish about it now, but must admit that in a crass and callow corner of my subconscious I pigeon-holed Dilys as an urban version of those mythical country wenches whose bosoms nestle in their bodices like ripe fruit on fertile ground and are willing for a shilling any time. It wasn't just her body that encouraged this perception, but her personality too – direct, unembarrassed, uncontrived. I'd never met a woman quite so warm.

Dilys had no time for refinement. She ate like a horse and lapped up large romantic gestures, the cornier the better – big boxes of chocolates, bunches of blowsy flowers. Though neither of us was wealthy she worked hard to have us both squander our disposable income, invading the West End or Kensington on Saturday afternoons and stumbling home at tea-time, laden with books and music and piles of preposterous garments that we sometimes even wore. 'You've got to go for it, you know,' Dilys would routinely assure me and when, now and then, my jaundiced side came to the fore I'd find myself upbraided without mercy. 'You arty types are all the same,' she'd scold, pinching a big chunk of my cheek. 'Cheer up, Picasso! You've got a gorgeous girl like me.'

It became a joke between us that old-fashioned language seemed to describe Dilys best: busty, brassy, bold . . . And me? Every stringy inch of me was horny. Our couplings were lurid and out loud.

'Give me a pearl necklace!'

'Tie me to the table!'

'Ram me from behind!'

And Dilys was no different.

'*Fuck* me!' she would smoulder. '*Fuck* me, I'm so bad!'

We had a lot of good clean fun between the sheets. Yet I came to reflect upon those days with deep disquiet: not with shame, nor with disgust, nor with nostalgia dipped in lust, but with a dark suspicion that the human part of me gradually ceased to be required.

'*Hello. My name is Joseph. I'm your server for today.*'

'*Fuck me, I'm so bad!*'

So bad at what, I started wondering. Car maintenance? Macramé? Documentary film-making? *Dilys, Dilys, darling*, I would inwardly intone. *To fail at floristry is not a crime!*

I could construct a grand cultural theory. We were, perhaps, deluded by the times. We were entering the era in which Marky Mark's almighty member bulged from bus stop adverts and Madonna exposed her private places to the public – in the photographic sense, that is. Fashionable young things lay awake at night worrying about not being gay. But even debauchery gets dull after a while. And I eventually decided that the reason Dilys left me was quite plain: I got on her nerves. That may sound a little feeble, but don't hold it against her. After all, she got on my nerves too.

All the same it seemed strange that our relationship failed for such a mediocre reason. Have I mentioned my ex-partner's profession?

She's a relationship counsellor.

Yes, the happiness of couples is her business. Honestly, it is. I would never joke about a thing like that. In fact, it may be to Dilys's credit that we stayed together for so long. Eleven years is quite a hefty stretch these days, especially when you've both worked out you should have called the whole thing off after three or four. But that's what children did for us. Too cynical, you think? Sometimes that's how realism sounds.

Nothing was planned. Certainly not by me. There's always been a blur of mutual convenience around Gloria's conception, a tacit understanding between Dilys and me that I wouldn't ask how it happened, and she wouldn't tell. Yes, yes, I've grasped that intercourse was centrally involved, and can even describe the pillowcase pattern on the night concerned – hideous green rococo swirls; I'd begun noticing such things while in the grip of sexual ecstasy by then. Between us, though, it will remain forever unasked and unsaid why Dilys forgot to swallow her pill. We'd only discussed having babies in a desultory way, side-stepping a subject we didn't wish to speak of frankly because to do so would have forced us to confront the bigger issue we both wanted to avoid – what we were doing with each other anyway. And once she was in the pipeline, Gloria gave us a fine excuse to

carry on avoiding it. We had a child to care for now.
Maybe things would improve.

They did, too, in many ways. Gloria gave us back
the passion for another person that neither of us could
any longer muster for each other; which is why we
proceeded to make Jed and then make Billy too.
The children gave us something new in common: a
deep love and commitment to their wellbeing. We did
domestic things together. We picked out cutlery and
curtains and squabbled about the details of the décor.
After we'd stopped squabbling, we marvelled at the
blossoming of our brood. And then into my world came
Christopher Pinnock, man of mystery. Nothing would
ever be the same again.

On that balmy, bloodless Monday I helped the men
from Pickford's carry out that kitchen table, that stereo
and those ancestral Babygros. I even spent the morning
loitering uncomplainingly as Dilys pottered round
the house, selecting certain artefacts from our to-be-
unshared possessions, ones that I've since realised she'd
calculated could be cleansed of all contamination, any
emotional links they might have had with me. She was
away by noon. Billy was with his childminder Esther,
and Gloria and Jed were at school. 'I'll call about
the children nearer the weekend,' Dilys said over her
shoulder, squeezing into a waiting mini-cab.

Fine then! Cheerio! Have one heck of a good day!

I closed the door.

Then I nipped down the garden and dug up the photo albums I'd buried in a bin bag late the previous evening when Dilys had had a sudden urge to do some late-night shopping (bizarre, but what did I care?). After that I took a shower. Before the full-length mirror I looked at myself: naked male, thirty-three, in reasonable condition for his age, blue eyes, fair hair sticking upwards as if in untidy surprise.

It was at that point that I shuffled off to Len's. Half an hour later I was waiting in the playground with a young mother called Lisa and another called Camille. 'What happened to your hair, Joe?' Lisa blurted out.

'Let's have a quick feel,' said Camille.

Some house-hubbies bleat that mothers blank them round the school gates. Never happened to me. It's all about communication, really. Sample dialogue:

'Hello, I'm Nibs's dad. He's in the same class as your Nellie. He talks about her all the time. And how are you today?'

'I'm very well, thanks. How are you?'

'What, apart from the hole in my tights and the awful price of peas?'

Hey presto, you're away.

I lowered my head and Camille massaged her palm on my new prickles.

'What's that in aid of then?' asked Lisa, looking on.

'I'm on the hunt for sex,' I said.

Camille jerked her hand away. 'You dirty devil!' she exclaimed, her eyes widening with her smile.

'I thought if I looked lean and mean it might improve my chances,' I explained. 'You know what us men are like: absolutely gagging for it fifty times a day.'

'I wish,' said Lisa wanly.

'I wish,' echoed Camille.

'Keep wishing,' I said, getting a bit reckless, 'and you just might have your way.'

'Woooh!' said Lisa.

'Woooh!' said Camille.

The 3.30 bell sounded. Gloria and Jed emerged into a world in which their father had gone bald and their mother had left home. Billy would join them shortly. I'm hell with the ladies, me.

chapter 3

True to her parting words, Dilys called me later in the week. But seeing Gloria, Jed and Billy wasn't all she had in mind. She'd rung, she explained, with her 'settlement suggestions'. I caved in to these completely and for that I accept full responsibility. I opted out of all the more bloody battles that I might have fought with Dilys at the time. I wasn't in combat mode. I went blank; I disengaged.

Dilys ran through her tick list. Firstly, there was the house. She said that I could have it – although she hoped I wouldn't mind paying the mortgage on my own. 'That sounds fair, doesn't it?' she informed me warmly. And I suppose it was fair. She'd put a lot of money into it, but didn't seem to want any back. I thought, this Chris guy must be loaded.

Secondly, the old Vauxhall Astra. I could keep that too. 'After all, it isn't worth much,' she explained, a bit too chirpily, 'and I don't need it anyway.'

This was true. As I would soon learn, the dashing Christopher Pinnock had a fully reconditioned chicken shit-powered, soft-top Morris Minor in which he pursued wildebeest across the open prairie before hurling himself, snarling, upon the fleeing creatures and ritually disembowelling them with his bare hands . . .

OK, OK, it was a slick new Volvo. Five seater, energy-efficient, all mod cons, green.

Where was I? Oh yes . . .

Thirdly, the children.

Oh, *them*.

'I'd like to take them out on Sunday,' Dilys continued, 'but I've decided not to bring them to my new home until it's in proper order. Just so you know.'

Oh.

'Are you listening to me, Joe? I'll collect them at eleven o'clock and bring them back at eight.'

Right. Goodbye.

So on the Sunday morning at five minutes to eleven I led Gloria, Jed and Billy down the long stairs to the street, and pointed them towards the idling Volvo which was waiting a sanitary distance down the kerb. It was too far away for me to make out the figure sitting behind the wheel. Standing on the pavement Dilys waved the children towards her and I watched their backs recede, Gloria holding Billy's hand, Jed trudging behind. I made a small attempt at cutting a tragic figure on the doorstep, a solitary daddy waving a painful farewell to his brood. It was my first and last excursion into mawkish posturing. At the time my mood was too good to perform with conviction. In the future, I'd be too angry to be arsed.

I passed the day at home, busy doing nothing. By 7.45 p.m. I was stationed behind the curtains, squinting through a crack at the darkened street below. The Volvo arrived precisely on schedule and, as in the morning, stopped twenty yards away from the shop. I watched the children spill out under the street-lights' eerie amber. I saw the silhouettes of kisses being exchanged. Scurrying down to the front door I opened it as Gloria reached up for the bell. She and the boys entered the hall and I saw that Chris's car was already pulling away.

Quietly, the children went up to the flat. Billy disappeared into the kitchen. The older two, still bunched up in their coats, perched awkwardly in the living room, Gloria on the settee, Jed on his favourite armchair in the corner. I took the Other Armchair as it was damningly known. 'So?' I said, smiling nobly. 'Have you had a lovely time?'

'We went to the Natural History Museum,' Gloria said.

'And was it good?'

'Yes. Quite good.'

'Only "quite good"?' Such descriptive inhibition was unusual in my daughter. 'Bit thin on detail, aren't we?' I joshed her edgily.

Gloria did her best. 'We played football in a park.' She looked to Jed for confirmation. 'Didn't we?'

'Yes,' said Jed, 'we did.'

I thought I might as well cut to the chase. 'So what is Mummy's friend like?'

'He's quite nice,' said Gloria quickly, giving the firm impression of delivering an answer she had prepared earlier. Let's hear it for *Blue Peter*. I turned to Jed.

'And what did you think of him, young man?' I sounded like a bishop at a prep-school sports day.

'Quite nice,' said Jed, clutching at Gloria's straw.

'Well, that's good, isn't it?' I said encouragingly. 'We wouldn't want Mummy's friend to be someone we didn't like.'

There was no comment from the panel. From the kitchen came the sound of tin cans rolling across the floor. Gloria spoke again. 'Mummy says we might go to the museum again. Chris really likes it there.'

I felt a jolt of adrenaline when she mentioned Chris by name. Until that point he'd been nothing to me but some fellow who was welcome to my ex. Now it hit me that to Gloria, Jed and Billy he was a real human being who had turned up in their lives and who, the older two had realised, planned on a long-term stay.

'Uh oh!' I blustered brightly, pretending I'd only just noticed the clatter of the cans. 'I'd better go and collar Billy. Can you two big ones get yourselves ready for bed?'

They pattered off, relieved. I went out to the kitchen, still surprised to find the chasm where the table used to be. As I tucked Billy under my arm and bent to put the cans back in the cupboard, I felt a little shard of iron enter my soul.

* * *

Weeks passed. Each Saturday or Sunday morning I watched Gloria, Jed and Billy climb into Chris's Volvo and each evening, spied on them climbing out again. Festive fairy-lights went on in South Norwood High Street. Then, at the end of November, Dilys wrote me a short letter suggesting that we meet to talk about the children's future. It seemed that the Dulwich Village dream home was almost ready to receive them. She felt we had some 'issues to resolve'.

We met during her lunch break in a non-romantic wine bar.

'You're not having them,' I said.

She lowered her eyelids and tilted her head demurely so that her dark hair, which she wore longer than before, hung like an ebony curtain to one side. It was not a mannerism I recalled.

'They're my children as well,' she pointed out.

We slapped bargaining chips on the table.

'You left the flat,' I observed sharply.

'You can't afford to live there.'

'Just watch me.'

'I will.'

For the first time since she'd gone away I felt resentment rise. I'd still learned very little from the children about Chris: he liked computers, he liked nature, he liked what he appeared to call 'seeking wisdom in the woods'. It wasn't much, but it was enough.

'You left me for a techy twerp in bush shorts.'

'You are so bloody offensive.'

'I can't deny I have a gift. I wonder what a judge would make of your affair.'

'You wouldn't go to court. You wouldn't stand a chance.'

'You're sure about that, are you?'

I was bluffing. In truth, I didn't have a clue where I might stand under the Law. Dilys, being Dilys, very likely did. And my guess is that this knowledge informed the compromise she then proposed.

'Perhaps we should experiment with sharing them,' she said, now flicking back her hair and looking up at me from underneath her lashes – another curious addition to her repertoire of charms.

'What do you mean, "sharing them"?' I asked.

Dilys had done some research: family break-ups were, after all, within her field of expertise. She said that such arrangements were increasingly common and sometimes worked extremely well. There were lots of ways of dividing your children's lives in two. You could rotate them every two days, three or four; you could split Mondays to Thursdays equally and alternate the weekends from each Friday, or you – that's to say I – could have them every other weekend and maybe one day in the week. 'That, of course, would not be equal,' Dilys said, 'but it might be easier for you, being . . . on your own.'

For two months I had slipped comfortably enough into being a lone parent, being a mum and a dad at the same time. It hadn't been so hard. The truth is that everyday life had carried on much as before. I knew the children missed their mother. Yet even though she'd disappeared from the domestic landscape, most of its daily features were substantially unchanged.

Even before Dilys left it had become mostly me who pulled Gloria, Jed and Billy out of their beds in the mornings, hassled them into their clothes and coaxed them through their Coco Pops. She had become the one who flapped around the house looking for her coat, her keys, her casework folders and bolted off to catch the early train from Norwood Junction, still smoothing down her tough-but-tender two-piece as she slalomed across the High Street through the crawling rush-hour traffic, her briefcase swinging at her side.

I'd also become the one who trotted Gloria and Jed to school before wheeling Billy round to Esther, his devoted childminder, while Dilys stood fretting at the platform looking at her watch, having a career. And as she had climbed the ladder, I'd become the one who almost always fetched the brood back in the afternoons, rustled up their tea, dealt with their end-of-the-day short tempers and used every trick and bribe to get them to the Land of Nod.

Now Dilys was sitting in this wine bar being the mummy who knew best. I didn't want to give an inch. 'You're obviously the expert. What do you recommend?'

'They could spend one week at my place and one week at yours,' she said, suspiciously quickly.

'Go on.'

'They could change over every Friday. After school.'

'Go on.'

'They'd become children with two homes instead of one. Mummy's Home and Daddy's Home.'

Everything else, she said, could stay the same: Gloria and Jed's school, Billy going to the ever-loving Esther until he was old enough for the school nursery.

I thought it over. Grudgingly, I saw advantages in Dilys's plan. I was weary and starting to feel the financial pinch. I needed working days that didn't end at 3.15. And I needed to get out more. Lisa and Camille were wondering if I, the great sex-hunter, would ever have a trophy to my name.

'How are you going to get off work to meet Gloria and Jed after school?' I asked.

Dilys had an answer. 'I can rearrange my hours. And Chris can sometimes do it too.'

'A whole week feels a bit long without my children,' I countered. 'You're used to it now. I'm not.'

That hurt her more than I'd expected. Her starchy manner fractured. 'Don't you realise I've been making them a *home* . . .'

'Sorry, sorry,' I said, startled by her tears. 'I'll visit the gents. You stay here and blow your nose.'

I stood at the urinal feeling ashamed. I hadn't come to the meeting intending to be hostile or to make myself look fragile too. This unwanted sighting of my deeply buried weakness had been heightened by the new version of Dilys. Being back in her presence stirred no carnal ripples. On the contrary, she struck me as a bit absurd. I had computed her transition from the lusty libertine who couldn't get enough of me to the head-strong Boadicea who simply had to get away. But now the dragonfly was behaving like a butterfly – albeit one still buzzing with resolve. Yet she was obviously blooming in her new relationship – and I was obviously very much alone. Turning to the basin, I felt mocked by the condom dispenser on the wall. Sexually, I'd been confined to an obscure corner of China – Wan-King, the lonely canton, more fun when you're fourteen.

I took a deep breath and rejoined Dilys at the table. She too had regained her composure.

'I was too sharp,' I said, the closest to an apology I could manage. 'Can I go home and think it over?'

Later I did quite a lot of thinking, not all of it friendly. Dilys, I was certain, had made a calculation that I would soon capitulate and she would end up with the children as good as by consent without the risky business of enriching a lawyer. Not a hope of that, I swore. But she was right about one thing: Gloria, Jed and Billy were her children too. And more importantly, the children knew it.

I spoke to Dilys on the phone the following day. 'All right. I'll go for sharing. One week at Mummy's Home, one week at mine.'

'And we'll see how it goes.'

'Yeah, we all will, won't we?'

You know that painting on my wall? The one of the bloke, the children, and the three-piece suite? I started working on it early in the morning of the first Boxing Day after Dilys decamped. During the phone call we'd agreed to delay starting the 'two homes' system until after the Christmas break. That was fine with me. But there had been some push-and-shoving over the holiday itself, especially Christmas Day.

'They ought to be with me,' I'd said. 'It's what they've got used to.'

'That isn't fair,' Dilys protested. 'And what about my mum?'

'*What* about her?'

I'd never really hit it off with Beryl Day who, as far as I could see, had spent too much time with Bette Davis in her youth. Her husband Raymond, Dilys's father, was a dour financial adviser who'd died of a heart attack a year before Billy was born, activating his exemplary life assurance provision in the car park of the South Mimms service station.

Dilys set out her case. 'Mum will be in Dulwich with Chris and me for the first time, and if she doesn't see the kids on Christmas Day she'll get into a state. She's had enough upsets lately, don't you think?'

'And my parents haven't, I suppose.'

My father George and mother Lana had been very fond of Dilys, and were naturally concerned for their grandchildren.

'Yours are stronger,' Dilys retorted. 'They can cope.'

This was true enough. And nothing lays on a guilt-trip quite like a worried, widowed granny. In the end a deal was done. Gloria, Jed and Billy woke up at Daddy's Home on Christmas morning, gratified to find that Santa had fulfilled his obligations: he'd pocketed the carrot left out for his reindeer, devoured the mince pie and, as Gloria observed knowingly, not only drained the tumbler of whisky we'd left out but helped himself to more from the bottle. Moreover, dear Saint Nick had left a small mountain of presents.

At eleven we made the short car journey to my parents' house, a large mid-market semi in Croydon's leafy hinterland where they'd moved when I was ten after the flat over the shop was starting to feel too small. There, Mum, Dad and my older brother Bradley, his wife Malika and my younger brother Charles made a fine job of pretending it was Stone Home business as usual. Then, at two o'clock, Gloria, Jed and Billy were transferred to Dilys's jurisdiction. It was, in every way, a diplomatic exchange. I didn't want to drop them off at her and Chris's place and she didn't want to fetch them from my parents', so we agreed to do the switch outside A Poor Man's Wealth as usual.

I had prepared a bag for each of them, containing toothbrush, pyjamas and a few small toys, though I persuaded them to leave Brian Lion, Geoff Giraffe and Neil Seal behind – I was afraid that if they went too, the children might never return. Dilys arrived in the car alone and took them off to Mummy's Home where Mummy, Mummy's mummy, Mummy's man and (I muttered cruelly) one other complete turkey lay in wait.

As I drove back to Mum and Dad's I thought of the kids exploring their second home for the first time that afternoon. I kept on thinking about it all through my mother's dinner, my father's deadly cocktails and my brothers' foolish jokes, and kept on thinking about it when the aunts, uncles and neighbours began turning up from eight o'clock.

I held out until eleven then hugged my parents goodbye. At home I slept extremely badly and woke at five to check the children's bedrooms – definitely not there. I said to Brian, Geoff and Neil, 'Guys, it's you and me against the world,' and then I dressed, went outside and drove the Astra through the drizzle up to Dulwich Village where for the first time I set eyes on the property where Dilys now lived. Mummy's Home: my children's other address. I sat for fifteen minutes in a handsome tree-lined street opposite a short gated drive. I noted the fairy lights twinkling round the porch and the Father Christmas silhouette on one of the upstairs windows. Then I went home to paint my picture. It's been there nearly three years now, but Billy still asks me about it now and then.

'Daddy?'

'Yeah?'

'You know that picture?'

'Yeah?'

'How did you do it again?'

'I worked from a photograph taken by your mother.'

'You copied it, you mean?'

'Not exactly copied. Every picture tells a story, and I made Mummy's photo say something a bit different, a bit more like the way that I was feeling at the time.'

Jed too takes an interest in the picture. I catch him looking at it and long to know what he is thinking. So I ask.

'What do you think of that painting, Jed?'

Jed shrugs. 'Dunno.'

Right, then. Nice weather we're having. Gosh, yes, I should say so.

I'd like to tell the boys the full story of the painting, but they're not ready yet. Gloria is ready, but only partly wants to hear. I explain that it dates from the time I started waking up wondering if she and the boys had been chopped into little pieces by a deranged intruder and I had slept through the whole thing. Or imagining myself answering a knock at the door to a shuffling female in blue saying, 'Mr Joseph Stone? I'm WPC Gentle. I'm afraid there's been an accident outside the school.' Or reaching for the ringing phone when I was at home alone convinced it would be Dilys calling long distance to say, 'Sorry to spring this on you, but Chris and I have bought a little ranch in Richville USA. We think the kids will be much happier out here. Oh, by the way, you can visit them at a neutral destination twice a year. The terms and conditions will be drawn up by our attorney who will be writing to you soon. Must fly!'

Gloria listens, then she says, 'Oh Dad, you are so sad.'

Yeah well. I've had my moments, I suppose.

chapter 4

Put yourself in my shoes, the ones that I was wearing at the time. After more than three months of solo steward-ing my brood I was suddenly spending whole weeks at home all on my own. It would have sent a lot of fellows loopy, but not me. When I wasn't in my studio commun-ing with my muse, I watched a few old movies, listened to a few old tunes on the radio and thought a few old thoughts. I saw in the New Year quietly. Brian Lion sat on the settee with his back resting against me. Neil Seal amused himself on the rug beside my feet. Geoff Giraffe kept his counsel in Jed's armchair in the corner. His self-absorption irked me and at one point I tried to needle him with a sharp remark – 'Hey, Geoff! Keep the noise down, eh?' He refused to be provoked.

Shortly after midnight I took the pets up to their beds and, before I too turned in, had a last look at the painting which I'd decided was complete. I was pleased with it, and felt I'd got on to the canvas the stuff that had been swilling round my head – a scene of sweet domesticity tinged with uncertainty: what an art critic might have called 'a screen for projected conjecture'. Or something.

My solitary sojourn offered some time for contemplation, a space for taking stock. I had some hard decisions looming: about money, about my home, about myself. Fearlessly, I opted to avoid them. Mostly I was just waiting for the children to return, and wondering if they had been just waiting to see me. They turned up as arranged on New Year's Day at noon. From the living-room window, I gave them the once-over. They looked the same as they had when I'd overseen their transfer to Dilys early on Christmas afternoon, wearing the same clothes, carrying the same bags, presumably containing the same bedclothes, toothbrushes and toys. But when they came into the house, something had changed.

Billy seemed much the same: he headed for his new toy phone and fell into conversation with a long-distance figment of his imagination. There was, though, a slight awkwardness about the other two. I picked Jed up and squeezed him, trying to sound relaxed when asking if he'd had a lovely time. He squeezed me back, but did more nodding than speaking. By the time I'd squeezed his sister he'd disappeared up to his room. Gloria, too, displayed a curious reserve, which I made it my business to dissolve.

'And how have you been, Daddy?' she politely enquired.

'I've been very well thanks, duchess,' I replied, gently mocking her formality, 'though the pets have been quite naughty while you've been away.'

'What have they been doing?'

'Well, Brian, to be fair, has been quite helpful as usual, though he hasn't done much roaring. He's seemed a bit down in the dumps.'

'Oh dear,' said Gloria drily, acclimatising slowly. 'Perhaps I'd better go and cheer him up.'

'As for Neil, I caught him trying to steal the fish fingers again. And Geoff . . . well, you know Geoff: disco dancing every night, staggering in the worse for drink at dawn. Giraffes were more considerate in my day.'

Gloria sighed. 'Ah well. I'll get Jed to have a word with him.' With that, she too trotted off upstairs.

It wasn't until later that I attempted a debriefing, prompted by the contents of a large envelope that Gloria produced for me from her bag. There was a short note from Dilys, hand-written but impersonal.

Dear Joe,

The children have had an enjoyable introduction to 'Mummy's Home'. I enclose some photographs taken during their stay. As you may gather from these, they have their own 'Mummy's Home' clothes, pyjamas, toothbrushes, toys etc, so there is no need for you to pack any such items on the days when they return here from now on. I look forward to collecting them after school and from Esther a week on Friday.

Yours, Dilys.

I read the note to the three children as bedtime approached and all four of us were squashed into my bed. 'No kisses on the bottom, eh?' I said. 'I'll have to find somebody else to give me those.' I scanned the watchful faces for signs of mirth. Not much doing, I'm afraid.

I moved on to the photos. There were about a dozen arranged in a mini-album, each well executed and carefully composed. An opening group shot showed the children, Dilys and Dilys's mother huddled, smiling, amid a heap of ripped wrapping paper and newly opened gifts. The rest were individual studies of Gloria, Jed and Billy, three of each child, arranged within the album in what was plainly meant to be a helpful sequence.

There was Gloria posing outside an internal door with a pink name plate saying *Gloria's Room*. She wore clothes I'd never seen before: a pair of turquoise flares and a strappy pink belly top covered in hearts. They were not the sort of items I'd have chosen. The next shot showed Gloria inside the room sitting on a bed hugging a giant white tiger, and I made a mental note to never let this image fall into the paws of Brian Lion to whom it would represent a cruel betrayal. The third picture of Gloria showed her standing beside the bedroom window. She was lowering her eyelids and tilting her head demurely so that her dark hair hung like a long ebony curtain to one side. As Dilys had remarked in the non-romantic wine bar, they were her children too.

The photos of the boys followed the same pattern. Each was posed outside a bedroom door in clothes I hadn't seen before – joggers and striped T-shirts – standing beside a little plate emblazoned with his name. The difference was that both were photographed by the same door – clearly, they would be sharing at Mummy's Home as well – and the name-plates were bright blue. Their walls were festooned with posters of Pokémon and Bob the Builder, and they displayed their fancy-dress outfits too. Jed stood a little stiffly in Davy Crockett fake skins and a furry hat – not his style at all. Billy's face peered out from an all-in-one Pooh Bear suit, possibly contemplating a ferocious growl such as Pooh himself had never to my knowledge ever made.

Of all the photographs, only a few to my mind had a spontaneous look about them. These showed the children exploring what appeared to be a fairly large and well-established garden, complete with combined climbing frame, plastic swings and slide. 'Are these things new as well?' I asked. Billy said nothing: he'd nodded off. Jed looked at Gloria. Gloria said, 'Yes. They weren't really Christmas presents. Mummy got them when she was, you know, away.'

'Yes. I know. And who made this lovely album?'

'Mummy did.'

'And who took the photographs?'

'Chris did. He's learning photography.'

'And learning very well,' I said, deciding for the moment not to pursue the reason why the album

42

contained not a single image of the ace snapper himself.

In the school playground on the first change-over on the Friday I said what I always said in the morning but did so with extra kisses and hugs.

'Gloria, be happy, be kind, be good.'

'Yes, Daddy. Kiss, kiss.'

'Jed, be happy, be kind, be good.'

'Yes, Daddy. I will.'

'Mummy will be fetching you today, and I'll see you both again in one week's time. You understand that, don't you?'

'Yes, Daddy,' said Gloria. 'I'll miss you. See you soon.'

Jed just nodded.

'In you go then.'

They headed for their lines, Gloria holding Jed's hand.

Then I took Billy round to Esther.

'Billy, be happy, be kind, be good.'

'*You* be good, Daddy.'

'Pipe down,' I said. 'You're only three.'

I went back home and opened up the shop. I had been offered work by an advertising agency – pop art illustrations, the kind of thing I'd done at school and college – and pretended to get on with it. I was completely used to spending the heart of the day alone but it was strange anticipating my solitude continuing for seven nights in a row. I knew about being a lone father. I wasn't sure I could get used to the idea of being free.

Free from what, exactly? Only the three people I loved best. To fill the void that I was dreading I'd asked my two best buddies to drop round in the evening. It was a nice idea in theory, though I'm not sure it is wise to let such people into your home.

Firstly, Kenny Flint. Kenny is the sort of man who walks through your front door, goes straight into your kitchen, makes a sidelong approach to your box of Mr Kipling's Eight French Fancies, wolfs down the last pink one with a single gulp and wears a laconic smile as you cry out in despair: 'You little shit! You know I only like the pink ones!'

That was exactly what he did when he came round. 'I'm sorry, Joe,' he murmured fondly, lounging against the new kitchen table, 'but I'm hard-wired to pinch your pink patisserie. It's written in my genes.'

'Call yourself a friend?'

'Just think of me as thrillingly untamed.'

Secondly, Carlo Bonali. He's not so dangerous as Kenny – your French Fancies are safe with him – but when Carlo is around you should be careful what you wear. Give him half a chance and he'll be rooting through your wardrobe, making rude remarks. Which is exactly what he did when he turned up just after Kenny.

'Mod retro meets late futurist minimalist,' he summarised when I unearthed him in my bedroom closet. 'The Eighties frayed around the edges. Sounds like my friend Joe.'

He and Kenny had decided to take me out.

'You need cheering up, mate,' Carlo informed me gruffly, holding up an ancient pair of loafers with distaste. 'Especially your feet.'

'I only bought them 'cos *The Face* told me I ought to,' I protested lamely.

Carlo's face was deadly straight. 'With footwear, always lead, never follow,' he growled fondly. 'That's always been my maxim, as you know.'

I looked down at the shoes he was wearing. To my eyes they were ordinary black Oxfords, but I didn't dare say so – he'd have spent the next half an hour explaining that they were one of only seven pairs of Wilbur Wolf Kasuals in the country and I should worship the welts of them right away. Instead, I kept my counsel until Carlo threw me some black trousers, a dark blue shirt and a tie hand-painted with a picture of a swift that he'd bought for my birthday.

'A work in progress, I'm afraid,' he tutted as I tugged the clothes on. 'But we'll just have to make do.'

'For fuck's sake, Carlo, we're only going to the Greek around the corner.'

He looked at me with pity. 'Some of us worry about standards,' he explained.

I didn't mind the mickey-taking. I didn't mind Kenny and Carlo treating my place as if it was their own because in their younger days it had been – and, in a small way, it still was. The three of us have a common history between these four walls; a history of laughter, parties, massive mounds of pasta cooked by Carlo's mum and plaster flying ducks hung with irony on the hall wall. We'd begun living there together after Mum and Dad got tired of letting out the place to people they didn't know. Although they'd kept running the shop after the move to outer Croydon, it had become more of a hobby than a business and the most interesting jobs started being done at home. They no longer needed the worry of unruly tenants. That's why I suggested that rather than let the flat rot, they keep it in the family by letting it to Kenny, Carlo and me.

'We'll pay you a fair rent and we'll smarten the place up,' I said.

By then I had my art degree and had spent a year bumming fruitfully around Paris. Now I was back and didn't want to be one of those blokes who can't leave home. My parents chewed it over. The shop and flat still meant a lot. They'd bought it when they were the reigning Jiving Champions of All Streatham and had arrived from Tooting Graveney bringing retail ambitions such as South Norwood High Street had not previously seen. For fifteen years their merchandise was mostly *à la mode* – kitchen chairs you could sit on backwards and Swedish coffee-tables with short legs. That changed in the late Seventies, when popular taste began to pilfer from the past and, as Carlo always puts it, everyone's flared trousers went missing overnight.

'Well,' said Mum, 'they're very tidy.'

'Who are?' I asked.

'These chaps like Kenny,' elaborated Dad, 'who are a bit . . . you know.'

'A bit "you know"?'

'I'm not being funny,' said my dad.

'Crystal Palace fans, you mean? He can't help it. It's a disease.'

'You *know* what I mean,' chuckled my dad. 'I mean he goes the other way.'

'There's no stopping him, the scamp.'

'Carlo's a nice lad, too,' said Mum. 'Always well turned out.'

'Italian,' said Dad. 'That explains a lot.'

My parents understood about panache and presentation. All-Streatham Jiving Champions do.

The three of us moved in with the spring – initially for free. We'd met at Croydon College where we'd been a bit arty, a bit barmy and – or so we'd desperately hoped – a bit cool, and our comradeship prospered nicely as we stripped and sugar-soaped, papered and painted the place where I had spent the earliest years of my life and where we'd live together cheerfully for about a year. After that we started growing up. Kenny got a posh job with a kitchenware company and bought a flat in Thicket Road overlooking the park. Carlo left not long after, taking his sewing machine and collection of tailors dummies to play house in Penge with his new wife Jill. By then Dilys had moved in. With help from the building society we bought out Mum and Dad on the most generous of terms. The rest is chequered history.

'I like this painting, Joe,' said Kenny, eyeing my new creation as we made ready to leave. 'Would it like a name?'

'Try me.'

'*Paternity Suite*,' he said.

'Pardon?' I looked a bit bewildered. I was having a long day.

'Try to keep up, Joseph,' Carlo said, taking my arm. 'You're letting yourself down.'

'Don't make me suffer,' I complained, straightening my tie and generally preparing to be seen out on the street. 'Don't you realise I've become a lonely, troubled man?'

'Bollocks,' said Kenny and Carlo, both at the same time.

I agreed with them, of course. In spite of everything I was still smiling – and still singing. Yes, I had found myself not switching on the central heating, the building society had told me my income was too small for them to take Dilys off the mortgage and I wasn't overrun with work. But never mind all that. When the children went to Mummy's Home I was glad to have a break, and yet I missed them anyway. If Dilys had imagined that I would swiftly fall apart she was seriously mistaken. I was totally dug in. Daddy's Home was not going away.

We were about two months into our altered situation when officialdom popped by to keep an eye. It took the pleasant form of a lightly-Jaegered woman in her middle fifties, who made polite enquiries in a smart Caribbean accent from behind lowered half-moon glasses.

'So, Mr Stone . . .'

'Call me Joseph, please.'

She sank into the Other armchair. I faced her from my end of the settee. Gloria sat close beside me, face half-hidden in the sleeve of my jumper, perhaps believing it would signify devotion. At my feet, Billy chattered intensely at a bunch of plastic pigs. Jed sat quietly in his armchair with Geoff.

'Very well, Joseph,' said our visitor. 'My name is Claudette. So . . . is everything all right?'

I knew why she was there. Claudette had got wind of the children's adjusted circumstances and quite properly decided she should give us the once-over. Had Dilys had a word? I might have felt insulted. I just showed off a bit instead.

'Everything is pretty much all right,' I said with a big smile. 'Hard work, I suppose. But nothing I'm not used to.' Shameless, but true.

'Yes,' nodded Claudette, 'I'm sure.'

Then one of the pigs spoke. You couldn't see its lips move, and it sounded a bit like Billy. But it was definitely a pig. 'Hello, lady. I'm a boy pig. I've got a boy pig willy.'

Claudette raised an eyebrow. I could feel Gloria stifling a guffaw. 'He'll draw a lovely picture for you shortly,' I predicted. 'Though hopefully not of a farm-yard animal's private parts.'

'I understand,' said Claudette mock-sagely, trying to

catch the mood. 'And how is the older boy?' She glanced
at the ring-binder lying open on her lap, and then smiled
at Jed. 'You're Gerard, aren't you?'

'Jed,' said Jed.

Gloria snorted and put a hand up to her mouth.

'Shut up, you,' I told her, half-seriously.

She giggled.

'Jed,' I explained. 'We all call him Jed – with a "J"
strangely enough, which is a bit of a long story. You're
OK, Jed, aren't you?'

'Yes,' said Jed.

Claudette went, 'Mmm, mmm,' to fill the silence and
made a note. Traffic noise and adolescent after-school
voices intruded through the double-glazing from the
darkening street below. I'd closed up the shop in honour
of Claudette's visit and I wondered how much money it
had cost me. Millions, probably.

'And you must be Gloria,' our visitor continued.
'Quite a clever girl, I see.'

'*Quite* clever,' said Gloria in a display of faked coyness
that I would torment her about mercilessly later. Then
Billy turned his attention to some felt pens and paper
lying on the coffee-table. He held his page of squiggles
up on high.

'Pig!' he announced. 'But not its willy.'

'Very *good*,' said Claudette, jotting approvingly. 'Does
this talent run in the family?'

I knew that she already knew the answer to that
question, but I obliged her anyway.

'It may do. I'm in that line of work.'

'Oh, really?'

'Yes. I paint for a living. Oils and watercolours, gloss and emulsion. Twenty-four hours, I never close.'

'It's *emotion* paint, Daddy!' Gloria interrupted.

'So sorry,' I chastised myself. 'I meant gloss and *emotion*. Silly me.' I looked down at my daughter. 'As you can see, Claudette,' I said, 'life with a know-all is never dull.'

Gloria punched me. Claudette succumbed to a small smile. 'So I see,' she said, lifting half an eyebrow and tucking her ring-binder back into her bag. I fished for a compliment.

'So, how are we all doing?'

'Well, there's nothing wrong with Billy,' Claudette said, before turning towards Gloria to add, 'and there's nothing wrong with you, young lady, either.'

'No,' Gloria concurred, 'or with Daddy, most of the time.'

'And I'm quite sure,' Claudette said reassuringly, getting to her feet, 'that Jed is fine as well.'

I showed her out down the long stairs to the street. Before leaving, she handed me her card.

'If you do have any worries, just give me a call.'

'I will.'

'These situations can be tricky.'

'Yes, that's what I've heard.'

I gave her a 'that's life' grin and closed the door.

51

chapter 5

I had memories of feeling sharp and sexy – false ones, as you'd expect, but I allowed them to beguile me as the sap rose with the spring. When the children were at Daddy's Home I thought of little else but them. I thought about them a lot when they were with Dilys too. But during those long, blank evenings I also thought a great deal about women: the pretty women at the bank with whom I flirted shamelessly; the cheeky women at the chip shop who called me 'love'; the saucy women in the playground like Lisa and Camille. But mostly I thought of women whom I had yet to meet. I wanted one to make love to but that 'hunting for sex' line was only a naff joke. I wanted warm and tender female company. I wanted it badly. But where was it to be found?

Kenny was quite sure that he could help me. I would, he leeringly explained, be considered quite a catch among the swelling ranks of women over thirty who were looking to replace the no-good loafers they'd divorced.

'Unattached, good with children, own paintbrush, nice ass – well, that's Rothwell's opinion.'

Rothwell was Kenny's Canadian steady. He was a visiting Professor of Medieval Literature and had never once said 'nice ass' in his life.

'Tell Rothwell I'm touched.' I'm no snob. I'll accept invented compliments from anyone.

There was only one problem. As Kenny put it with meaningful understatement, to hook up with such women I would need to, 'Er, go out. Familiar with the concept, Joe?' And, of course, he had a point. Apart from seeing him and Carlo I had no social life. Kenny promised me that he would put that right. And, true to his word, he invited me to a trendy business function to take place one Friday night: a Friday when Gloria, Jed and Billy came back to Daddy's Home after a week in Dulwich, rather than the other way round.

'Bad timing, Ken,' I scolded when he came to pick me up.

'Have you got any cakes?' he asked distractedly, rifling through a cupboard in the kitchen. 'Not even a sponge finger or a bit of Battenburg? Just how sick and twisted can you get?'

This was classic Kenny: devoted but disruptive. Fortunately, my parents said they'd look after the children and keep them for the night. Where might I end up sleeping? It was time to visit Len.

* * *

'Hello, Joseph . . .'

'Hello, Len.' I climbed into the chair and waited.

'Anyone special . . . ?'

'Who?'

'The lucky lady you're seeing . . .'

'There is no lucky lady,' I protested.

'There is, Joseph, there is. She just doesn't know it yet . . .'

'Thanks, Len. I'll bear that in mind.'

I'd dropped the crop by then. Len layered and gelled. I admired myself freely in his mirror. I was about to pay and make good my escape when he looked at me and said: 'Something for the weekend . . . ?'

I was amazed. 'Do barbers still provide that service?'

'No, Joseph,' replied Len. 'But I do enjoy *saying* it every now and then . . .'

Two hours later I was dropping off Gloria, Jed and Billy, making sure they understood that I'd be back to see them the next day. Four hours later I climbed into Kenny's car and mentally prepared myself for an experience I'd forgotten how to have; socialising with fellow humans, some of them female.

The Fandango Galleria was one of those ripped-out, souped-up, stripped-down somewhere-in-Soho reception joints regularly over-stuffed by members of what Kenny called the 'blab-blab-blaberati' of domestic design. Their excuse on this occasion was the launch of a new range of chi-chi tableware 'created for' the Homelove

Company by the S&M sculptor turned non-stick sauce-pan guru Den McMurphy. The floors were painted green, the walls were tinted mint and the pictures hanging from them were of winsome yuppies disrobing next to scarlet lobsters and bulbous artichokes. People stood yakking madly, balancing plates of petits fours and clutching slippery Homelove brochures under their arms. It was groovy. It was gruesome. What was I doing there?

I'd been to shindigs like this before when I had been with Dilys, usually in the hope that they might generate some work. That never occurred. They did, though, bring a touch of gratis luxury into our lives. Grateful, amused and cynical in roughly equal measures I would maintain a demeanour just the polite side of aloof as Dilys mingled with her customary zeal before we trundled home. This, though, was my first excursion into glitz of the post-Dilys era and the difference was profound. I viewed the occasion through eyes of hopeless longing.

There were so many women there, doing all those woman things: checking coats and hats at the cloakroom, swanning in threesomes to the bathroom, lighting up, laughing, confiding, dipping into their handbags for . . . well, I would never know. I was seized by a panicky compulsion. I had to speak to them. I wasn't driven by desire, more by a fear of feeling a coward if I didn't somehow amuse them, get close to them, breathe some-thing of them in. I became a risky cocktail of angst and

ardour. Three glasses of bubbly, a dash of quiet desperation and all of a sudden I'd turned into Cary Grant.

'I'm Joseph. Who are you?'

'I'm Lucy. This is Louise and this is Linda.'

'Hi.'

'Hi.'

'Hi.'

'Hi.'

'Erm. What's your connection here, then?'

They were in retail consultancy, or marketing advisory
or advertising strategy or something. And what was I in,
by the way?

'Interior upgrading. Painting and decorating, as it's
more usually known.'

'Oh, really?'

Yes, really. Well, I couldn't say I was an artist.
What would they have asked back? 'What sort of artist?
Graphic, con or piss?' And the awkward truth was this:
the sort of artist I'd become was 'struggling'.

I soldiered on. 'Hello, I'm Joseph. And you are . . . ?'

'I'm Sonia. This is Saskia, and this is Sandra . . .'

'I'm Joseph. Sorry, I didn't get your name . . .'

'I'm Marnie. This is Maeve and this is Maggie . . .'

I wasn't talking to these women. I was interviewing
them. And the more I wittered on, the more long and
difficult the road from 'how do you do?' to 'I love you
too' appeared. The noise level reached the point where
even making small talk meant a sore throat in the
morning. And the bubbly that first buoyed me now

started to deflate me. Cary Grant moved over. Jack Nicholson stepped in. I was ambushed by a walking toothpaste commercial playing the zany front man for some cable TV crew.

'Hello, you look interesting.'

I said: 'Jesus, no.'

This seemed to please him a great deal.

'Nice tie,' he schmoozed. It was Carlo's birthday gift again, the one with a picture of a swift.

'Thank you.'

'What's your name?'

'Claude. Claude Monet.'

'So, Claude, what do you do?'

'Oh, you know, I go to parties where I don't know anybody and stand around waiting to be pounced on by blokes like you.'

'Ha ha! Looks like you struck lucky, Claude.'

'I feel lucky to be alive.'

'What do you think of the beautiful creations on display here?'

'You're including yourself in that category, I presume?'

'Ha ha! Ha ha! I meant the Homelove tableware collection by Den McMurphy. You know, Claude: pots, pans, soup tureens. You've seen a soup tureen before?'

'To be honest with you,' I said, suddenly feeling very tired, 'soup tureens don't get my juices flowing.'

His smile tightened slightly, but his ring of confidence remained. 'So tell me, Claude, what does?'

'Please. Leave me alone.'

'Fine, Claude, suit yourself.' He oozed away to bother someone else.

'What a cunt,' said a female voice behind me.

'Delicately put,' I said with such *sang froid* as I could muster.

She laughed, tipsily. Her accent was refined Estuary English. Red wine tilted in the tumbler in her hand. 'This place is full of arseholes,' she elaborated. 'Present company excepted, naturally.'

Had she meant only herself or was I exempted too? The question still returns to nag me now and then.

'We're going home now,' she continued. 'Want to come?'

'Who's "we"?'

'Who's we?' she mocked, then pressed her palm against my chest. 'Me and a few friends.'

'You've got some of those then?'

'Oooh, Prince Charming . . . Nice tie, by the way.' She took it between her fingers, then let it drop again. She was in her mid-twenties, thin, with fair, highlighted hair that flopped over her left eye. Clutch bag. Red cardigan. Pretty little black dress. Pretty little nose.

Another young woman barged over: taller, darker, less frugally-fleshed. Above the low-slung waistband of her purple trousers a jewel glinted gaily in her navel. Her tight red T-shirt announced *Cray-zee Bay-bee, Yeah!*

'Are we going? Are we going?' she demanded.

'Any time,' said my new buddy. 'Where's Kelly?'

'Over there with Phil. Who's this?' The newcomer tipped her glowing cigarette my way.

'I don't know. Who are you?'

'I'm Joe.'

'Daisy, this is Joe. Joe, this is Daisy. She's one of those modern, go-get-'em women. She'll shag anything.'

Both of them convulsed. Then the one in the red cardigan tugged me over to the table from where the wine was being served, helped herself to two full bottles and pulled me out through the front door. 'Come on, Daisy!' she called over her shoulder. Daisy joined us shortly, towing Kelly and Phil. Kelly was high-heeled, pale and taciturn. Phil was tall, dark and unsmiling. I'd been looking round for Kenny, but couldn't see him. Never mind. It was understood that he wouldn't hold my hand if I got a better offer. I decided to find out if such a thing was being made.

'What's your name?' I asked the woman.

'Priscilla.'

'What happens next, Priscilla?'

'We all go back to my place, then we all go out again.' She broke off. 'Well done, Phil!'

Phil had hailed a cab. Priscilla took my hand and we all climbed in together. Priscilla sat in the middle, me on one side of her, Daisy perched unsteadily on the other. Opposite us on the fold-down seat, Kelly said nothing. Next to her, Phil said a great deal. He said, for example, that Den McMurphy's tableware collection was, 'Tat, total tat, total fucking ratarse tat,' that the Fandango Galleria was, 'Bumwipe drivel, total ratarse crap,' and that all the people there had, 'Not a titful of integrity between them.'

Daisy and Priscilla sniggered helplessly at every word.

After a mercifully short ride, we piled out of the cab into a narrow street. Where were we? Holborn? Clerkenwell? Bloomsbury? I hadn't kept an eye. Priscilla slid a key into a shiny black door and led the way up a dozen stairs with fine fitted carpets into an anonymous but smartly-furnished flat. Phil barged into the lounge as if he owned the place – as possibly he did. 'All right,' he scowled to himself, taking a mirror from the wall, a banknote from his wallet and a crisp fold of white paper from inside a book on a shelf unit in the corner.

He snorted up the powder with ostentatious indolence. There is a saying about people who are crazy for cocaine: it makes them even bigger arseholes than they were before. I tried to keep an open mind, as the others took their turns at bending to the powder. Kelly stood in the corner. Daisy announced that she was going off to spew. Only when she'd inhaled did Priscilla seem to remember I was there.

'Do you want some?' she said sweetly enough, wrinkling and sniffling through each nostril.

I smiled. 'I wish I could, but tomorrow is a busy day.'

'Oh, that's a shame,' she said, and I found myself melting absurdly into meekness, so grateful was I for this small gesture of compassion. I was perching at the end of some kind of basket-weave bench. She came and sat beside me, emptying the last drops from one of the bottles she'd lifted into a glass. She smelled decadently lovely: of perfume, booze and Daisy's cigarettes. 'Isn't she a lush?' she said, nodding towards the corridor her friend had disappeared through. 'What do men think about mad birds like her?'

I realised that I had nothing to say. Then Phil glanced over at Priscilla. Her eyes were ready and waiting and, having met them, he swiftly looked away, his lips puckering in a millisecond of private mirth. Phil strode over towards me. I wanted to go home.

'I didn't get your name,' he drawled, jerking his hollowed features round towards me.

I weighed up a few options: 'Picasso – Pablo', or 'Gogh – Vincent van'. But I didn't think that trick would work out quite so well with Phil.

'I'm Joe.'

'Ordinary Joe, eh?'

'If you say so.'

'So what do you do, Joe?'

Back at Fandango Galleria being a painter and decorator had at least made me feel novel. It made me feel pathetic now.

'This and that,' I said. 'I'm often pretty busy with my children.' I said it in the hope that it might soften him somehow. But I was wrong.

'You've got kids then?'

'Three.'

'Like to shag them, do you?'

I heard a sharp intake of breath and looked around. It had come from Priscilla. The bottle she had emptied was still standing at my feet. I bent and took it by the neck, got slowly to my feet and pushed the end of it into Phil's face.

'Like cosmetic surgery, do you?'

In the movies people cheer at moments such as these. But this wasn't the movies. I was flooded with fury and bravado; fury at what this fuckwit Phil had said, bravado because he'd said it in front of Priscilla, a woman I hardly knew, but a woman who had been holding my hand and a woman I suspected quite liked Phil. I was never going to hit him with that bottle. And I did try to make my words just on the hard side of light-hearted, hoping to avoid the impression that I'd completely lost it. But I must have looked and sounded as if I was ready to kill. Just as well, really, because if he'd said that thing again I would have broken down and cried.

He didn't say anything though, for a moment. He looked at the bottle, then looked at me, and then looked quickly towards the stairs where Kelly now stood waiting.

'Sorry, man, sorry. Just joking. Anyway, we're leaving.'

Keeping one lazy eye on me, he picked his coat up off the floor. 'Ciao babes!' he shouted. Together, he and Kelly slunk downstairs. The door slammed shut behind them.

'I'd better go and mop up Daisy,' said Priscilla and disappeared after her friend.

She was still gone twenty minutes later. I found a remote unit, switched on the television and pretended to be watching *Bareback Biker Boys From Belgium*. Then I got up and padded down the same hall as Priscilla. The bathroom door stood open, and I looked in on Daisy curled up on a mat beside the toilet. The adjoining door was closed. I knocked softly and walked in. Priscilla lay under bedclothes, softly snoring. She stirred, stared up at me and reached for my hand again. Then she went back to sleep.

That's the last thing I remembered until I woke up in the small hours with a screaming bladder and an erection Batman could have hung his cloak on. I was still on top of the duvet, and still wearing all my clothes. Priscilla snored beside me, only her face and hair visible. It was a pretty face – but not the face for me.

I slithered off the bed and felt my way to the bathroom. Daisy was still there. First, I heaved her away from the toilet bowl, then bent my rigid member downwards and released a little urinary pressure. Stepping back over Daisy, I slunk back to Priscilla, pulled a pocket sketchpad from my jacket and composed a careful note.

Sorry To Rush Off. Family Business.

I placed it on her bedside table. I didn't sign my name. Then I escaped into the dawn and went looking for the night bus that would carry me back to where I belonged.

* * *

63

Among the glories of South Norwood is the pedestrian subway that runs under Norwood Junction station. A straight, narrow tubeway it is a claustrophobia-sufferer's nightmare and a mugger's paradise. It is also a great place for letting off a lot of noise.

It was about seven-thirty when I pushed open my parents' front door, met my mother in her nightie making the morning tea and told her I had the car and was taking the kids out for an egg and bacon breakfast treat. I could hear the children stirring, and I didn't want to do any explaining. I went straight up to their rooms, lifted each one from their bed, led them to the toilet and thumbed the sleep out of their eyes. I got them dressed, put them in their coats and told them we'd be going to their favourite greasy spoon a short walk from A Poor Man's Wealth. But first there was a ritual to honour.

We gathered at the top end of the subway.

'You go first, Jed,' I said. 'As fast and as loud as you can. I'll count to five, then Gloria can go. I'll go last with Billy in the buggy. It's not a race, remember. You just run and you roar.' I looked once more down the tunnel. No one was around. 'OK, Jed! Go!'

One, two, three, four, five . . .

'OK, Gloria! Go!'

Gloria sprinted after Jed.

'Run, everyone! Run!' I bellowed, pushing off with Billy. Jed and Gloria's footsteps echoed, the buggy's wheels set up a rattle right behind.

'And now, Stone children,' I shouted, breaking into a run as well, 'let me hear you roar!'

'ROAR!'

'ROAR!'

'ROAR!'

Inside, I was roaring too.

chapter 6

Let's come up to date . . .

'Gloria?'

'What, Dad?'

'Don't be cross with me.'

'But you're not being nice.'

'Oh don't be so pathetic.'

'*You're* the one who's pathetic. *You're* the one who can't be nice.'

'*I'm* not the one giving off all the attitude.'

'I'm not listening to you!'

'That's life. Deal with it.'

'*I'm not listening to you!*'

'So you can stay or run away.'

'I'M NOT LISTENING TO YOU!'

Stomp, stomp, stomp. Up the little wooden hill to bedfordshire she goes, never to be seen by her pig of a pop again – at least not until it's time for tea.

Forgive me for exposing you to that unseemly scene.

But I had to underline what I explained right at the start – that Gloria and I no longer get on quite as smoothly as we used to when she thought a sanitary towel was one I hadn't dried my feet on, and I was either half-silly with post-Dilys excitement or half-mad with despair.

Those were the days . . .

I approached my first summer as a half-time single father with a nasty build-up of unpaid bills and not enough cash in the pipeline to be sure I wouldn't have to sell my body on the streets. Overdraft country was just beyond the next horizon. One evening, after the boys had gone to bed, I discussed the situation with my daughter. She had just turned nine and was a woman of the world.

'Don't tell anyone, Gloria, but I'm going to have to send you up a chimney.'

'You're so silly, Daddy.' She was curled on the settee enjoying jolly Alan Titchmarsh and the gang. I was lying on the carpet looking up at her with my feet propped on Jed's armchair. Brian Lion lounged imperiously on my chest.

I went on, 'We need a lot of money, Gloria. Would you find someone rich and stupid who will give me loads of work?'

'Yes, Daddy.'

'Find them for me tomorrow, would you, please?'

'Yes, Daddy.'

'And tell me I'm the best dad in the world.'

'Huh!'

'Right. That's it. I want a divorce.'

Gloria was munching on a chocolate biscuit. She seemed content, smelling of bath bubbles, her lavishly self-powdered toes peeking from the bottoms of her flannelette pyjamas. Yet the chocolate biscuit told a troubling tale. It was a Safeway Savers chocolate biscuit, significantly cheaper than a standard Safeway's own brand chocolate biscuit and still less of a deluxe snack than a McVities Milk Chocolate Digestive Biscuit, arguably the field leader among mainstream chocolate biscuit brands. The Safeway Savers, by contrast, was the chocolate biscuit of the financially stretched, and fooling absolutely no one by masquerading as the shrewd choice of the admirably thrifty – except, just possibly, a primary-school-age child.

'I'll give you some money, Daddy.'

'How much have you got?'

'Nine pounds and seventeen pence.'

'Thanks.'

Budget-range products were appearing in my super-market trolley more frequently. They represented the ongoing erosion of my financial empire as the post-separation numbers began crunching. In addition to the burden of running the home on my income alone, I'd hardly sold a picture or been asked to paint one since Christmas. Meanwhile, the ad agency work was becoming soul-destroying. One account manager acting for a male fashion chain asked for a set of illustrations showing a bunch of skinny young women laughing at a weedy bloke in really cheap trainers. In the brief the awful trainers in question were described in minute detail. I had a pair just like them, which may explain the lukewarm reaction to my pitch.

'The chicks need to be more sassy,' the voice on the phone whined, 'and the guy should be more sad. The story is that he's a total loser.'

Shame. He seemed like a terrific bloke to me.

I kept on looking on the bright side. If neither art nor commerce would bless me with a glorious future I would take the Dulux road to solvency. Mindful of the onset of the home improvement season, I compiled a portfolio of my greatest feats of bespoke decorating: my living room, which I had tarted up in mauve two years before and looked extremely chic with the period-piece suite; Kenny's flat, a vision in its many shades of blue; my parents' earth-shades-tiled kitchen; a couple of nice snapshots of exterior doors and windows I had done to pay my way during my sojourn in France. I put fliers in shop windows and placed adverts in the local papers. I told myself that I was a gentrifying yuppie's dream.

Meanwhile, I economised with care. Some things were easy to go without: after the Fandango Galleria fiasco I'd almost given up on going out, even for a quiet drink at the pub. It had gradually sunk in that a round of fashionable lagers could cost more than it did to feed the children for a week. Other areas of domestic spending, though, I was determined to maintain. These were often about keeping up appearances, a concept that had not previously disfigured my life. When my parents came to tea, I hid the Safeway Savers biscuits and wheeled out the fancy shortcake. Mum and Dad aren't daft. They knew I must be struggling, but there was no way I was going to let it show.

The stakes were slightly higher when it came to Dilys. We had remained on cordial if distant terms and, to my relief, the 'two homes' rotation system did not seem to be upsetting the children – they were as eccentric as ever. Yet our relationship was becoming subtly marked by competition. I caught myself getting touchy when Gloria revealed that the tooth fairy – in which she no longer believed – had been summoned to Mummy's Home for the third time in a row. There was clearly a conspiracy in the mytho-orthodontic world. I'd been wiggling at that molar for a week.

Still, at least it saved me a quid. That would come in handy when Gloria kept her regular hair appointment down the road at Sindy's Salon. This tradition was rooted in the pre-separation era, but thanks to the salon's proximity to Daddy's Home, I'd managed to become the parent who maintained it. It was now a special thing that Gloria and I did together, and that made it worth every penny.

It was an afterschool ritual on the last Friday of each month. After dropping Jed round with Billy at Esther's place after school, Gloria and I would sashay into the salon, and the glass door would ease shut behind us, sealing us into a teeming theatre of womanliness-in-progress: banquettes padded with black plastic, a shin-high chrome-framed smoked-glass table topped with shiny slabs of *Glamour*, *Company* and *Vogue*, the long curve of the reception desk; the hot whirr of hand-held dryers; cascading plastic foliage and floor-to-ceiling mirrored walls; a chemical kick in the air; white, powdered ladies in black clothes, quick and crimped and plump and far more sexy to my interloper's eyes than any of them knew.

The routine never varied.

'Hello, Gloria darling,' Sindy would say. 'With Daddy again today?' Sindy had yet to catch on to my domestic situation. Her intelligence network was less advanced than Clip-Joint Len's.

'Yes, it's Daddy. As usual.'

Gloria's eyes would roll in presumed solidarity over the uselessness of men, and Sindy, a sleek siren in her fifties, would roll hers in return before sending a secret wink my way. A teenage trainee would appear and chirrup, 'Gloria? Would you like to come this way?' And off Gloria would trot, oozing confidence, towards the line of basins at the far end of the shop, there to be propped up on a cushion then shampooed and conditioned while I picked at the magazines and let the girly vibes and vapours seep into my pores. Then the hairdresser herself would call me for a consultation. Sometimes it was Vicki, sometimes it was Jan, occasionally it was Sindy herself. Then, one day, it was Marina.

'Are you Gloria's daddy?'

Marina was new to me. I noticed her hair first: shortish and dyed blonde with a single dark highlight expertly swept across her brow.

'I am that lucky man.'

She gave a short laugh. Clearly, Gloria had already worked her charms.

'I'm Marina. I'll be cutting her hair today. What would you like done?'

I looked at Marina more closely. Had I met her somewhere before? She was blithely voluptuous, her facial features round and soft, though they were hardened by plucked eyebrows and concealed behind a high wall of foundation. I felt a faint wave of nostalgia for girls I'd known at school: precociously sexual, painstakingly turned out, too grown-up for me.

'What would I like done?' I sighed, by way of a reply, closing an article on perfect blow jobs and letting the magazine flop back on to the pile as casually as I could. 'I'd like you to give me a million pounds. Would that be all right?'

Marina glanced at the magazine's cover as it fell: *SEX! SEVEN WICKED WAYS TO MAKE HIM BEG!*

She said, 'If you can make do with a cheque.'

'Will it be the type that goes "boing boing"?'

'Yep,' she said.

We walked over to Gloria, gowned and gleaming on her special high stool. I dragged my fingertips through her damp locks, sensing Marina standing near.

'This is the first time you've had the privilege of making Gloria even more beautiful, I think.'

'It is.'

'Shut up, Daddy,' Gloria said, beaming.

'She wants it shorter at the back and sides,' I said, inexplicably recalling that Dilys's tresses were getting longer and longer. 'But keep the fringe please. She's very fond of that.'

'Fine,' said Marina.

I stepped to one side. Marina took up her scissors and comb.

'Now, Daddy, go away,' said Gloria.

This took me by surprise.

'But I like to stay and watch. You know that.'

'Daddy, just *go away*.'

I screwed Marina for the first time the following Thursday afternoon. Does that sound impressive? You know: six days from eye-contact to primary penetration? Whatever, that isn't how it was. My relationship with Marina was needier and kindlier from the start but I can't deny that, to me, it felt like a victory too. I had ventured fearlessly into that foreign, female field and got myself a girl. Thank you, Gloria – you little minx.

'*Daddy, just go away*.' Girls' talk came to her effortlessly.

'All right, Cheeky Spice. I'll be back in a while.'

I'd taken an agitated saunter round the neighbouring shops, browsing distractedly, gripped by what I'd half-

73

recognised as a truly desperate longing to sweeten up this Marina, a probably entirely unsuitable woman whom I'd only just met. I had returned, knowing I couldn't stop myself from trying, and found that Gloria had laid on an *entrée*.

'So you're a decorator, then,' Marina said.

'Some of the time, yeah.'

'Gloria has told me all about you.'

'Leaving out the bad bits, I hope.'

'There weren't *many* bad bits, really.'

'Not *many*?' I felt a certain slippage in my seducer's smile. Marina would later say she hadn't noticed. Had Gloria? One of these days I'm going to ask her.

'Nothing *too* serious,' Marina had said, as anxiety made my fingers fiddle round Gloria's ears.

'Don't do that, Daddy! Marina hasn't finished yet!'

'Sorry, boss. It won't happen again.' Had Gloria mentioned Dilys? Chris? The Safeway Savers chocolate biscuits? The solitude in which half my life was sexlessly immersed?

'I need a decorator,' Marina said at that moment.

'You don't say!'

'My lounge needs doing.'

'My' lounge, not 'our' lounge. I glanced at her left hand as she wielded the comb. Was that a wedding ring?

'I can come round on Monday.'

'I'll meet you there during my break.'

I'd thought about her all weekend: while at the park

with the kids, at the cinema with the kids, at home with the kids for Sunday dinner. Come Monday at midday I was waiting at Marina's gate.

'You remembered me then,' she said when she arrived five minutes later. I couldn't tell if her surprise was genuine.

She took her key out of her purse and let us in. Inside her prosaic South Norwood terrace it was all Homebase surfaces and plum-coloured plush. I thought about the children dragging their mucky fingers down my staircase walls. I'd shown Marina my portfolio. She'd shown me her colour scheme and we'd agreed a fee. Our intimacy had progressed as we'd shifted her lounge furniture to one end of the room. A photo of a young man stood on a mock-Georgian sideboard.

'That's my son Gary. All grown-up and gone.'

She'd given me a spare key and her blessing to let myself in the next morning. I'd cleaned down her walls on Tuesday, put a coat on the ceiling on Wednesday and accepted her offer of lunch in her kitchen on Thursday, her day off. Two peppered mackerel and a bottle of sweet wine later she'd taken me to her bedroom where we'd made love without frills. Afterwards, she'd brought me tea. As I'd sipped it she'd noticed my frequent glances at her bedside clock.

'You look like a man who thinks he should be somewhere else.'

'I'm sorry. I'd love to stay, but I've got to pick the kids up.' Feeling bad, I'd added: 'They go back to their mother's house tomorrow.'

'So, I'll see you then, shall I?'

'That would be good.'

I'd taken her hand and squeezed it, noticing the angled edges of her sculpted fingernails. It was eighteen minutes past three. I'd dressed quickly and sprinted to the school. 'How's the decorating going?' Gloria enquired in the playground. 'A bit slowly today,' I'd answered. 'And how's my favourite girl in all the world?'

It was three weeks before I told a soul about Marina. I chose my words with care.

'I'm seeing someone,' I said.

'Aha!' said Kenny and Carlo in perfect unison, nodding to each other and tapping index fingers on the sides of their noses.

'What sort of "seeing" might that be?' Kenny asked lewdly, tilting an ear towards me and wiggling its lobe.

'And what sort of "someone"?' Carlo enquired, gesturing in what he probably thought was a Mediterranean manner. 'Tell me everything. We Italians understand *amore*.'

'Her name's Suzie,' I said. 'She's a beautician from Brixton. I met her in a bar.'

I had to lie, didn't I? You see, there were some complications. There was no problem with Kenny, who was my friend more than Dilys's. He revelled freely in my news. 'Suzie!' he purred, narrowing his eyes and framing strips of imaginary neon in the air. *Making Over Suzie – A Film by John Walters*. I can see it all now.'

It was harder, though, to share such confidences with Carlo. Carlo himself wasn't the problem, but his connections were. He was still married to Jill, the girlfriend he'd moved out of my flat to set up home with. They were happy, and had two children, and I was a friend of Jill as well. Unfortunately, Jill had long been very close to Dilys. In fact, it was through Jill that I'd first met my ex-to-be. Kenny, Carlo and I had thrown an over-the-shop party to celebrate finishing decorating and Jill had brought Dilys along. They had both recently completed their psychology degrees. Where I was concerned, Dilys graduated with full marks.

'Joseph – that's a lovely name.'

'I'll bet you say that to all the boys.'

'Only the nice ones.'

'So why make an exception for me?'

Now I was the one in need of mind-game expertise. I was worried about Carlo feeling torn. Jill was sure to ask him how I was getting on, and he was sure to feel obliged to tell her. Yet he would also know that I wouldn't want Jill to know about Marina because, of course, Jill would feel obliged to pass the news straight on to Dilys. And *I* didn't want Dilys to know too much about the 'someone' I was 'seeing' – whatever that meant – because *she* might tell Gloria, Jed and Billy. I wasn't sure I wanted Gloria to know that I was having it away with her hairdresser. What's more, if anyone was going to tell her or her brothers anything about my sex-life, it was going to be me.

dave hill

My calculation was, of course, that a white lie –
inventing Suzie the beautician from Brixton – would
at least ensure that whatever information might be
imparted to the children by way of Carlo, Jill and Dilys
would at least be safely false. But there was an irony in
this. The person I most wanted to 'tell all' to was Gloria.
She had rapidly become my closest confidante. Even
when playing basketball.

'Gloria.'

'Yes, Daddy?'

'I've got a sort of girlfriend.'

'A girlfriend?' Her face brightened. 'Ooh la-la!'

'Ooh la-la?'

'Ooh la-la!' she said.

We were shooting hoops against the back wall of the
house. She was better at it than I was.

'Come on, then,' she said. 'What's your girlfriend's
name?'

'Suzie.'

'That's a nice name,' she said. 'Does Mummy know?'

So if Carlo had told Jill and Jill had told Dilys, Dilys
hadn't yet told Gloria.

'Do you think Mummy would like to know?' I ventured.

'Mmm. Dunno.' She stood studying the mini-
basketball.

'I think I won't tell Mummy yet,' I said. Then, realising
that I was asking Gloria to do to Dilys what I'd asked
Carlo to do to Jill, I added: 'You can though, if you
want.'

78

'She might feel funny about it,' Gloria said.

'She might. She might not.'

'I'm very happy for you, Daddy. Can I meet her?'

'I don't think so, no. At least not yet.'

She let it pass. Already she was acquiring the diplomat's arts. I felt a need to know how far I could go.

'Do you play basketball at Mummy's Home?'

'Sometimes, yes.'

'Who with? Dilys or Chris?'

'Either, I suppose.' She shrugged, still holding the ball.

'Does it feel funny telling me about what goes on at Mummy's Home?'

She nodded, eyes cast down. I went over and hugged her, sensing a resistance in her shoulders that was usually not there.

'I'm sorry, Gloria darling. I'm sorry. I was wrong.'

chapter 7

Remember how I sat on the settee the other day imagining ringing Dilys to tell her Jed was dead? Knocked flat by a car? Right outside his school?

Well, I snapped out of it. First, I watched ten minutes of *Aerobics Oz Style*. Then I knocked back half an inch of Scotch. And *then* I walked back to the school, fished Jed out of his classroom and got him to sit beside me on the corridor floor.

'Are you all right? That car nearly hit you.'

'No, it didn't. I saw it coming. It slowed down.'

'Are you sure?'

A nod.

'Look at me. Are you sure?'

Another nod.

'Please will you look at me.'

Reluctantly, he turned his face my way.

'I believe you, Jed. It just looked different from where I was. Do you understand? Do you understand why I had to come to see you? Do you understand how frightened it made me feel?'

His eyes drifted towards his classroom door.

'I'm here because it made me think about how terrible I'd feel if that car had knocked you down. Do you know how terrible I'd feel? More terrible than anybody else would. More terrible than *anybody* else.'

He was desperate to get away.

'Please look at me, will you?' Was I being cruel? Cruel to be kind? And, if so, kind to whom? He half-turned and I felt bad as I so often do when Jed tries to block me out and I keep pushing anyhow.

'Have a tissue,' I said as a tear tumbled down towards his chin. 'I always have a pocket full of tissues. Proper daddies do.'

The tears came faster now. Sorry, Jed.

I worry about Jed. Something happened to him. That's really all I know.

His proper name, Gerard, was the middle name of Dilys's late father. Right from the beginning we shortened it to Ged. But when he started at school nursery he began learning letter sounds, and one day he objected to the spelling.

'My name should start with the letter "j",' he announced out of the blue, 'because it sounds like *juh, eh, duh* not *guh, eh, duh.*'

He was getting on for four, a sweet, serious boy, very cuddly, very grave.

'The letter "g" has a *guh* sound,' he expounded, 'like in goldfish.'

'Or like in "awkward git",' I pointed out.

'So my name should start with a *juh*,' he persevered.

'Did your teacher say that?'

'No, Daddy. *I* said it!'

'Sorry, sorry, sorry! *You* said it, Jed. It was definitely you.'

Dilys was there too, sitting beside me in the kitchen, the two of us impersonating family good cheer. The episode entered Jed folklore – why else do you think he's got a giraffe called Geoff? – and he shone so brightly that day. But there was already a dark side. Dilys and I dubbed it his Precision Thing. It could emerge at any time. At meal-times, for instance.

'Daddy! I need some ketchup.'

I leaned across the table, aimed the plastic bottle and squeezed.

'No, no, not *on* the sausages, *next to* the sausages!' Crash! He threw his fork on to the floor.

'Sorry, Jed. I'm sorry, I didn't understand.'

'*Next to* the sausages! I want it *NEXT TO!*'

'All right, Jed. All right, calm down . . .'

'*I SAID NEXT TO THE SAUSAGES, NEXT TO THE SAUSAGES, NEXT TO THE SAUSAGES . . . !*'

'And I said "please will you calm down." '

'*NEXT TO THE SAUSAGES, NEXT TO THE SAUSAGES, NEXT TO THE SAUSAGES . . . !*'

'I'm not going to help you if you shout.'

'*I SAID NEXT TO THE SAUSAGES!*'

'RIGHT! THAT'S IT! THEY'RE GOING IN THE BIN!'

Slam dunk. Goodbye to Jed's din-din.

Something happened to him. Was it that? Maybe, although there are other contenders.

'Daddy, we have to make a telescope.'

'I'm busy, Jed. Be careful, this saucepan is very hot.'

'But Daddy, we *have* to make a telescope.'

'But how, Jed? How?'

'We *have* to, Daddy. We *have* to make one *now*!'

We found an empty toilet roll. We impaled it on the handle of one of my old brushes. We splayed the bristle end out and secured it to a dinner plate with Sellotape, with Blu-tack and with glue. That's how we made a telescope, my biggest boy and me. Then we positioned it *precisely* where Jed wanted it positioned, *precisely* in the middle of the topmost stair from where Jed could peer down from an impregnable position and where Billy later found our magnificent creation and sent it crashing to destruction on the half landing below.

'*Dad-ee! Dad-ee! Billy broke my telescope!*' Jed rolled in fury among the remnants of our father-son achievement. I reacted with dignity.

'*Fucking* telescope! *Fucking* telescope! *Fuck, fuck fuck!*'

Dilys walked in from work.

'What's going on up there? Why are you shouting at him, Joe?'

83

'I'm not shouting. *He's* shouting. I'm raising my voice in controlled exasperation. It's not the same thing.' I was raising my voice in controlled exasperation. Dilys was not impressed by the distinction.

'It sounds like shouting to me.'

I had a pair of floral oven mitts hanging off my shoulder. I had paint on my fingers and, I fear, a wild look in my eye. I said, 'I'll deal with this, Dilys. Why don't you go and hoover something? Do yourself a favour. Calm yourself down.'

'Don't talk to me like that, Joe.'

'OK. I'll talk like this instead. Fuck. Off. Dilys. Leave. Us. Alone.'

Dilys went off and hoovered. Jed cried. I sighed.

Sausage Fury.

Telescope Hell.

Precision Thing.

Why?

Dilys and I had already gone with him to a child therapist – that's why Claudette had jotted in her file. There had been tests, observations, some advice on how to defuse him, but otherwise a clean bill of health. 'He's probably anxious about something,' the therapist had said. 'That's why he's so insistent and particular. He's trying to get things under his control. It might be related to having a new baby brother. And he may simply have a pedantic side to his nature. He might be a perfectionist, and that may actually help him when he's grown up.'

Dilys and I were thankful. Our son might be worried sick but at least no one could say he was defective. Now we could get back to Precision Thing as usual.

'But Daddy, *I* have to put the toothpaste on the brush.'

'Oh Jed, we'll be late for school!'

'*I* have to do it! *You* have to wash it off so *I* can put the toothpaste on!'

'No, I don't! This is crazy!'

'WASH IT OFF *NOW*, DADDY! WASH IT OFF *NOW*!'

I could go on – and on, and on – as I very often did in my own mind both before Dilys ditched me for Chris and after; especially after, and even more especially as I lay awake just after 3 a.m., the time when Jed and Billy made those nocturnal migrations from their own beds into mine.

('Come on in then, one each side . . . Ouch! I've only got two of those, you know.')

They wrapped themselves around me and went quickly back to sleep. But where Billy would roll over and keep himself to himself Jed would cling on like a limpet. I didn't dare move. Plenty of free time then, for me to mull a few things over. Like . . . will he ever forget the day of Sausage Fury? Did my demented loss of patience mark his psyche for life? And as he writhed with rage among the ruins of the telescope, did I seem more or less disturbing for those greasy floral oven mitts hanging off my shoulder? Is their pattern forever imprinted on his subconscious, inexplicably disabling him every time he encounters a similar textile design?

Imagine: the summer frock that scares him; the pillow-case that triggers erectile dysfunction; the tea cosy that reduces him to unexplained despair. Was he the same as before Dilys left or worse?

Ask yourself those questions. Ask them a few hundred million times. Have a dream about a faceless woman in a long white coat coming towards you holding a hypodermic and speaking soothing words.

'There, now, just a little prick.'

'Yes, but I've got a lovely smile.'

Jed had always been a bed-hopper – far worse than Billy who usually only joined his older brother for the ride – and it had never really bothered me before. But as he got older without getting any better and Precision Thing showed no sign of retreating I began more and more often to look into his so-serious face and ask: did I do this to him? Did Dilys? Or should she and I graciously share the credit for our older son's neurotic disposition? I couldn't ever really know the answers to those questions. I felt I had to seek them anyhow.

Children grow so quickly that recollections can dissolve into a blur. But some things stick for ever.

'It's better at Mummy's Home,' Jed said.

Mum and Dad had come to tea. The question 'Cake, anyone?' would not have filled the silence very well. I shattered it instead. 'What's better about Mummy's Home then, Jed?'

'I'm going to have my own bedroom at Mummy's Home,' he said.

'Are you?'

'When I'm older. Mummy says.'

'That'll be nice. What else does Mummy say?'

'Mummy says she's going to have a baby.'

Gloria intervened. 'No, she doesn't.'

'Yes, she does!'

'She isn't going to have one yet. She says she's going to have a baby *one day*. And anyway, Jed, you've hurt Daddy's feelings.'

'I haven't!'

'You have!'

'I HAVEN'T! AND I DON'T CARE!'

He had. Everybody knew it. Even Billy. My dad rushed to my rescue.

'Jed?' he said.

'I'm not talking.'

'Jed, come with me. I've got a secret to tell you.' He offered Jed his hand. Jed thought about it – he liked his grandad. His decision, though, was plain. 'I'm going away,' he said, getting down from the table. He went straight up to his room and slammed the door. I followed him half an hour later.

'What's the matter, Jed?'

'Go away.'

He was lying on his bed behind a barricade of boxes and pillows. Geoff Giraffe lay splayed upon the ground.

'Don't you want to come back down now?'

'No.'

'Oh, come on.'

'Go away.'

'I'm sorry, Jed.' What was I sorry for? Something I didn't understand.

'Go away.'

'I said, I'm sorry.'

Silence.

'Shall I leave you alone now?'

Silence.

'Shall I go away?'

'Yes.'

'Are you sure?'

'Yes.'

'You know I love you, don't you? Honestly. I do.'

'Just go away.'

Jed became more and more the main object of my concern, especially straight after his returns to Daddy's Home. The day at school or, in Billy's case, with Esther provided an effective sterile zone between the different households and made the children's transition back to my care easier. But where Gloria accomplished it with diligence and care – she was a model of fairness to both sides – and Billy, being younger and being Billy, took the whole thing in his stride, Jed had a harder time adjusting.

'It's better at Mummy's Home,' he'd said.

More than once I asked Kenny for his theory – he'd been a boy outsider too. For once in his life, though, he was stuck for a smart reply. 'He's always had that streak in him; that bit of him that's so particular. But it's hard for me to know if he's got worse. The Mummy's Home thing might have just been him trying it on. He's not stupid, is he?'

'Very true.'

'But Joe, I'm just a kind of silly uncle to him. You're his loving daddy. What do I know?'

Anxiety about Jed made me feel more and more alone. I couldn't speak to Gloria because it might have left her loyalties divided. I couldn't speak to Carlo because of Dilys's connections with Jill. I couldn't speak to my parents because they would be still more worried. Marina might have qualified as a dispassionate party, but I couldn't talk to her about it either.

Our relationship had taken on a settled shape by then. When my children were at my place we didn't see each other, and spoke only briefly on the phone. When the children were in Dulwich I saw her three or four days of each week. She never came to my flat. Nor did we go out much together and when we did we stuck strictly to each other's company. At her place, we took turns preparing meals: she cooked, I ordered pizzas. We had companionable sex, after which I usually went home. We agreed that someone else would cut Gloria's hair at Sindy's Salon from now on. We talked about our lives without providing too much detail; the need for this was not discussed but understood. So when I asked her about her son, when thinking about mine, I took a calculated risk.

'Where's Gary's father?'

We were in bed in the dark.

'He's abroad.'

'Where?'

'In Spain.'

'Bank robber, is he?'

Marina laughed. 'No. Electrician.'

'Did he live here? In this house?'

'For a while.'

'Were you married?'

'Strictly speaking we still are.'

'What, are you divorcing?'

'It's still not quite official.'

'What about the boy?'

'He's doing OK. He doesn't see his dad much, but he's always had me.'

'Does he miss his dad?'

'No. You're a bit nosy tonight, aren't you?'

'It's the artistic genius in me.'

'Oh yeah. That must be it.'

Finally, I tried talking to Jed. It happened when he wandered unannounced into my half-redundant studio when I was sorting through some sentimental junk. I was nearly thirty-four. He still wasn't six. I was wondering how much of his old life he remembered.

'Here, Jed,' I said, 'here's one I did of you when you were two.' It was just a pencil sketch, but quite a nice one: Jed sitting in the garden leaning against his mother's side. 'There's you and a bit of Mummy. And look, there's Geoff Giraffe. He wasn't called Geoff then. He'd only just been born.'

Jed took the pad from me and considered it with care. No response.

'What do you think, then?'

Eventually . . . 'Why isn't it painted?' A pause . . . 'It would be better if it was painted.'

'Blimey, two whole sentences in a row.' I meant to say it as a joke but he saw the exasperation behind my phony smile. And that was that. Unnerved by his retreat, I got back to sorting out. Then I stole a glance over my shoulder. He'd already left, leaving the sketchpad on a chair beside the door and me ashamed to find myself relieved that he had gone.

There was nothing for it. I'd have to talk to Dilys.

We met in the same non-romantic wine bar as before Christmas. I soon cut to the chase.

'I'm worried about Jed.'

She thought about that for a moment. 'He seems all right to me.' She threw her hair back off her face. It was longer than I'd ever seen it, a great shimmering drape that reached way down her back. There's a job for her, I thought, advertising Timotei.

'He still does Precision Thing,' I said. 'At least, he does with me.'

Dilys made a puzzled face, which then cleared

91

suddenly. 'Oh, I remember,' she said. 'He does have that fastidious streak.'

I didn't believe she'd forgotten. 'Fastidious?' I said. 'Not obsessive, then?'

'Not in Mummy's Home. Not really.'

'And he's gone very quiet lately,' I continued.

'Has he?'

Dilys was drinking Perrier. I was drinking whisky. But I'd have lost my patience anyway.

'Are you being straight with me, Dilys? This is our child we're discussing. Our funny little boy, the one we used to lose sleep over, both of us, not just me. The one we took for therapy. I don't think he's happy, but I'm not sure why. I don't know how it connects with how things have been between you and me. I don't know if he's only unhappy when he's with me.'

'Don't start shouting at me, Joe.'

'I'm not shouting. I'm being honest with you here. Gloria seems fine, Billy seems fine, but I'm frightened that Jed is getting all torn apart.'

Dilys said nothing.

'How does he get on with Chris?'

'They get on very well.' She shook her hair aside again. It enabled her to look somewhere other than at me.

'Do you think he prefers being with you to being with me?'

'I don't think so, no.'

'When he's at your place, does he say "Daddy says this" or "Daddy says that"? And does it get on your nerves?'

'No, he doesn't say that. Is this about Jed or your wounded ego, Joe?'

'Oh, you psychologists . . .' I reckoned she was rattled. I took a deep breath. 'Does he prefer Chris to me?'

'And what if he did?'

'And what if you answered my question?'

'I've had enough of this.' She got up from her chair and walked away.

chapter 8

Let me tell you more about Billy, nowadays six-and-a-bit
and well on the way to hosting his own chat show. When
this television treat is put before a grateful nation it will
break new ground for the genre: Billy will talk and talk
and talk until his guests all beg for mercy. He's been
practising on me for years.

'Daddy?' he says.

'Yeah?'

'D'you know what?'

'What?'

'You know Beckham, yeah?'

'Yeah. He's the one who cleans our outside toilet.'

'Daddy?'

'Yeah?'

'We haven't got an outside toilet.'

'I know.'

'Daddy?'

'Yeah?'

'You're silly, you are.'

'I know that too. So tell me about Beckham.'
He goes straight into a tune:

> *'David Beckham,*
> *Got no hair,*
> *Puts on ladies' underwear.'*

Reciting this ancient favourite has him hooting with happiness. One day I'm going to take him back to Little Boys R Us and swap him for one with an 'off' switch.

'Billy?'

'Yes, Daddy?'

'Do you ever belt up?'

'No. Give me a piggy back.' He stands before me on tiptoe.

'I'm very old and frail, you know.'

'Please, Daddy, please!'

He's so beautiful. He drives me mad. He's also had me asking myself a big, big question – can this child really be mine?

I began pondering Billy's provenance with greater urgency around the time his repertoire of alter egos was enlarging.

'Daddy?'

'Yes?'

'I'm a puppy dog.'

'You're a puppy dog?'

'Yes, woof woof.'

I blinked. Then I said, 'Would the puppy dog like a biscuit?'

'Daddy,' he replied. 'When I'm a puppy dog I want you to say "woof woof", woof woof.'

'Woof woof, woof woof.'

'No, just one "woof woof", woof woof.'

'Aaah! At the end of every sentence, woof woof?'

'Yes, woof woof.'

'All right, woof woof.'

'Can the puppy dog have the biscuit now, woof woof?'

Well, *excuse* me. Not just a puppy dog, but a puppy dog that speaks about itself in the third person.

'Is the puppy dog suffering from delusions of grandeur?'

'Daddy, you forgot to say "woof woof", woof woof.'

'Sorry, woof woof. It won't happen again . . . woof woof.'

For sure he didn't get *that* from a sardonic soul like me, and Dilys isn't nearly so surreal. How could it be explained?

'He's a one-off, Joe,' my older brother Bradley said as the puppy dog cavorted at my parents' house one Sunday afternoon.

'He's from outer space,' added my younger brother Charlie.

I told him I agreed. I explained that Billy was, in fact, not my child at all, nor the child of Dilys. The truth was that he was conceived by aliens on the distant planet Babble, smuggled to Earth by special pod and implanted in Dilys's womb at dead of night. My brothers liked this theory – we'd had a pretty liquid lunch – so I went on. The aliens, I explained, had long been studying our species and were eager to learn more about humankind's capacity for tolerating endless prattle. It was comforting to know that my suffering was adding to the sum of extra-terrestrial wisdom.

'One day they'll replace you with a robot,' Bradley said. He knew about these things. He was a marketing manager for a toy retail chain. His two sons Jake and Vinny knew about Beyblades before Hasbro did.

'They already have replaced me with a robot,' I replied. 'How else can you explain why I haven't lost my mind?'

'Joking aside, though,' Charlie said, 'he doesn't look much like either of you, does he?'

It had got easier to talk about Dilys by then. Charlie continued, 'I mean, Gloria's just like her mother and Jed has definitely got a bit of you about him. But Billy's, well . . .'

'Entirely his own bizarre creation,' I'd said, 'in every single way.'

I didn't give these exchanges a second thought at the time. But they crept up on me later. How *could* my youngest child's extreme uniqueness be explained? Perhaps the foetal Billy had overheard Dilys and me speaking in a drab, dutiful way through the uterus wall and, constantly a-fidget in his amniotic fluid, decided he was going to be different. Or perhaps, he really *wasn't* the fruit of my own dear loins. He was, after all, conceived at the point in Joseph-Dilys relations when I was mostly trying to avoid her and she was frequently late home from work. We weren't really fighting – we never really fought – just reminding ourselves that we were at our happiest being parents in A Happy Family. Well, it beat kidding ourselves we were in love. Rather than face this awkward fact we agreed that we would like to add to Gloria and Jed, and rutted accordingly, though not very frequently, and with me guiltily wishing that I was somewhere else.

And Dilys? Maybe she'd been secretly wishing that I was some*body* else, a somebody with whom she had already shared her favours at some secret location after all the other relationship counsellors had packed up their dispassion and their understanding faces and pushed off to be thoughtless towards their loved ones at home (just kidding with that last point, by the way). Could it be that the heroic little sperm-in-a-million granted sole access to Dilys's orbiting egg was processed in some other fellow's prostate? Could it have emerged from one of Christopher Pinnock's very own tremendous testes? Could the seed of destiny really have tail-lashed its way through *his* venerable *vas deferens* and surfed up *his* urethra on that white tide of desire?

It seemed pretty unlikely. But, I wondered, how long had her affair with Chris been going on before she told me? I still knew so little about him, but I had found out that he had curly hair. OK, it was dark where Billy's was blonder than Blondie's. It was wiry, though . . .

I began to speculate more frequently. It was a useful way of making myself mental. When Billy was asleep I started studying his face – it was the only chance to do so without it asking a daft question or bursting into song – and scrutinising it for signs of me. His nose? Just possibly. His eyebrow architecture? I couldn't rule it out. Hardly a clear-cut inheritance, though. But so what, I told myself. DNA testing would be surplus to requirements. If he turned out to be the spawn of Santa, Billy would always belong to me.

I mean: the two of us had been through some serious guys-together stuff when he was very young. I found it deeply satisfying that I had been the parent who had persuaded him to say goodbye to pull-ups and step boldly into pants. One of my proudest missions had been to march him down to a kiddy clothes emporium with a clear object in mind. I pounced on the target merchandise and stooped to buggy height, the better to impress its virtues on the prospective wearer.

'Look at these ones, Billy! Teletubbies on the front.'

Billy studied the multi-pack with care. He recognised his tubby chums and smiled.

Back home, Gloria, Jed and I applauded loudly as Billy paraded in his historic purchase. He progressed impressively. Within a week Esther and I agreed that he was day-time dry. My pride in his achievement was almost as great as his was. But not quite. I, after all, did not take it upon myself to stand up in the shopping trolley at the supermarket check-out, solemnly lower my elastic-waisted joggers, smile widely at the woman sitting at the till and announce 'Pants!' at the top of my voice.

The woman gaped, barked a laugh, then looked away. Tinky Winky stood proud and purple, his red handbag swinging boldly at his side.

They say a child's first five years are the most formative. They also say a child remembers almost nothing from before the age of five. I don't know about the first 'they', but I can relate to the second. I don't think Billy really noticed his mother's sudden departure. I don't think he gave a second thought to the onset of his double home rotation situation. I don't think it damaged him not having Mummy always handy. He seemed content that I would do. He's just carried blithely on in his own delightful way, charming the world's socks off, blissfully bending its ear. All that distresses me about him is his absence of distress. Has he turned himself into a nonstop one-boy cabaret as a way of lessening some agony of loss and betrayal? Is he talking, talking, talking only to stop himself from thinking about things he cannot bear?

If so, he's making a fine job of it. Since he was old enough to speak he's been able to conduct a jolly conversation in an empty room. Long before he could construct sentences, abstract mutterings could be heard coming from behind the corner of the living room: that was him and Neil Seal planning an assault on the yukka palm in the corner. Soon, families of catatonic polyester fibre rabbits were being warmly thanked for asking him to tea. A selection of glass animal ornaments found themselves frequently engaged in sympathetic dialogues about the perils of captivity (the dolphins), hibernation (the porcupine), the nuisance caused by mice (the cats), Olympian feats of urination and excretion (the elephants) and the death of Bambi's mother (the deer).

By the time he started at nursery, breaking poor Esther's heart, Billy had developed a wide range of interests. High diving, for example: 'Daddy! Watch me jump into this puddle!'

Recycling: 'Daddy! Look at this bit of rubbish I found!'

Improvised music: 'Daddy! Listen to my bottom go parp parp!'

And then there was his love affair with radical couture. He got into this big time when the school held its summer fête. The children went in fancy dress. Gloria was a witch, Jed was a pirate. And Billy?

'I want to be Snow White.'

There was no deflecting him. He'd already rummaged in Gloria's dressing-up box for the replica frock: that bodice, those puffed sleeves, that plastic wig to top the ensemble off.

'Why Snow White?' I asked.

'She's twirly! She has lipstick too!'

I tried to reason with him: 'Those dwarves, they never lift a finger round the house. You'll be a bored housewife, a drudge, forever darning Grumpy's socks.'

Billy was unimpressed. 'Rabbits like her. And birds.'

Billy's mother picked his name. She was thinking of Just William, evidence of a sentimental streak I used to tell myself was charming but was beginning to admit I had found deeply nauseating all along. Funny, how things change. I concede that my boy and Richmal Crompton's have a certain urchin energy in common. However, I don't think that other guy shared my Billy's passion for cross-dressing. Or cooking. Even as a toddler he was at home in the kitchen. When he was ragged with fatigue at the end of the afternoon, clinging to my hip as I stirred the bolognese was the only thing that calmed him down. Oh, the times we had hanging out over those hot plates! Oh, the deathless dialogue!

Billy: 'Daddy is the cooker!'

Daddy: 'Yes, Daddy is!'

Billy: 'Can I help you, Daddy?'

Daddy: 'Oh, God. Yes, if you must.'

'Helping' me with the cooking gave Billy insights into life that his older siblings lacked, especially after his mother left. On long winter evenings, while Gloria sat marvelling at *Oprah* or *The Naked Chef* and Jed disappeared up to his room, Billy would watch me doing the old loaves and fishes routine. Jesus did it His way. I did it with Tupperware. Several months of penny-pinching had taught me a new respect for food. No plate of baked beans was too congealed to be scraped into an airtight container and warmed up for my lunch the following day; no boiled potato was too old to be hammered into mash and passed off as brand new; no egg was too far past its 'best before' date for me to cook and eat it in the name of the domestic economy. Nothing got thrown out, as Billy sometimes noticed.

'Daddy, this apple is changing to another colour. That's all right for leaves when it's the autumn time, but it's not all right for apples, is it, Daddy?'

'No.'

'Daddy?'

'Yeah?'

'I'm cold.'

I'd got meaner with the central heating. The mortgage had begun to grind me down.

Billy looked at me with wide eyes and an open heart. There were no complications. Although precocious he was too young to feel torn in the way I knew Gloria and Jed did some of the time. The full significance of this hit me one weary evening as he graced my washing-up with his by then customary stream-of-consciousness commentary. Now that he could speak coherently, he also spoke extremely freely.

'Daddy?'

'Yeah?'

'You know what?'

'What?'

'You know Chris?'

'In a manner of speaking.'

'You know what Chris did?'

'He carried off your mummy.'

Billy looked puzzled at this. 'No, he didn't, Daddy.'

'Didn't he?'

'No, he didn't carry off my mummy.'

'Oh.'

'No, he didn't.'

'What did he do then, Billy?'

Billy looked very serious indeed. 'You won't *believe* this, Daddy . . .'

'Probably not,' I smiled. 'Go on.'

'He knows a man, yeah?'

'Spit it out, son, I know you can.'

'Well, this man, yeah?'

'Yeah?'

'He was a hairy man, yeah?'

'Yeah?'

'And he lived in a lake.'

I finished wiping clean the table and sat down. I realised this could be a special moment.

'A hairy man who lived in a lake? Sounds a bit funny.'

'No, Daddy, it isn't funny,' Billy said.

'Speak to me,' I intoned, going all *basso profundo*, 'of this hairy man in the lake.' I was trying for Charlton Heston, but that was lost on Billy.

'He is made of golden,' Billy said.

'Made of golden what?'

'No, no, Daddy. He is made of golden. And he is fierce.'

'He is fierce?'

'He is very fierce.' Billy paused for a moment there and stuck his finger up his nose. He chewed on what he found there for a moment. Then he said: 'That's when he found his iron.'

'His iron?'

'Yes. His iron.'

'You mean his shirts had been all creased?'

'His iron, Daddy. His *iron*.'

'And Chris told you all this.'

Billy nodded: 'It was in the olden days.'

'The olden days, eh?' There was no point pursuing this one. 'The olden days' could mean any date in human history up to and including the day Billy was born. 'Is this a bedtime story?' I asked.

'Yes, Daddy, it is.'

'Does Chris read to you at bedtime?'

'Me and Jed, yes. Lots of times. But it isn't a book story, Daddy. Chris is very clever. He makes it all up.'

I absorbed that little body blow and kissed my sweet boy on the nose. I said, 'You'll have to tell me more things about Chris.'

'Daddy!'

'Yes, Billy?'

'I'm a puppy dog, woof woof.'

'OK, puppy dog. Speak.'

'Daddy, you forgot to say "woof woof", woof woof.'

'Sorry, woof woof.'

'At Mummy's Home, there isn't a puppy dog.'

'No puppy dog at Mummy's? What a shame.'

'At Mummy's Home, the puppy dog's a bear.'

'Oh yeah?'

'A big, scary bear!'

'Why a big, scary bear?'

'Chris says I'm a scary bear. A big, scary bear.'

'Is the scary bear fierce? Like the hairy man who lives in the lake?'

'Yes, woof woof.'

Christopher Pinnock.

Chris the Pillock, more like.

My relationship with Marina ended in mid-summer. She told me it was over the same day that she called the estate agent in.

'I'm going out to Spain,' she explained.

'To see your husband?' A good guess. It was almost like I'd seen it coming.

'Gary's out there now. We all think me and his dad should try again.'

I'd never really figured out Marina. She was a bit older than me and yet she made me feel surprisingly protective: surprisingly, because she fostered an impression of such worldly self-possession. She derided her ripening pear-shape yet saw the increasing fullness of her figure as no reason to not pamper it and clothe it with the best she could afford. She took care of herself, just as she took care of her home. Just as she took care of me. It was she who set the terms on which our affair was conducted, and yet I sensed that she perceived her first womanly duty was to give rather than receive. With a surprisingly old-fashioned maidenly decorum she'd place a restraining hand upon my head if it strayed below her navel, yet would occasionally fellate me with selfless dedication, rinsing directly after with a glass of flavoured water positioned for the purpose in advance.

SEX! SEVEN WICKED WAYS TO MAKE HIM BEG!

Marina had read that feature before I did.

Gary, she revealed, had got a degree in leisure and hotel management. He'd worked hard, and she was proud of him. His first job was out in Malaga and once he'd found his feet there, he'd got in contact with his father after a two-year gap. One thing had led to another. She'd given in her notice at Sindy's. She was catching a flight out the next day.

'I'll miss you,' I said.

'No you won't. Not for long.'

'Keep in touch though, won't you?'

'You just take care of that little girl – and her brothers. You're a decent person, Joe. You'll find someone better than me.'

Better than her? I later tried placing Marina in the montage of my past. She'd always seemed too hard-bitten to have been the hopeful offspring of those frayed white-collar couples who lined the district's residential avenues with net curtains and Ford Sierras, one of those dutiful daughters who dressed just like her mother, got engaged on the same day that she turned twenty-one, got married one year later and bitterly regretted it five years after that. Yet she didn't seem hard enough to be one of those curvy, scary girls I used to be in awe of at my secondary school, the ones who were dating older boys at fourteen, having sex with them at fifteen and, in some celebrated cases, bearing their children at sixteen without a great deal of hope – or desire – to ever again set eyes on the shrugging lurches who had screwed them in the bushes. And yet Marina did seem to have something in common with those girls – the sad conviction that, to win status as women in the circles they were trapped in, they would first have to consent to being used.

Marina kissed me on the cheek. I could have acted hurt and angry, but what would have been the point? I wished her well instead. Then I went back home to be alone.

chapter 9

When was it that I started to unravel?

There is a demon DJ who sometimes jumps into my head. He always picks a track from the same album: *Daddy Loses It – His Greatest Hits*. One popular selection goes like this . . .

The four of us are on the road, off to Brockwell Park. The sun is shining! It's a cheap outing – hurrah!

Billy starts things off: 'Daddy, the car's all dirty.'

Jed joins in: 'Dad, the car's all old. Can we buy a new one?'

Gloria, in the front seat, turns to the boys and makes her contribution: 'You know what our dad always says.'

One verse apiece. Now, the collective chorus:

'We can't afford it.'

'We haven't got the money.'

'You'll have to go without something else.'

Mount Etna gives a warning. She and I differ in that way.

'You horrible, ungrateful, selfish little SHITS!'

My voice flies out of pitch like a spotty adolescent's, my fist thumps the steering wheel. 'SHUT UP! SHUT UP! SHUT UP!'

I veer off down a side street, screech to a halt, climb out and swing the door shut violently with both hands. I turn and kick the bastard Astra, kick it two times, kick it more, then walk across the road and sit down on somebody's wall. A garden gnome observes me as I fume. The little shits. All my sweat and all my tears and all they do is laugh. Now Daddy has erupted. The village is destroyed. Hot ash and lava everywhere. I peer between my fingers and see three worried little faces looking at me through the glass. Just like Sir Elton said, 'Sorry' seems to be the hardest word.

I get back into the car. 'We're going home.'

Silence. Scorched earth. Scars.

One midsummer Sunday Gloria, Jed, Billy and I went round to Carlo and Jill's place – the new place by Croham Hurst they had recently moved into – for lunch and, we grown-ups hoped, a long afternoon of relaxing in the garden in the sun. Carlo and Jill were thriving. His business was in good order. She was moving up the health management scales. Their new house was clean and light. I looked wistfully at the painting I'd done of them and their children Paulo and Emily when they'd lived somewhere much more poky and small.

'Good piece of work,' said Carlo, joining us in the hall.

'Not bad,' I sighed. 'Must be worth all of ninepence now.'

'Oh come on,' Carlo said. 'You're good. We all know that. Even you.'

They were being kind. But I was feeling sad and nervy. When we sat down and ate I was more than usually grateful for my children's good behaviour at the table and more than usually relieved when they scurried off amicably to play. Emily was two years younger than Gloria and worshipped her accordingly. They headed for Emily's bedroom. Paulo was the same age as Jed. They ran down the garden to where there was a climbing frame and a tent. Billy and Neil Seal immersed themselves in conversation. We three grown-ups carried our coffee out to the patio, settled round a wooden picnic table and hoped the peace would last.

'Your children are remarkable,' said Jill.

'In what way?'

'They're so capable. They've done very well.'

I liked Jill. She was obviously better at psychology than her old friend, my ex.

'You've seen them with Dilys too, of course,' I said, 'which in some ways makes you a better judge than I am.'

'I shouldn't think so, Joe,' she said.

Carlo offered me a brandy. I was already full of wine and would be driving back home later, but I was grateful that we'd slipped so easily into the sort of conversation I'd been dreading. Perhaps Carlo and Jill had calculated that if they avoided the whole subject of the split with

Dilys they'd look like they were blanking me, or taking her side. I accepted the brandy.

'So what's he like, then, this Chris guy? You know, I've never laid eyes on him. Not even a photograph.' I looked over at each of them as they looked over at each other.

'Well,' said Jill, 'he seems quite nice.'

'A bit intense,' said Carlo.

'Intense?'

Carlo laughed and glanced at Jill, who failed to join in with his laughter.

'Well . . . he's very into his particular sort of thing. What can I say? His computer thing, his spiritual thing . . .' Carlo laughed again. 'Sorry, Jill,' he pleaded, palms upturned. 'You must admit, he laid it on quite thick.'

I could feel the pair's discomfort. 'Well, he's certainly quite serious,' Jill cautiously allowed, remaining firmly serious herself, 'but I don't think that's a bad thing in a man. So many of them are so juvenile these days.'

'True, very true,' I said. 'And speaking of which, how tall is he?' We could return to the 'spiritual thing' later.

'About average height,' said Jill.

'Is that more average or less average than me?'

'A little less, I suppose.'

'Excellent news. And how old?'

'A little less average than you, Joe,' Carlo said. 'I don't think he's quite thirty yet.'

'OK. Don't rub it in. How old, exactly?'

'I didn't like to ask.'

'How about you, Jill? I bet Dilys has told you.'

Jill hesitated over that one: 'I don't think she *has* told me, actually.'

'Yeah, yeah . . .'

'She hasn't, honestly.'

I raised the stakes a little. 'Is he lightly bearded?'

'Oh Joe, stop it! Actually, he is.'

'Hah! That was a trick question. I already knew the answer. Does he wear desert boots?'

'I didn't look.'

'And I'll bet he showed you his palm pilot.'

'Jesus, man,' said Carlo, turning out his hands in mock amazement, 'you must be psychic!'

'No, he *didn't* show us his palm pilot,' tutted Jill.

'So he has *got* one then,' I said. 'He just didn't show it to you.'

'As it happens, Joe,' said Carlo, reaching into his breast pocket, 'I showed him mine. This one.' He laid the black wafer of techno-foolery on the table.

'*Et tu, Brute,*' I said. 'And does he support Chelsea, like a certain person of Italian extraction I could mention?'

Carlo had been a nominal Blues fan for years. His dormant interest had been reawakened by the latterday influx of 'my people' as he called them into the club. The suits, he said, had come on in leaps and bounds.

'No,' said Jill, smiling now.

'Really? I'm amazed! Who does he support then?'

Carlo answered this time. 'He supports Old Brookham Wanderers. They're an amateur team from

113

Surrey, near where he lived when he was little.'

'Ooh, really nice. I bet they have half-time carrot cake and everything.'

'Hey, hey, hey,' said Carlo, placing a hand on my shoulder, and giving me a glimmer of the heavy eye. 'You're sounding a bit sore.'

And I was feeling sore. It had gradually become a too-familiar feeling.

'I'm sorry. I'll stop being embarrassing now . . .' I looked down the broad strip of garden to where the boys were playing. 'It's just that . . . I'm not some lost soul. I know what I'm doing – or what I'm trying to do. But, you know, I've got a real battle on my hands. Even when they're with Dilys I've still got to look after them. Got to make sure their clothes are cleaned, got to get the food in, got to stop the flat falling apart. I'm treading water, but you can't do that for ever. Eventually, you get too tired and then you drown.'

I didn't mention money: they'd have written me a cheque, and I could not be having that.

Nobody spoke for a while. Then I said, 'What chews me up is I don't know what goes on over there. In Dulwich. What the kids are like when they're with Dilys and Chris. I don't know how she treats them compared with how I do. I get mad at them sometimes. I got mad with them the other week driving to Brockwell Park . . .'

I didn't mention that I lost it so badly we never even got there. I hoped the kids hadn't mentioned it to anyone – Dilys, especially.

'. . . and I don't know what his game is.'

'What do you mean, his game?' Carlo asked the question.

'I'm not sure, really. Is he their stepdad? Is that the deal? What should a stepdad do that's different to what I do? Does he want his own kids? Mine say they think Dilys is going to have another baby, but not yet. And she's still got lots of time. But if that happens, what will it mean for mine?'

My two friends listened politely. Almost impassively. I could hear my voice getting an edge to it again. 'I think Dilys and I ought to discuss some of these things. But she doesn't want to know. And by the way,' I added, anxious to lighten up the tone, 'what is this "spiritual thing"?'

Carlo grinned at Jill. She declined to respond. 'I don't think he's, you know, *weird* or anything, Joe,' said Carlo. 'There's a touch of the Zens about him, that's all. Personal growth, getting in touch with the soul, all that business. You ought to get together. You could go off in the forest and do ju-jitsu in the nude.'

'Great idea, Carlo.' I turned towards his wife. 'What do you think of him, Jill? Is he an attractive man? If you'd been Dilys, would you have fancied him?'

It was as if Jill had been expecting that one. Perhaps Carlo had asked her the same thing. Perhaps she'd asked it of herself.

'I wasn't her, though, Joe. I don't think I can help you there.'

* * *

The first summer holiday under the two homes regime brought my financial failings sharply into focus. Dilys and Chris had booked a fortnight in Provence from the middle of August. I took Gloria, Jed and Billy on the slow train down to Hastings for the day, an improvised picnic in my battered Nike hold-all. Down at the water's edge we settled by a groyne.

'It's smelly here,' said Jed.

'Please be happy, will you? I'm half dead just getting you here.'

The three of them amused themselves throwing pebbles into the sea. I unpacked the picnic: sweaty cheese sandwiches, bruised apples, crushed crisps, melted Safeway Savers chocolate biscuits. I sat in the shade with my legs stretched flat and watched the children eat and play. For the first time since I'd started parenting alone I caught myself contemplating giving in. The unthinkable seemed plausible: that Gloria, Jed and Billy would enjoy better lives if they spent all of them in Dulwich with Dilys and the pillock, Chris. I'd see them, I supposed, every other weekend, like almost every other separated father. I would find that hateful but I glumly speculated that the kids would cope. After all, what would they be missing?

'Daddy, I don't like this picnic,' said Jed.

'No. Neither do I. We could try eating a seagull.' Jed didn't laugh. 'Come on,' I sighed, climbing to my feet. 'Let's go and buy some chips.'

Gloria helped me pack away and we trudged back over the pebbles up to the promenade again. I had a plan to walk into the arty part of Hastings after lunch. Jed, though, only had eyes for the amusement arcades.

'We can't go in there, Jed.'

'Why not?' That level gaze. He had his argument all ready, I could tell.

'Because it's much too crowded and it's throwing money away.'

'But I've got my own money.'

I should have been more patient with him.

'If it was only you and me it might be different, Jed,' I said. 'But it's not.'

'But that's where I want to spend my money.'

'I'm sorry, Jed, we can't.'

'But Daddy . . .'

'No, Jed. The answer's no.'

'But Daddy . . .'

'*For God's sake, Jed! I said the answer's no! No! No! No!*'

Another gem for the demon DJ. He's got quite a collection now.

'*All right, all right, Billy, we'll make a bloody chocolate cake. You just do the washing-up, that's all.*'

'*Earth calling Jed, Earth calling Jed. Come in please, over.*'

'*Gloria, princess, angel, totally top girl. When I look like Charlie Dimmock, can swing an axe like Charlie Dimmock and have as much spare time on my hands, then we'll build some sodding decking in the garden. That OK?*'

'*You horrible, ungrateful, selfish little SHITS!*'

* * *

See those anxious little faces? Hear that car door slam?

The boys fell asleep on the short bus-ride to the little niche of Hastings that is all pretty gift shops and antiques. I switched Jed into the buggy and threw Billy over my shoulder. It made walking exhausting, but it gave Gloria and me a chance to talk.

'You're a painter, aren't you, Daddy?'

'Yes. I ought to do it more.'

'Yes, you should. I like that one on the wall at home.' Then Gloria asked: 'Have you still got a girlfriend, Daddy?'

'No.'

'What happened to Suzie?'

'She went away.'

'Do you miss her?'

'Yes and no.'

The journey back to London was laborious and slow: the inevitable cancellation, the inevitable bus detour. To get home to South Norwood quicker we queued for a taxi from East Croydon station, me fishing out the emergency tenner I had tucked into my sock. I pulled the cab door open, bent down to lift Billy and looked up to see the foot of an unknown adult resting on the running board. She was about my age and about to steal my cab.

'Oi!' I said, hard-eyed. I shoved Billy inside and hustled Jed and Gloria after. Only when I too had climbed into the taxi did I realise the woman had been holding the door open for me. Now she was swapping faces with a friend.

'I'm sorry,' I said weakly, through the window. 'I'm sorry.'

I wasn't certain if she'd heard me. I felt guilty and ashamed. The jolly outing to the seaside had become one of those days and it wasn't until later when I watched over the children as, at last, they slept that a handful of golden oldies crept into my head.

'It's emotion *paint, Daddy.'*

'Golden slumbers kiss your eyes . . .'

'If we do lots of bedtime singing, Mummy will come back sooner from her voyage.'

They don't write them like that any more.

I lay down on my own bed, fully dressed. I felt as if I could sleep for ever. Drifting off, I remembered what Kenny had said more than a year before.

Unattached, good with children, own paintbrush, nice ass. Quite a catch.

Fat chance.

part ii: loving it

chapter 10

I met her when she walked under my ladder.

'That's bad luck, you know,' I told her, looking down. Looking down into her eyes. Looking down at her breasts.

'Not necessarily,' she said, declining to look up. She was inspecting a plug socket above the skirting board, making no effort to conceal that she was checking to see if I'd papered round it neatly.

I flirted too hard in those days. I was badly over-wound.

A widow called Mrs Rose had given me the work and this woman was visiting. She walked in unannounced during the best part of the job. The old paper had been stripped away, the crumbling plaster made good, the liner cut to shape and pasted. And now it was just me, my brushes, my sheepskin roller, my perfect walls – cool, clean and aquamarine – and the delicate white glosswork in progress. Secretly I watched her as she gazed around – unhurried, standing arms folded in the middle of the room. She was quite tall and rather slight. Her skin was fair and faintly freckled, her short hair reddish-brown. She wore a denim jacket over a green semi-see-through top with lots and lots of buttons down the front. Poking from the turn-ups of her khaki trousers were a pair of flat brown brogues, the sort of shoes I might have worn myself. I looked up from the brogues and saw she'd finally decided to look up at me.

'Mrs Rose is very pleased,' she said, her voice bearing a faint trace of somewhere north of Watford. She let the statement fall between us. It might have lain there like a challenge, but something gentler came across. I curbed my usual urge to be facetious.

'That's good,' I said, sounding more grateful than I'd meant to.

'You live nearby, don't you?' she enquired.

'Just a short walk from here, yeah.'

So Mrs Rose and she had been talking about me. My heartbeat shifted up a gear. It was a year since Dilys had gone.

'If I dropped round,' she went on concisely, 'could you show me the charts and photographs you showed to Mrs Rose? I'm looking for someone to do my flat.'

'Sure,' I said. 'Later today?'

'Yes,' she said. 'If that's all right. What time?'

I was still up the ladder. I had a fleeting thought of what a fool I'd feel if I should fall.

'I have my children to collect. Four-thirty, maybe? After that, it's tea-time and confusion.'

'That would be *lovely*,' she said, smiling for the first time.

I liked the way she said 'lovely'.

I clambered down and picked an offcut of lining paper from the floor. On it, I wrote my address – and my telephone number, just in case. I walked across the room and handed the paper to her. As she took it, I noticed that her eyes were perfectly level with mine.

'*Lovely*,' she said again. 'I'll see you later on.'

She turned and left the room with a slightly gawky walk. I stood looking at the door, wondering what it was about her that made me feel so enthralled and yet so calm at the same time.

I left Mrs Rose's at three o'clock, fetched the children, brought them home, and left them to their own devices. Upstairs in the bathroom I got clean, rubbing my fingers with white spirit to dissolve the gloss, then with washing-up liquid to dissolve the white spirit, then with soap to take away the washing-up liquid smell. Then I stripped off my overall and washed under my armpits. I listened hard for signs of sibling squabbles down below.

Standing sideways at the mirror I held my stomach in and caught myself calculating feverishly. 'My flat' meant that she was unattached, or at least semi-detached. Mrs Rose being pleased had to be more than a comment on my decorating skills, it was a sign that she considered I was safe – otherwise this acquaintance of hers, this so-collected woman, wouldn't have invited herself over. I found to my surprise that I had jumped under the shower. I found to my surprise that I was shaving. Mindful of time passing I dashed, dripping, to my bedroom and found a half-clean shirt. The bedside clock informed me it was nearly half past four. I rummaged for fresh underwear, pulled on my favourite jeans, tugged the shirt over my head and heard a ring on the front bell.

Gloria got there first. I lurked up on the stairwell, listening.

'Hello. I'm Gloria.'

'Hello, Gloria, I'm Angela. I'm very pleased to meet you.'

Angela: I hadn't known her name before.

Gloria said, 'Hello, Angela. I'll tell Daddy you're here.'

It was time to announce my presence: 'Hello! Come on up!' Lightly, brightly, sprightly! Totally relaxed!

Angela followed Gloria up the long stairs to the flat. A carpet-style bag hung from her shoulder.

'Hello again. You've met Gloria already, I see.'

'Oh yes. How old are you, Gloria?'

'Guess,' challenged my girl. Cheeky.

'All right then,' said Angela. 'Let me see . . .' We were all together on the landing now. Pursing her lips very slightly, Angela appeared to fall into deep thought. Finally: 'I'd say ten and a half.'

'Nine, actually,' said Gloria, coolly concealing her triumph. 'I won't be ten until next year.'

'Oh!' said Angela, faking surprise. 'I must remember to send you an expensive birthday card.'

Angela could have left it there and turned instead to me, defusing any social awkwardness by discussing Gloria as if she wasn't there.

'Isn't she grown-up?'

'Well, she's quite mature for her age . . .'

'And so beautifully behaved!'

'Not all the time she isn't, ho ho ho!'

Yet Angela knew better. 'Well Gloria,' she resumed, affecting a confiding tone of resignation. 'I suppose I'd better talk to your daddy about wallpaper and paint.'

Mentioning decorating was her first mistake, or so I'd thought. Now she'd never get shot of Gloria who was, after all, already a world expert on interior design.

'You're Angela, is that right?' I asked, leading the way through to the kitchen.

'That's right,' said Gloria before Angela could reply.

'Take a seat,' I said. Gloria pulled a chair back from the kitchen table. As she did so it hit me that I'd long ago stopped noticing how shabby the kitchen was. Angela said, 'Thank you,' and sat down, placing the shoulder bag beside her on the ground. Gloria pounced.

'Have you got any interesting make-up in there?' she asked.

'Oh Gloria,' I groaned, burrowing in a drawer for my decorator portfolio.

'Actually, Gloria, I have. Would you like to see it?'

I'd made my token intervention. I now let Gloria alone. My motives were not noble: I too wanted to know what Angela kept in that bag.

She lifted it up to the table. 'I know,' she said, 'let's get the good stuff out where we can see it properly.'

Deep September rays slanted through the window. I leaned against the worktop and looked on. I had become invisible; excitingly so.

'That's a very tiny eye-pencil,' Gloria said. She knew about eye-pencils from her mother. That and lipstick, which Dilys had always used to great primal effect.

'I've had this one for years,' Angela laughed, regarding the eye-pencil like a long-lost friend. 'I don't think I've used it since I was fifteen.'

'What else have you got?' asked Gloria, peeking.

'This is face cream,' Angela said, 'for when my skin gets tired.'

'Can I have some?' Gloria offered a cheek, but Angela made her laugh by dabbing some on her nose instead.

'And this,' resumed Angela, 'is blusher.'

'What's blusher?'

'It makes your cheeks red. But I don't use it.'

'Why not?'

'Because I don't believe in blushing.'

My daughter snorted in solidarity, then asked, 'Why have you got it, then?'

'It was a present from another girl I know – a bit younger than you.'

'Why did she give it to you?'

'For finding her and her family a home.'

'Is that what you do?'

'Yes.'

'I have two homes, you know.'

If she was surprised by this piece of information, Angela didn't let it show. She replied, 'I'll bet that's good.'

Enthralled by the pocket drama developing before me, I heard the sound of my own breathing as Angela's fingers dipped into the bag again.

'And this is my compact. See, it opens up just like a shell.' She raised the hinged lid part and explained, 'There's the mirror, and there's powder in the bottom half. But I don't use that much either. I just like the case.'

She closed the compact and tapped twice sharply on the shiny chrome with a clean, unvarnished nail. 'That's all the good stuff, I think,' she said.

The good stuff was spread out like items in a memory game. Looking at the bag, I wondered if there was any bad stuff in there too and what it might reveal about its owner. But I said nothing. Then Angela looked up at me and said, 'Yes, we are extremely girlish. But we are not ashamed.'

Gloria giggled. 'Daddy's a bit girlish.'

'Oh, tell me everything!' said Angela.

'He cooks. He does the laundry. He sings.'

'He *sings*?' said Angela.

'All over the house.'

'Extraordinary!'

'And he paints,' Gloria added, glinting at me slyly and letting her voice drop low. The part about the singing was a gross exaggeration. But this was the dirtiest little detail of them all.

'I know about his painting.'

'No, no. *Easel* sort of painting. He has a secret room downstairs. He does it in emotion paint.'

'She means emulsion,' I corrected. 'That is just our little joke. What Gloria says is true, though, I confess. I lead a secret life as a great artist. More secret, as it happens, by the day.'

Gloria flicked a glance at Angela and smirked: as if she, the brilliant sophisticate, hadn't worked out that 'emotion paint' gag centuries ago.

Angela feigned severity. 'I'm sure your daddy paints extremely well.'

'But he cooks extremely badly,' I put in, 'and that reminds me – I ought to turn the oven on.' I plonked my portfolio under Angela's nose. 'Why don't you look through that? We have pizza and baked beans on the menu this evening. If you want to risk it, you're very welcome to stay.'

'Please do,' said Gloria.

'I'd love to,' Angela replied. I didn't think she was just being polite.

What happens is you lose your bearings. You get over-excited, imagine something's happening on the girl

130

front when it's not. You don't realise until much later that you were dicing with disaster: like I did that night with the silly lush Priscilla; like it might have been with Marina if she hadn't marked her boundaries so clearly. Now here was this Angela. We'd only met that afternoon, yet she seemed utterly at home in my home. And me? I felt at ease. Now *that* was a novelty.

'What a wonderful suite,' she said. Gloria had led her into the living room.

'Of what? Furniture or children?'

'Oh, children, of course,' she smiled.

Jed and Geoff Giraffe were burrowed in their armchair in the corner watching Bart Simpson make a monkey of his father.

'You all right, Jed?' I said.

'Hmmm.'

'Educational, is it?'

'Mmmm.'

'I'll take that as a "yes". This is Angela, by the way.'

Jed forced himself to raise a hand.

'Hello Jed,' said Angela. 'Don't let me disturb you.'

I shrugged an apology, but Angela seemed amused. I turned then to my other strapping lad.

'And how are things with you then, Billy boy?'

Billy was on the rug entertaining Neil Seal and an impeccably nuclear Sylvanian Family – Mr and Mrs Non-Specific Rodent and their brood. Billy wore Gloria's pink tutu, Barbie's red lipstick and a gash of green felt pen on each eyelid. His *pliés* were exquisite and his posture, sheer delight. He was a model little dancer, though what Degas would have made of him is difficult to say.

'I'm a princess, Daddy.'

'Yes, yes, you are. And one day you may even be a queen.'

'This is Angela,' said Gloria. 'She's our guest. Say hello.'

'Hello Angela,' said Billy.

'Hello Princess Billy,' Angela said.

We ate the pizza on our knees and spread the colour charts out on the rug, where Gloria and Angela pored over them. I learned about Angela's job with a housing charity – Mrs Rose was a beneficiary – and joked that we could do with some of that round here. I revealed just enough about my work – my *real* work as the man whose mighty brushworks would eventually be hailed across the world – to sound fairly interesting rather than deluded and defeated. Angela listened. Still she didn't flirt. Then Gloria made a decisive move after she and her brothers had shovelled down some ice cream. Safeway Savers ice cream – I dished it up out in the kitchen so Angela couldn't see.

'You will come up and see my bedroom, won't you?' she asked our visitor.

'Of course I will. I've just got time before I go.'

They disappeared and I crooned the boys to sleep. It was nearly dark outside when I crept back down the stairs, and found Angela peering in the fridge.

'Everything all right?' I asked, more quivering than casual now we were alone.

'Yes, she's fast asleep. Is this milk OK? I hope you don't mind if I make myself a cup of tea.' Before I could say anything she turned towards me, holding up a small plastic container. 'What's this in here?'

'It's a very small quantity of leftover skipjack tuna.'

She levered the lid back and sniffed. 'It's disgusting,' she said, wrinkling her nose.

'Actually, it's lunch . . . tomorrow's lunch.'

'You can't eat *this*!'

'But it's skipjack,' I said, struggling to stay afloat.

'Do you even know what skipjack means?' she returned, stepping accusingly towards me.

'Does anyone?' I said, backing away.

'Sit down, will you.'

'Oh . . . all right.'

'Don't cross your legs like that.'

'Why not?' I said, uncrossing them even as I spoke.

'Because I think I want to kiss you and I can't get near enough if you do.' She squatted down and eased my knees apart. Then she reached up and placed the palm of her right hand against my cheek. What I said next surprised me.

'I need a kiss, quite badly.'

'I think you're absolutely right,' Angela said.

I lowered my mouth to hers . . .

'That was *lovely*,' she smiled, looking up. 'I thought it would be, somehow.'

'I like the way you say "lovely".'

'Does it sound funny, the way I say it?'

'That wasn't what I said.'

'No, no, you didn't. I'm sorry.'

'What are you sorry for?'

It was her first moment of awkwardness. I stood up, lifting her by the elbows, conscious once again of our closeness in height. We stood there near and still, her inside my home, me inside the boundary of her personal space.

'*Lovely*,' I said. 'The way you say it sounds so nice.'

She regarded me and said, 'You're a *kind* man, aren't you.'

It was a statement not a question and we might have kissed again, but I'd thought suddenly of Dilys for whom I'd felt so little kindness lately. I half-turned my face away and spoke instead.

'You know, I get even kinder when I'm lying down.'

'You know, I think you probably do.'

We tiptoed together up the stairs. I looked in on Gloria, I looked in on the boys. I knelt in front of Angela as she sat on the bed and watched her watching me as I undid all those buttons. Soon our skin touched under the covers and my head telegraphed 'Yes!' though down in the southern regions the signal was weak. Was it the children being close by? Was it that Angela was too good to be true? I cleared my throat.

'As you can tell, I'm out of practice.'

'Honestly, you're doing fine.'

Her crotch fitted precisely in my palm.

'You're all liquid,' I purred.

'I'm actually quite shy.'

'You're perfect.'

'I'm *not* perfect.'

'I love your cunt.'

'You're so *rude* . . .'

'Should I stop?'

'No, no. Keep holding me that way.'

'I want to tell you that I love you. I shouldn't do that yet, I know.'

'That's all right, you can say it. Say whatever you need to, Joseph Stone.'

'Can I say I have a problem with cunnilingus?'

'Do you?'

'Yes. I just can't get enough of it, you know.'

By midnight I'd convinced her. Then, at 3 a.m. I vaulted lightly to the floor and intercepted Jed and Billy zombie-walking on the landing, for once turning them back to their own beds. I settled them quickly then slipped back under my own duvet where Angela's lips and fingers lay in wait.

'You feel so *big*,' she breathed.

'Don't make me laugh. It'll go back into its shell.'

'Just lie close to me; I want to see your face.'

I lay close, keen to please. I let her gaze right into me.

'I heard you singing earlier,' she murmured as we fell asleep.

'Oh shit,' I murmured back.

* * *

I woke again at six. In the half-light I watched her kneeling up beside me, fastening her bra. 'I wasn't sneaking off,' she whispered. 'I just think I should be gone before the little ones wake up.'

I reached out for her hip as she went on, 'And anyway, I can't go into work dressed the same as yesterday. Everyone will guess what I've been doing.' She paused before adding, 'I don't do this with just anyone, you know.'

I saw her down the long stairs to the front door. We hissed like thieves in the gloom of the grubby hall.

'When will you come back?' I was anxious. There were less complicated men to get involved with. There were more convincing penises as well.

'Tomorrow? On the late side?'

'I'll be here.'

chapter 11

'*What are you doing, Daddy?*'

I was scanning the darkened High Street from the living-room window. It was after 10 p.m.

'I'm searching for truth and beauty in a contaminated world. What else would I be doing, Gloria?'

This was a fantasy conversation. Gloria wasn't really there. I'd said goodbye to her that morning, one of those every other Friday mornings when the children's days at school served as a buffer zone between the end of a week at Daddy's Home and the beginning of a week at Mummy's; between life with the frayed and penny-pinching Joseph Stone and the nearby land of plenty where Chris and Dilys lived – a land I had at first ignored, then envied and now begun to fear as my spirits had subsided with my bank balance in tow.

They'd come down in their usual order shortly after Angela left at dawn: Billy first, shiny-eyed and hungry; Gloria second, washed and dressed already; Jed third, reflective. They were reliably angelic. All three understood that if bad moods disfigured these bye-bye Friday mornings it would sentence me to seven days of gloom. 'Listen,' I would upbraid them when tempers became frayed. 'I look after you. But I need looking after too.' Maybe Gloria had this in mind when she took me to one side.

'Is she your girlfriend?' she'd asked.

'Who?' Behold my crap attempt at ersatz innocence. Put it down to happiness.

'*Angela*, that's who. Is *Angela* your girlfriend?'

Could thirty-five-year-old part-time lone fathers of three have free-and-fancy things like 'girlfriends'? Such circumstances surely demand a different word. How about 'lover'? Hello to you, world. This is Angela, my lover. But could it really be?

Gloria was still waiting for my answer. 'I don't know if she's my girlfriend. What do you think?'

'I don't think she's your girlfriend *yet*. But I think she's *going* to be. I hope so.'

'You do, do you?'

'And you don't, I suppose.'

Things had changed since my day. Back then, children didn't do sarcasm until puberty.

The four of us had walked to school. Gloria had gone in alone. She had started in Year 5 and I'd given her my usual sign-off: 'Gloria, be happy, be kind, be good.'

'Bye, Daddy. Give Angela a kiss from me.' *So* advanced for her age . . .

Then I'd seen Jed into his Year 2 line.

'Jed, be happy, be kind, be good.'

'OK, Daddy. Bye.' Unreadable . . .

Then I'd taken Billy into nursery.

'Billy, be happy, be kind, be good.'

'Hug, Daddy, hug!'

Irrepressible . . .

'Bye, bye, Billy. Come home soon.'

I'd turned away to start my working day assailed by the usual confusion of farewell feelings: on the one hand I would miss them, on the other, solo parenthood is heavy work. And I was bubbling with thoughts of Angela. I'd sat like a sap on Mrs Rose's floorboards reliving our first encounter of the day before. In my head I had rerun the kitchen scene about the 'good stuff' in her bag. Nothing seemed to wipe out her aroma. I'd raised my fingers to my face and breathed her in.

10.17 p.m.

A whole minute had passed since I'd last looked at my watch. My heart was pumping. I had no breath. My mind careered between amorous anticipation and romantic angst in a way it hadn't done since I was twelve. My breath had clouded up the window. I cleared it with my shirt cuff and spoke to the vaporous Gloria again.

'She's gorgeous, isn't she? Although not in a *Baywatch* way.'

'*What's* Baywatch, *Daddy?*'

139

'Before your time, sweet thing. OK, you know Atomic Kitten? Angela's a different sort of gorgeous. Do you see?'

'Yes, I think I do. I hope I'll be tall like her one day.'

'I don't think you will be.'

'I suppose I'll be more like Mummy.'

'To look at, probably.'

'Is Mummy gorgeous in a Baywatch *way?'*

'Sort of. Or used to be. Those days seem so far away . . .'

'Daddy?'

'Hmm?'

'Daddy! Wake up! That's Angela at the door!'

The bell rang a second time and I peered down at the porch. Angela was looking up and waving. I leapt down the long stairs and let her in.

'Sorry, sorry, sorry. I was looking so hard I didn't see you!'

'I could tell. I was about to throw a stone up at the window.'

I scanned her carefully as if to make quite certain it was her. As well as the 'good stuff' bag slung over her shoulder she held a little overnight case in one hand. I squinted at it. She saw.

'I brought some clean things for the morning,' she explained.

'I hope you're not suggesting I'm an easy lay,' I blurted out suavely.

She laughed, and then considered me unhurriedly; appraisingly. She seemed to see through to the disquiet in my face. 'I'm sorry it's so late.'

'Well, I was starting to worry.'

'I hadn't seen Denise for ages. She's a very old friend. You know how it is.'

'I know. Did you have a good time?'

'Very good, thank you. But not as good as I am going to have now.'

We climbed the stairs together and I unplugged the phone; shyness swiftly receding; signals to the south in sharper order. We pushed the bedclothes to one side. No need to hide from one another any more.

Go on: ask me a question. Whatever you want.

Those orgasms she had – anything to do with you, Joe?

As it happens, yes. I won't go into the details, but I think it's fair to say I played my part.

And Joe. Her warm hand on your belly when you woke up in the morning. How did it make you feel?

It made me feel so wanted. She was tucked in close behind me, sleeping serenely. I lay listening to her breathing and longed for her to wake.

You're gushing, Joe. Aren't you embarrassed?

Embarrassed, nuts. You don't despise romantic clichés unless you're too scared to enjoy them. Or if you've never had the chance.

OK, OK. But while we're on the subject, what happened to those strawberries she'd brought in her 'good stuff' bag?

We fed them to each other in the bath. And while we ate, we talked. Sweet talk. Silly talk. Lovers' talk. You had to be there, really. I was. Lucky me.

So . . .

So there we sat, face to face, up to our chests in Safeway Savers bubbles.

'Angela's a good name,' I said. 'A Sixties sort of name.'

'Is it? I'm not much of a swinger. Just a nice girl from Derby.'

'Oh really? So who was that I made love with last night?'

'I'm not sure who she was either.'

'Whoever she was I fancy her like mad.' My name is Stone, Joseph Stone – Sultan of Smooth, Master of Repartee.

'Well,' said Angela, 'when I bump into her again I'll ask if she fancies you too.'

I had my heels hitched round her middle. I pulled her closer. 'Thanks,' I said. 'What can you tell me about her?'

Angela was thirty-three years old. Her second name was Slade. She'd moved south to deepest Croydon to work for the housing charity eight years earlier. She lived in a flat in Broad Green, on her own.

'No bloke, I hope,' I said.

'No bloke.'

'How about an ex-bloke?'

'None I've ever lived with. I have kissed a few frogs, but they turned out not to be princes.'

I felt ridiculously jealous.

'Don't worry,' she went on. 'Some of them were very nice, but not as good at sex as you.'

'Stop reading my mind, will you? We've only just been introduced.'

'I think I should get out,' she said. 'I'm starting to go wrinkly.'

I jumped out in front of her and took a towel down from the peg behind the door. She pulled herself out of the water, and I tried to look at her without seeming to stare. Her body was long and boyish. I clocked the freckles on her shoulders, her toenails painted blue.

'I hope you don't mind Disney merchandise,' I quipped, shivering slightly as I draped the Lion King around her back. I suddenly felt very naked. I wondered how she was feeling about me.

'Nobody's wrapped me in a towel since I was little,' she remarked lightly. 'It comes from having children, I suppose.'

'Sorry. Force of habit.'

'I'm only teasing. It's OK.' She took a pace forward and kissed me deliciously. I was familiar with the theory that men who care for children are irresistible to women. In periods of desperation I'd even tried to make myself believe it. I wasn't desperate now. There was, though, something I needed to know.

'What do you make of them? Gloria? Billy? Jed?'

'I think they're beautiful. They're lovely. You must be very proud.'

'Yes, I suppose I am, though I can't take all the credit.'

143

She fastened the towel above her breastbone and placed one hand on my shoulder. With the other she reached down.

'Tell me I'm not dreaming,' I whispered, hardening helplessly in her hand.

'What do you mean?'

'You're here with me alone. You're grown-up and you're female. All over.'

'You're not dreaming,' she said. 'Let's be grown-ups some more.'

What was I like?

A dog with two dicks.

The cat who got the cream.

I was an animal, you know, a beast. Especially when I got behind that shopping trolley and unleashed myself among the fruit and veg.

'Bananas, Angela? Do you like them large or small?'

'I much prefer a small one. Couldn't you tell?'

'You can go off people, you know.'

'Oh! And you've been *so* charming so far!'

Yes, I was Prince Charming himself, getting ripe with the rude food: the soft round peaches, the sweet cascades of grapes, the blushing mangoes, the fragrant figs . . .

'You've been watching too much *Supermarket Sweep*,' Angela said. She was right. I had been deeply penetrated by the Dale Winton Within. We swanned together down the groaning aisles.

'Cadbury's Creme Egg?' I enquired.

'I don't do that sort of thing.'

'Stop being more smutty than I am,' I complained, tugging her towards me by her trouser belt. 'And another thing. Stop being the same height.'

'You're so masterful, aren't you?'

'It's true. And yet I can be soft and yielding too.'

And a little later on, after we'd packed away my provisions and I was driving Angela and the contents of her carriers over to her place, we fell into a more reflective mood. We climbed to the second floor of her low-rise block and I watched her, longingly, as she fished for her keys in the pocket of her denim jacket and fiddled at the lock.

'You've got the job, by the way,' she told me, flicking through the junk mail on her mat.

'Job?'

'Decorating my flat. Don't tell me you'd forgotten.'

'Don't worry,' I said. 'I've thought of nothing else since Thursday afternoon.'

She led me through to her main room, a kitchen-lounge affair. I quickly warmed to what I saw: paper lampshades, a curling floor rug and a self-assembly bookcase; half-stacked CDs and a compact stereo, bits of a Sunday broadsheet and work-related bundles on a cluttered coffee-table; a noticeboard crowded with reminders and postcards. I'd learned to be wary of homes without children – too many tense encounters amid the just-so furnishings of consumerist couples and supercilious singletons. I felt as comfortable in her home as I did with her. And yet I hovered awkwardly as she put away her shopping. I'd become a poor spectator of domesticity. As if sensing this she said, 'Why don't you look round?'

There were two other rooms, both emanating a solo girlishness that sent a lovely shiver through me. In her bathroom, a goldfish bowl of tampons stood upon the cistern lid while handwashed bras and blouses hanging from a drying rack dispensed occasional drips on to a tea tray resting on the vinyl floor. In her bedroom, I let my fingers walk along an open rail of clothing and resisted a strong urge to peek into her bottom drawer. Guiltily, I scanned the surface of her bedside table for insights into her womanly world. Her bed was a brass double. Above it hung a print of Gustav Klimt's *The Kiss*. It was the bedroom of someone who knew better than I did how to live alone. And I only had to do it half the time.

'What do you think, then?' Her voice came from nearer than I would have anticipated. She'd leaned into the hall to avoid shouting.

'I'll do it,' I said, walking quickly back to join her.

'Why don't you sit there?' she said, indicating an ageing futon. I did as she required, accepting a cup of tea. She placed her own cup on the coffee-table and settled herself beside it, on the edge, facing me.

'It won't be difficult,' I said. 'I couldn't see any damp corners and your plaster isn't crumbling, like mine is –

not so old, you see. All you've got to do is pick your shades.'

She'd taken off her shoes and socks. I wanted to devour her and spoil her.

'That all sounds wonderful,' she said, folding her bare ankles round my calf. 'But first you'd better tell me about Dilys.'

chapter 12

Remember how I used to be? Remember how I filled in my free time? I was the guy whose mind's eye contemplated the mutilated corpses of Gloria, Jed and Billy after the mad axeman had popped by; I was the fellow who didn't know how to disable the crocodile savaging my children as they tried and failed pitifully to scramble up a tree; I was the one always expecting a shattering phone call from Ranch Pillock, USA.

'Hello, Joe. It's Dilys here. Chris and I have run away with those you hold most dear. The weather here is wonderful. Have a nice day now!'

'Tell me about Dilys,' Angela said. She waited.

I scratched my head. Unburdening: discuss.

'What do you want to know?' I hedged.

'Everything you think I ought to.'

'And then?'

'Everything I need to know that you'd rather not tell.'

Angela already knew the basics: about the break-up, the parenting arrangements, the evolving enigma of the unseen Chris. That much I had already been happy to volunteer. Now, though, she was asking to gaze upon my soul. I considered my position, then enquired, 'Do I get to ask a question at some point?'

'About me, you mean?'

'You guessed!'

'Anything,' she said.

'What sort of answers will I get?'

'Truthful ones.'

'I'll bet you say that to all the boys.'

'Actually, I do. And none of them ever realises I'm lying.' Her ankles gripped my calf a bit more tightly. I succumbed.

'I think Dilys decided that what she really wanted was a different kind of man.'

'What kind of man was that?' Angela asked.

I pondered for a moment. 'I can provide a choice of answers to that question.'

'Oh really? Please go on.'

'Well, there are several options from my bitter, twisted range, or madam might prefer something more measured and forgiving.'

'Measured and forgiving has more obvious appeal.'

'Well,' I said, 'it's hard to judge someone you've never even clapped eyes on, but my impression of Chris is that he's terribly earnest, and terribly neat.'

Angela's frown was sweetly disbelieving. 'You're telling me that Dilys left you *and* her three young children *and* the home the two of you had made together because she preferred a man who was more earnest and more neat?'

'That's one way of putting it. Another is to say that she went weak at the knees over a bearded geek midget with a poncey house in Dulwich and great big pot of gold. But that would be bitter and twisted, and we're not interested in that.'

'No,' said Angela, 'we're not.' Her self-possession tickled me. Thrilled me, even. I tried again.

'It wasn't as dramatic as it sounds. She just got sick of me, you see. She used to come in from work and complain about the mess. The first thing she did was hoover the living room. She couldn't settle down until she'd done it. My disorderliness disturbed her deeply.'

'Typical man,' Angela said.

'Who? Me?'

'No. Her.'

'What do you mean?'

'My friend Denise told me her husband is like that. He comes in from the office and the first thing he does is plump up all the cushions. She says it feels like he's rebuking her for not keeping the house tidy enough. It seems there's quite a lot of it about.'

'Ah well,' I shrugged, 'it served me right, loafing around the place all day in my dressing-gown and fluffy slippers with a roll-up hanging off my bottom lip.'

Angela laughed. Then she asked, 'Did you ever cheat on her?'

'No. I suppose I might have, given half a chance. I didn't get out much in those days. Even less than I do now.'

'You're sure she doesn't want you back?'

'Totally.'

'Do you ever wish she did?'

'Not ever.'

'Did you ever hit her?'

'No, though there was some pushing and shoving now and then. She hit *me* a few times, actually, out of sheer frustration. It never hurt, which made her very angry. I don't hold that against her. I deserved to be hit. I deserved it for refusing to be earnest.'

I hoped she'd laugh again, but she looked reflective instead.

'Maybe she thought you didn't take her seriously.'

'Maybe.' I wasn't keen to wander down that path – too many guilty tripwires down there – so I was relieved when Angela led our dialogue elsewhere.

'What does she look like?'

I considered, carefully. 'What Gloria will look like twenty-five years from now.'

'Lucky Dilys . . .'

'Gloria is beautiful, isn't she?' I offered niftily.

'Yes, she is. She's going to be a babe, as the men's magazines say.'

'Stupid word for a woman,' I said. 'Stupid word for a girl.'

'Am I a babe?' Angela asked with a pout, her cheeks

sucked in absurdly, a coquette's hand perched on a waggling hip.

'Oh, definitely, yes.'

'No, I'm not,' she said, with an amused defiance. 'I'm too lanky and about fifteen years too old.'

'We artists see things differently.'

'I bet you say that to all the girls.'

I shrugged. 'You're very, very gorgeous. Trust me.' *Go on. Trust me . . .*

She asked, 'How badly do you hurt?' She said it half-teasingly, as if giving me the option of swatting the question away.

'Because of Dilys leaving?'

'Yes, that's what I meant.'

'I was OK with it at first. Almost relieved, in a way, that all the pretence was over. I've hurt a bit more since. Well, not hurt exactly. A bit bashed up and tired.' I flinched. 'Boring. Let's stop talking about me.'

Angela persisted. 'Do you hate her?'

'No. It isn't hate. Sometimes she annoys me.' It was an honest answer. But there was more I had to say; there were darker passions involved that I knew I'd be a coward to conceal. 'I'm not always very nice, you know,' I said.

'To Dilys?'

'Well, *about* Dilys . . . and Chris.'

'Go on.'

'And sometimes I'm not nice to the children. I don't mean I beat them up, or anything . . .'

'Oh no, no, of course not.'

'But I explode sometimes. I blow my top. I don't think they forget.'

Angela said, gently, 'Do you miss them when they're gone?'

'Yes and no. I think about them. I wonder what their other lives are like. But I'm glad of the extra time – not that I make much use of it. I think I'm a bit weird when I'm on my own. All my systems shut down. I stagnate.'

'It must be hard for you,' she said.

'Not as hard as it is for a lot of people. It's a struggle sometimes but I know what I'm doing.'

'I can see that.'

'Which? The struggling or the knowing-what-I'm-doing?'

'Both.'

I said: 'You seem very comfortable with kids.'

'My older brother Stephen has two,' Angela answered easily. 'I see a lot of them.'

We tossed around some family information. Her father Ralph was a senior secondary school teacher, her mother Blanche a GP. I gave her a brief account of the flat above the shop and everybody else who'd lived there with me. She asked about A Poor Man's Wealth and I recalled its heyday, when Mum and Dad were dedicated to the salvation of domestic objects of quality and distinction.

'Who do you get your artistic genius from?' Angela asked.

153

'I don't know. Dad used to collect big books on art and artists and I loved looking at those. And we had a hip art teacher at school. He got me into the territory I operate in now – figurative, modernist, a bit of age-ing pop. As for my genius, I've a feeling that's dried up.'

'Isn't that one of yours above Jed's favourite armchair? Three children in a living room that looks a lot like yours and a man who's not as good-looking as you?'

'Hmmm. Yes, that's one of mine. It's not too bad.'

'You did that after Dilys left, I expect.'

'Oh yes. My ambition is to be thought of as a tragic figure.'

Angela nodded empathetically. 'I promise to regard you as more pitiful in future.'

'That's awfully decent. Thanks.'

She laughed again (to my relief), then stretched out her arms and legs and sighed. I sat quietly. She said, 'What are you thinking about now?'

'Gustav Klimt,' I replied.

'You mean that picture above my bed?'

'A very famous picture. Very erotic, Klimt.' I suddenly felt flooded and heard the words gush out. 'Angela.'

'Yes?'

'I've really loved these last two days. I've loved being with you. Seeing that picture, thinking of it hanging above you and whoever you might have slept with there makes me feel very anxious.'

'Anxious about what?'

154

I struggled hard to sound light-hearted. 'I don't want to be another frog – like the ones you kissed who didn't turn out to be princes.'

I paused. She looked me over.

'Stay here with me tonight,' she said. 'I don't think I'll be hearing any croaking in the morning.'

chapter 13

I called Dilys on her mobile. 'Hello, Dilys. It's Joe.'

'Yes, Joe. I know.'

'There's something I want to talk over. Could we meet?'

'Oh God. Won't it wait?' Our pre-Christmas conversation was due in a few weeks' time.

'It's quite important,' I said. 'It's about—'

'I think I know what it's about, Joe. Let's leave it until we meet.'

Our telephone relationship was always fairly brittle but I'd never been fobbed off this way before.

'Suit yourself,' I said. 'Anything else helpful to tell me?'

'No,' said Dilys briskly. 'They're all fine.'

It was Friday afternoon, a time when we often spoke. The children were transferring back to me and I was calling from home having wrapped up work early to get the paternal nest in good welcoming order. My employer was understanding – indeed, we'd be ravishing each

other in a shameless manner later and joking that it was
in lieu of my fee – and I would be meeting the children
out of school within the hour.

'Any message for the kids?' I pressed.

'Just send them my love, all right?'

I sat back on the sofa and picked over the bones of
our exchange. It was Angela I'd wanted to discuss. Five
weeks had gone by since she'd walked under my ladder,
and since then my life had changed in many ways. There
was, for example, the carpet of rose petals that formed
beneath my feet every time I walked along the street;
the fabulous rainbows that filled the skies above my
head; the sparrows and robin redbreasts that perched
upon my hands chirping 'You Are the Sunshine of My
Life'. And that was just the dull part. Since our first
night together Angela and I had spent only one apart –
one too many for my liking – and she'd been a regular
presence when Gloria, Jed and Billy had been at Daddy's
Home. And like everything else that moved on South
Norwood High Street this had not slipped under the
radar of Clip-Joint Len.

'Seems like a nice girl . . .'

What drew me to the world's nosiest barber in periods
of powerful emotion? A longing to retreat into a conventional male enclave? An appetite for intellectual tussle?
A deep-seated craving to confess?

'Who seems like a nice girl, Len?'

'Quite tall for a lady, narrow sort of build, attractive
smile . . .'

'OK,' I said, 'I give up. That sounds like someone I know.'

'Tomboy sort of cut. Brown shading to gold. Natural colouring, I'd say . . .' He was asking me if Angela's matched. Cheeky sod.

'As it happens Len, I have a question for you.'

In the mirror I spotted a nerve twitching at the corner of Len's mouth, the nearest he ever came to smiling. 'Please Joseph, go ahead . . .'

'Have you found out her name yet?'

'Well, there you have the better of me . . .'

It was a bitter pill for Len to swallow. I generously freed him from his pain. 'It's Angela.'

'Very nice,' said Len. '*Very* nice . . .'

'Thanks, Len. I'm glad you approve.'

'Any gel for you today . . . ?'

'Just a dab.'

'Pickford's job, perchance . . . ?' The master interrogator had recovered his poise! I stalled, unconvincingly.

'Now let's not get ahead of ourselves here.'

I had a smoother ride from Gloria. But not much.

'She is your girlfriend, Daddy, because she lives with us, doesn't she?'

'Well, sort of.'

Sort of? She ate breakfast and dinner with us and kissed us all goodnight. She had a toothbrush in our bathroom, a coat hanging in our hall and spare underwear stashed in my chest of drawers. In no time she'd taken a special place in each of our lives.

'When I came round that first evening were you hoping that I'd sleep with you?' she'd asked.

Valiantly, I'd understated. 'I suppose so. I was prepared.'

'Prepared?'

'A quick blow-torch of the toenails, a squirt of herbicide up the nose, a little Shake n' Vac under the foreskin. Nothing untoward.'

To Gloria, meanwhile, Angela had become an informal image consultant.

'Angela? Will I be tall, like you?'

'Maybe not quite so tall. You will be beautiful, though.'

'How do you know that?'

'Because your mummy's beautiful.'

'How do you know my mummy's beautiful?'

'Because your daddy told me so.'

To Jed she was a catering assistant of foresight and subtlety. 'Jed, I need your help. Do you like your ketchup next to your sausages or on them?'

'Next to the sausages, please.'

'Just there?' She pointed to a small space on his plate.

'That way a little bit.'

'Between the sausages and the egg?'

'Yes. And not on the mash.'

'How's that?'

'That's it. That's exactly right.'

And finally, to Billy she was a fellow participant in surrealist discourse – notably when he dropped in on us at dead of night as he still occasionally did.

'Hello, Billy,' she said blearily. 'Did you fall out of bed?'

'It wasn't me what did it,' he insisted.

'Who was it, then?'

'It was Mr Push.'

'Mr Push?' said Angela.

'Yes,' said Billy. 'He got in next to me and . . .'

'Let me guess,' she said.

I pretended not to wake. I knew what was coming next.

'Can I get in the middle?'

'Of course you can, Billy. But first you should meet my good friend Mr Pull.'

'Who's Mr Pull?'

'He's Mr Push's brother – and he's magic.'

'Is he *really* magic?'

'Yes. Let's go back to your room and see what magic he can do.'

Yes, Angela was my 'girlfriend' but already much more. Dilys, I suspected, had figured that out too. '*I think I know what it's about, Joe.*'

Which of the kids had told her, I speculated as I tidied up their bedrooms ready for their return. Jed? Unlikely, although with him you never knew. Billy? His alien creators had equipped him with an indiscretion overdrive module. It wasn't hard to imagine the kind of conversation he and his mother might have had.

'*Mummy?*'

'*Yes, Billy?*'

160

'Do you know what?'
'What?'
'You know Angela?'
'No. Who's Angela?'
'The lady in Daddy's bed.'
'I see.'
'Mummy?'
'Yes?'
'You know Mr Push?'
'Mr Push . . . ?'

And what about Gloria? I hoped she hadn't turned informer. For one thing, I didn't want her sharing confidences about me with her mother. More nobly, I was concerned about her feeling torn. A woman Mummy didn't know was sleeping with Daddy and helping her pick out her clothes. Would Mummy be worried? Would Mummy be hurt? I didn't want such questions preying on Gloria's mind.

At 3.15 I headed for the school. In the playground, Lisa and Camille pounced.

'We've heard a secret about you,' said Lisa.

'A secret,' echoed Camille. They exchanged nudge-nudge smiles.

'Oh yeah. What secret's that then?' (Hellcats, both of them. Born to be divorced.)

'Your Billy told us this morning,' Lisa said.

'Come on then, out with it.'

' "My Daddy's got a girlfriend",' chimed Camille. 'That's what he said.'

161

'Did he say it in front of his mother?'

Lisa and Camille made *uh-oh* faces.

'OK, I get the picture. How did his mother look?'

'She's looked happier,' said Lisa.

'If looks could kill,' added Camille.

The bell for home-time rang. One by one the three children emerged. I slung Billy over my shoulder, took Jed by the hand and stooped to peck Gloria on the forehead. As usual, I clandestinely looked each of them over. Everything seemed to be in order: no sign of unauthorised haircuts (coiffures were my territory; Dilys had dentistry) and they wore the same clothes I'd dressed them in the previous Friday morning. We alternated swap-over day clothes every term. I quite liked it when Mummy's Home washed Daddy's Home clothes because they came back smelling of fabric conditioner.

So much for appearances – time to delve beneath them. I laid off Gloria for the time being – I'd be shining my desk lamp in her face a little later – and decided against activating some unmanageable stream-of-consciousness from Billy. That left Jed.

'So, Jed. How's it been at school?'

'Good.'

It was the nearest I would get to a satisfactory answer to a lightly loaded question. The Dulwich area was rife with Toytown prep schools and I'd ascertained from Billy that some of the kids he knew who lived near Mummy's Home were sent to these bizarre and dinky places. I doubted Dilys would be tempted but then she was Dulwich Dilys now.

'Excellent, Jed. How's Mummy?'

'Fine.'

'How's Chris?'

'Fine.'

'And what's the weather been like lately?'

He looked at me witheringly.

'What's the matter?' I asked nervously. 'Lost our sense of humour while we've been away?'

'Ho ho, Daddy,' he replied, looking straight ahead, and not for the first time I reflected that a week was far too long. We trudged the rest of the way home, the children unusually quiet. We had reached the flat before Angela was mentioned. 'Is she coming over tonight?' Gloria asked when the boys were out of earshot.

'Yes. She's bringing fish and chips.'

'Oh, right.'

'Is that OK?'

'Yes.' Gloria was fiddling with her fingers. I reached gently down and stilled them.

'Does Mummy know she's been staying with us?'

'I think so.'

It hurt me, grilling Gloria this way. Violating her neutrality was the ultimate crime.

'Did Mummy say anything about it?'

'Not really.'

'Should I tell her about Angela?'

'I'm not sure. Maybe.'

'Would you like me to?'
'I think so. Yes.'

I wrote Dilys a letter. It took a while getting it right.

> *Dear Dilys,*
>
> *I have recently become romantically connected with Darth Vader, the well-known Jedi Knight. He and I would like to recruit Gloria, Jed and Billy to the Dark Side of the Force so they can enjoy the full benefits of The Empire's boundless power. Feel free to reply with any comments or concerns . . .*

I tried it out on Angela. She responded gravely, 'Since when has the Force been with you, Joe?'

'Only since I started dating Darth. It comes from swallowing his reproductive fluid, I suppose.'

'Oh! You are *so* disgusting!'

'Sorry. It's a guy thing. And he was so *flattered* and so *grateful*, exactly like the manuals all say . . .' I conceded that this approach was not up to the task. I tried a different line.

> *Dear Dilys,*
>
> *After much consideration I've decided to domicile my own personal harem in the shop below the flat. Founding members will include the Spice Girls (excepting Sporty, more's the shame; and not a word to Becks, mind), my old South London flame Naomi Campbell, TV's Xena,*

Warrior Princess, those toned and lissom lovelies on Aerobics Oz Style *and Her Majesty the Queen. The aforementioned females have agreed to settle my outstanding financial debts to you in return for regular and vigorous high-grade sexual servicing. Feel free to reply with any comments or concerns.*

'Where do I fit into this scenario?' Angela asked.

'You'll be upstairs doing the housework and amusing the children,' I explained.

'Being your little slave, you mean?'

'I'm sure that could be arranged.'

'Eunuchs can be arranged for harems too.'

This was going nowhere. I switched tack again.

Dear Dilys,

I want to reassure you that Angela could not be a more helpful or agreeable overnight guest in the little family home you were so anxious to evacuate a year or so ago. She is kind to the children, does the washing-up and has quickly become expert at locating my prostate. Yes! Even in the dark!

('Trust me,' she'd said, probing playfully. 'I'm a doctor's daughter.')

. . . Feel free to reply with any comments or concerns.

Still not right. I persevered.

Dear Dilys,
   Chris the Pillock is a wanker. Feel free to reply with . . .

Even I can detect in this idiotic conduct what Dilys would call a 'coping strategy' at work: phase one, a flight to foolishness; phase two, a drift towards aggression; and finally phase three, in which the emotional nettle is finally grasped. I sat with pad and biro one more time.

Dear Dilys . . .

The two words in combination felt odd and unfamiliar. Again it hit me hard that my former partner had become a remote and rather irritating figure, somebody I'd known a long, long time ago and was unhappily obliged to allow a half share in the raising of my children. As when addressing a stranger I found myself adopting an oddly formal tone.

As the children may have mentioned, I have begun a serious relationship with a woman named Angela. Over the past few weeks Angela has been a regular visitor to the flat and formed warm and affectionate friendships with each of our three children. After careful consideration she and I have decided we would like to live together. I'm hoping you'll have no objection to her moving in . . .

I waffled on for a bit longer, narked at having no choice but to ask for her approval. It wasn't the niceties of home ownership that bugged me (Dilys, remember, was still my co-mortgagee) but the injustice arising from my own grudging belief that Dilys was entitled to run a maternal rule over anyone I wanted to shack up with under my own roof. As far as I could see, I was her equal as a parent by any measure except financial. Yet even I believed that as the mother of my children she had the right to give Angela the once-over, despite neither of us ever thinking that I might be entitled to any kind of veto over Chris. What was more, Angela believed Dilys had that right as well. 'If I were her I'd at least want to meet me. We all ought to meet – the four of us together.'

And so my letter continued.

Angela and I both feel it would be a good idea if we met you and Chris some time before Christmas. That way everyone can get to know each other and we can talk about the future in a constructive way. I look forward to your reply.

Yours faithfully, Joe.

Nice touch, that 'faithfully', I felt.

I met Dilys again in the non-romantic wine bar. It was exactly a year since the first time I'd met her there. The décor made me feel almost nostalgic: same artificial spruce, same artificial reindeer, same seasonal tape loop. Same condom dispenser in the gents' toilet too, though my attitude to that was more robust now. No longer did it goad me with its teasing ribs and ticklers. Instead I'd contemplated it in blissful reverie as I'd stood holding my hands under the drier.

Angela: 'Safe sex is both partners' responsibility, you know.'
Me: 'OK. I'll tear, you unroll.'
And so to Dilys.
'Thanks for your letter,' I said coolly.
Her reply to it had been a classic of Dilys-type directness.

There's no need for a meeting of the sort that you suggest and I'm sure your sleeping arrangements aren't any concern of mine.

I continued: 'I was trying to make a constructive suggestion. It seems a shame that we can't all be more co-operative. For the kids' sake, you know.'

Dilys jumped in smartly: 'I think we're meeting the children's needs perfectly well.'

Which 'we' was that, I wondered. 'We' as in she and I, or 'we' as in she and Golden Geek Boy? I took a sip of wine and inspected her across the varnished table. She seemed different again. There was less make-up and less career woman attire. She looked a little wild and frayed, triggering an obscure memory of Raquel Welch in *One Million Years BC*. 'Is something amusing you, Joe?' she said.

'No, no,' I protested, 'I was just thinking about Billy. Something he said the other day.'

Dilys became a vision of affronted suspicion. 'What did he say?'

'Well, you had to be there really. You know, he's a funny boy.'

'Well,' Dilys said, 'we are rather concerned by the cross-dressing.'

'Oh we are, are we?' I wasn't bothered at all by Billy's fondness for a frock but it seemed to have Pillock Central in a righteous froth.

'Aren't *you*?' Dilys asked. Or was it an accusation?

'Nope. It's a phase loads of boys go through. He likes dressing up, that's all.' I thought about his stories about Chris: *He says I'm a big scary bear; he found a fierce man under the lake.*

'And how are you finding Jed?' I asked, trying to move things on. Dilys sipped a non-sparkling mineral water and shook back her shaggy mane. Him Tarzan, I thought. You Jane.

'He spends too much time in his room,' she pronounced.

'Not at my place,' I lied.

'He ought to be outdoors more, playing with other boys. He's getting to the age of separation. Can't you do more to encourage him?'

The age of separation? What psycho-hokum was

169

that? I decided I would sooner not be told.

'I'm not that worried about him at the moment. He's fit and he's bright and he's got good friends at school.'

He was still coming into my bedroom at night though. And none of those schoolfriends came round to Daddy's Home to play. I wondered if they went round to Mummy's Home but was afraid to ask. Dilys and I were not communicating. We were circling each other like two nervous scorpions, each of us too fearful to chance landing a sting. I felt my mood lurching towards depression.

'Gloria's growing up,' I observed weakly.

'Yes,' Dilys allowed.

'I wonder which of us she'll hate first.'

'Well, that's a cheerful thought,' Dilys replied. 'We'll be working hard to protect her feminine essence. I don't know about you.'

Her *feminine essence*? I'd have to get back to her on that one.

'Listen. Angela is willing to take your place on the mortgage.'

I'd felt edgy about saying Angela's name, as if doing so would make her susceptible to scorn. But Dilys's response was reasonable.

'That sounds sensible. I'll put my solicitor in touch.'

Encouraged, I raced on. 'She has a buyer for her own flat. She'd like to move in soon.'

'All right.'

'And we're going to get married. In February.' I said it looking Dilys in the eye.

'Very nice,' she said.

'Do you mind if Gloria's a bridesmaid?'

Dilys shrugged. 'If that's what she wants.'

We'd been in the bar no more than fifteen minutes. Already we had nothing left to say; or rather nothing we were ready to risk saying. I got up to leave and on an impulse said, 'Dilys, you're not the same.'

I was surprised by her reaction. What I expected, I don't know. But it was definitely not the sudden look of pain that spread across her face and seemed to consign her whole spirit into shade. 'All right, Joe,' she said. 'I know.'

chapter 14

It wasn't really a Pickford's job at all but a self-drive Rent-A-Van affair. Angela had lived light all her adult life and the two of us moved her belongings on our own. In my bedroom – *our* bedroom – she nailed *The Kiss* above the headboard then propped herself against a pillow to contemplate her trunk.

'I'll unpack you,' I announced.

'What shall I do?'

'You watch.'

I lifted out her shoes – four pairs, two brown, two black, all flat – and arranged them neatly on the wardrobe floor.

'Have you ever gone in for heels?' I asked, ever curious.

'No. I'm enough of a beanpole as it is.'

I took out jumpers, T-shirts, blouses, trousers, jackets, jeans and dresses, of which she had just two.

'Pretty isn't it, that blue one?' she remarked.

'Very,' I agreed, mounting it on a hanger. 'Don't let

Billy see it, though.' I reached in a little deeper. Out came a hard, round jewellery case with a glitzy casing. 'Can I be nosy?'

'I'm too tired to stop you.'

These were her special trinkets, more for keeping than for wearing: earrings, bracelets, a brooch that had belonged to her grandmother. I placed the case on top of the chest of drawers and reached into the trunk again. I came up with a pristine white vibrator.

'Oh dear,' said Angela. 'I'd forgotten about that.'

I kissed it wetly on the tip and buried it among her underwear.

'You're *terrible*!' she breathed.

'Be grateful,' I breathed back. 'Some things you just don't get with Russell Crowe.'

In the space of fifteen months I'd been deserted by Dilys, passed up by Priscilla and marooned by Marina. Lacking in confidence, energy and drive I had all but given up being a talented exponent of wry and stylish bespoke domestic portraiture (yes, I've double-checked and that was definitely me) and become instead a semi-desperate painter and decorator whose profits were made more meagre by my burning determination to meet Gloria, Jed and Billy out of school. For all my staying power I'd turned into a man fighting a losing rearguard battle. My boxer shorts had holes in them. My studio was lined with dust. And when my children were with their mother their cuddly toys became intimate friends.

'Geoff Giraffe, I was just wondering. Have you tried new quick-dry wood stain from Ronseal? Are you interested in cheaper car insurance? When did you last check your testicles for lumps? Speak up son, I can't hear you . . .'

But now I'd found Angela and I was mad for her. She was cool-headed and compassionate, captivating and shrewd. To me she was a masterpiece, a jewel. I placed her on a pedestal and unveiled her before selected members of the public. I blazed in reflected glory as they took turns to admire.

'Lovely girl,' whispered my mother as we stacked dishes in her kitchen. It was after the Sunday lunch where she and Dad met Angela for the first time.

'Lovely girl,' hissed my father, taking a jelly from the fridge. It was a Daddy's Home weekend so the children had come too; I was that eager about Angela, that sure.

'Lovely outfit,' mouthed my mother.

'Lovely posture,' undertoned my dad.

This was high praise indeed. All-Streatham Jiving Champions aren't impressed that easily.

Kenny the cake-fancier liked her too. He whispered words to that effect as the three of us meandered at Tate Britain.

'Would she pose for me?' he wondered, eyeing her covetously as she wandered among the Turners. 'I bet she looks fantastic in the nude.'

Kenny had forsaken art for household ceramics, but he liked to keep his brush hand in. As a student his speciality had been depictions of women: big women,

174

small women, sad and solitary women, very happy women with their legs up in the air. The boy had a unique angle on the female condition. He was wasted on crockery.

'You have noticed, haven't you, Kenny, that she is not, in fact, a bloke?'

'I can dream, though, can't I?' he replied.

From each of those near and dear to me I wanted something different. From my parents I required a tacit reassurance that they saw the same good things in Angela as I did. From Kenny I craved a generous stroking of my ego, his endorsement of my engulfing desire. From Gloria, Jed and Billy I hoped for their indulgence as yet another grown-up worked out how to belong in their lives. Christmas focused the issue with a special clarity. The kids began the day in Dulwich and were delivered to us at one o'clock. As ever, I spied the Pillockracer from the upstairs window. As ever, it parked some distance from the door. As ever it was gone by the time I reached the front door to let the children in. This ritual preservation of Chris's anonymity was becoming a festive tradition.

'Daddy and I thought that you should each have a special present just from me,' Angela said. Both of us were nervous, scared that we couldn't compete with Mummy's Home. But the stakes were higher for her. I saw her smile tighten as she rummaged behind our Christmas tree, the first we'd dressed together as a new stepfamily. For each child she'd bought a teddy bear.

Billy's was bright orange. He examined it carefully then asked, 'What's the teddy's name?'

'You choose,' said Angela.

I held my breath. We all did.

'The teddy's called . . . Beautiful Lettuce,' Billy said.

Angela sustained an immaculate straight face. 'Beautiful Lettuce it shall be.'

Jed's bear was yellow. He opened it in silence then sat it in his armchair next to Geoff Giraffe.

'What should yours be called, Jed?' Angela ventured.

'I don't know,' Jed replied.

Expecting this reticence, Angela had scared up a suggestion in advance. 'How about Germaine?'

Jed brightened. 'How do you spell that?' he enquired.

I was relieved to see my sons conform to type – it suggested they were taking Angela's arrival in their stride. Gloria's reaction to her bear – a green one – was equally welcoming, yet different in a significant way. I'd spotted the change coming. When she was five she'd had a bunny rabbit rucksack. She'd recently retrieved it from Billy's dressing-up box and begun wearing it again as an ironic fashion statement. She responded to her bear in the same spirit.

'It's, like, *so cute*,' she enthused. 'It's, like, *really, really cool*. I think I'll call it Brad.'

Nine-and-three-quarters going on nineteen. Gloria's childhood was moving on to a new plane. Her bedroom walls were covered in whales that needed saving. Gareth Gates would be joining them soon. Was this in keeping with the 'feminine essence' Dilys had in mind? Did I know what was going on in Dilys's mind at all? My life had moved on with such lightning speed and big implications for our children, yet Dilys's response was indifference.

In keeping with our whirlwind romance Angela had sold her flat and sunk her profit into my debt. She'd sent a card to Dilys thanking her for making the transfer of shared ownership so easy, but Dilys had not replied. Her delivery of the children halfway through Christmas Day was conducted with the same bloodless efficiency. To me, the lack of sentiment seemed pointed. The same went for Angela. It helped spur our decision to ask Jill and Carlo over during the lull before New Year. I needed their steadfastness. I also needed their co-operation – especially Jill's – in signalling to Dilys what Dilys had declined the chance to find out for herself – that Angela would be a stepmother she didn't need to fight against or fear.

They arrived early one lunchtime. It was a day for firsts: the first time they'd met Angela; the first time Angela and I had received guests as a couple above A Poor Man's Wealth.

'Carlo, Jill. This is Angela.'

They shook hands in the hallway. Paulo and Emily, the Bonali brood, ducked by in search of Gloria, Jed and Billy. Three pairs of eyes performed rapid top-to-toes.

'Angela,' said Carlo. 'There are some things you need to know.'

'Oh?' Angela said.

'About the man you're going to marry.'

'Good things?' Angela asked.

'Strange and disturbing things,' continued Carlo. 'About his wild and sordid youth. About the many squalid secrets of his past. About his dreadful taste in clothes.'

'Shut up, Carlo,' Jill said fondly.

'It's all right, Jill,' said Angela, catching the other woman's eye. 'Better let him get it off his chest.'

Over chocolate Viennetta and lasagne I began to get the hang of turning into someone else. Carlo sweetly embarrassed me with tissues of half-truths about what I was like at college ('a purist, a weirdo, a rising star') and when I came back from France ('swivel-eyed and full of mad ideas'), yet that version of Joseph Stone now seemed a remnant of the past. Carlo steered deftly around my early days with Dilys, a time when he was wooing Jill with an ardour and commitment that had, at the time, been far beyond me. Kenny and I had joshed him for it at the time, yet hindsight made his purposefulness seem noble and mature. While my relationship with Dilys muddled on then died, he and Jill grew into a model happy couple. I had some catching up to do, and I hoped that with Angela I might be able to do it. Later in the day, as we stomped through Crystal Palace Park, I stole a word or two with Jill.

'Do you like her?' I asked.

'Yes. I really do.'

'So do I,' I said. 'I'm putty in her hands.'

'I think she's very brave,' said Jill.

'Why? To get mixed up with a deadbeat like me?'

'You're not a deadbeat, Joe. You've never been one of those.'

'OK. To get hitched to a failed artist with three children?'

'You're not a failed artist, either. You're a good one – remember?'

'Dimly. Do you think the children like her?'

'They obviously like her. Anyone can see.'

We were coming to the lake with the model dinosaurs, a place of pungent memories for me. I asked Jill another question. 'Will you be coming to the wedding?'

'I don't suppose Dilys will try and stop us coming, if that's what you're wondering, Joe.' When I made a gargoyle face, a caricature of bravado, Jill laughed. She said, 'Wedding bells, Joseph Stone. I'd never thought getting married was your style.'

Nor had I, although I don't really know why. I think Carlo had it right when he likened the institution to the zip-up cardigan: sometimes it was something only your grandad got into, other times it seemed the height of style.

'Do you think it's Dilys's style?' I asked out of the blue.

'Oh,' said Jill too quickly, turning her head away. 'I really wouldn't know.'

* * *

179

'I'm getting married tomorrow, Len.'

'So I hear, Joseph . . .'

'You can come to the reception if you like.'

'At your parents' home in Croydon, I understand . . .'

'Your intelligence is impeccable, Len.'

'. . . and then you're off to Venice for a week leaving your three delightful children in the care of George and Lana . . .'

How did he know that? Special Branch?

Len continued, 'You can't beat Venice for romance . . .'

'You're so right. Just one Cornetto.'

'Presumably, Joseph, the, er, timings are in order . . .'

He was nosing about The Curse. I produced my deftest footwork. 'Yes, Len, we've got the taxis booked and everything . . .'

'Very good, Joseph, very good . . .' And those timings were in order. Angela had insisted. She'd said, 'Nice girls don't bleed on their honeymoon.'

My stag night was insightful. You know the dreary old conventions: you down a yard of ale and heave into someone's hat; you are stripped and spanked by three half-naked rent-a-harlots and detained by the police. Forget all that. My boy buddies came up with something vastly more profound.

'*Mauve?*' I gasped. 'You're making me marry in *mauve?*'

Carlo had promised to unveil the suit and it was sumptuous. Perfect for a walk-on in an Austin Powers movie. With my jaw resting on my plate, I watched Carlo make weighing gestures with his hands. 'I gave a lot of thought to apricot, but that is more *my* colour. You've always been a mauver man than me.'

He pulled impassively on a ridiculous cigar. I looked along the restaurant table: Carlo, Kenny, Rothwell, Bradley, Charlie and Angela's big brother Steve all beamed back expectantly. 'So tell me,' I demanded, 'what makes one man mauver than another?'

'Call it a tailor's instinct,' Carlo said. 'And don't forget the added bonus that if you stand very still you can make yourself invisible in your own front room.' My front room is mauve, remember?

'Now try it on, will you,' Carlo continued gruffly. 'I may need to let out the waist.'

I stood up and dropped my trousers. There was a gentlemanly cheer and I became aware of Kenny whispering in my ear.

'Joe?'

'What?'

'I'm homosexual as you know, and you're . . .'

'Lacking in that department.' Carlo handed me my wedding strides. I was naked below the navel except for my pants and socks.

'You're lacking, that is true,' Kenny agreed. 'Well, the thing is . . .' he continued.

'Yes?'

'This is an emotional moment.'

'Yes?'

'We've known each other a long time and I think you ought to know . . .'

I was all attention now. I had one leg in the mauve trousers. The other became frozen in mid-air.

'I think you ought to know that I have never fancied you.'

Carlo had been earwigging. 'Bad luck old son,' he said. 'Looks like you're stuck with sleeping with your wife.'

Kenny, Carlo and me – what a team. We slouched up the Town Hall steps together the next morning, Mr Mauve, Mr Apricot, and Kenny, Mr Turquoise – the gay Reservoir Dogs. We were the pastel musketeers. We were the groom and two best men who befuddled the registrar.

'Erm, *who* is the gentleman getting married?'

A gentleman? Me? With my bastard brood of three?

They stood with their grandparents. Gloria wore a glimmering green skirt and matching jacket. She reached up and kissed me.

'You look very handsome, Daddy.'

'And you look very beautiful.' (And more like her mother every day).

Jed fiddled in his chino pocket. What did he have in there? A stegosaurus? A set of worry beads?

'Jed, are you OK?'

'Yes.'

'You're sure?'

'I'm sure.'

'You won't forget I love you, will you?'

'No.' (Try to get out more, son. Your mother wants you to.)

And finally to Billy, his eyes wide, his face gleaming, his wig not on quite straight.

'Hello, Daddy!'

'Hello. You're looking gorgeous, Snow.' (How proud your mother would be feeling if she could see you now.)

And then the bride, hanging on to the arm of her beaming father. She looked perfect: the jacket, the trousers, the mauve. Wedding days are usually so kitsch. Not ours, though, no sireee.

'You're a picture,' I whispered.

'Who'd want to buy me?' she smiled.

'Call me Saatchi. Name your price.'

Kenny held open the ring box. Carlo handed me the ring. I slipped it on to Angela's finger. Then I said 'I do'.

It rained in Venice. Hunched in Pac-a-macs we bolted between downpours from café to café. We ate outrageous mounds of ice cream as sodden tourists queued along improvised wooden ramps that traversed the flooded San Marco Piazza and converged on the famous church. It was the only way short of swimming to get a gander at the inside of the famed Renaissance pile.

I said to Angela, 'Will they flock from far and wide to look at my interior wall décor in four hundred years' time?'

'For sure,' she replied.

It was a romantic scene. Waiters sloshed between the tables, confirmed in their conviction that the English are insane; a pianist picked out a melody as rogue waters lapped around the legs of his imitation Steinway; we celebrated Angela's thirty-fourth birthday; we thought about the future; we held hands.

'I'd like to get back to the canvas,' I remarked.

'You ought to,' Angela said. 'It's the only way we're going to get rich.'

She was right. With our newly combined incomes we were getting by fine, but people in our lines of business didn't own too many yachts. I envied my big brother Bradley who'd been laid off from his job with the toy company, and had decided to go into business with his wife. Malika was an excellent cook from a catering background in Marrakesh. Armed with Bradley's redundancy money, the two of them were opening a Moroccan restaurant in Stockwell. I could do with some of that entrepreneurial conviction. My little brother Charlie had it too, although his took a, shall we say, more *nebulous* form. After the wedding he'd approached me with a business proposition.

'I may have a nice opening for a man of your abilities,' he'd schmoozed. 'Specialist niches in developing markets overseas. Special order quality artworks, substantial remuneration – *if* you can deliver what the client requires.'

We were ensconced in the nerve centre of Charlie's business empire: his bedroom at Mum and Dad's where he still lived. He claimed to be involved in import-export ventures all round the Pacific Rim. He was twenty-seven years old. He owned one Armani jacket and a mobile phone.

'Don't tell me,' I'd said. 'Pneumatic blondes draped over phallic dragsters; wild horses galloping through ocean spray.'

Charlie had gaped at me in wonder. 'At last I understand why everybody says you're brilliant.' In the attic of his existence he had discovered a Vermeer. I was less enthusiastic. I have this funny thing called pride.

Angela and I chewed all these matters over as we roamed the damp alleys and swollen canals.

'You could give it a try,' Angela said. 'Do a few things for him, see how it works out.'

'A few might be too many,' I replied. 'How big is the Hong Kong market for lissom biker lesbians with bullwhips? How many devotional studies of Manchester United in soft-focus scoring action does a shadowy Malaysian gambling godfather need?'

I had been half-captured, though. I tried to think of it as creative recreation: one's muse may be titillated by crass short-order commissions; one is fruitfully diverted by such trifles; one is kept amused; at around two grand a throw and not too much effort required one can kick a few big lumps out of one's mortgage. I resolved to sort out my studio when we got back home. In the meantime the decision gave Angela and me the chance to dream.

'We could buy a car that starts on winter mornings,' I suggested.

'Good idea,' said Angela. 'Or we could spend some fixing up the home.'

Another good idea: the place had got a little tatty and rundown. What I said next surprised me.

'Or even buy a new home, one with a bit more room.'

Angela was surprised too. She knew all about my emotional investment in A Poor Man's Wealth and Daddy's Home. She gave me a sideways look. 'What do we want a bigger house for?'

'Oh,' I said, 'I dunno.'

Our final night arrived at the right time. In our hotel room we prepared to pleasure one another on the absurd bridal fourposter one last time.

'So Angela,' I said. 'What brand of vile, unnatural practice takes your fancy this time?'

'Let's do it the old-fashioned way,' she said. 'I love the way we fit together. It makes us feel so close.'

Trembling with tenderness I rifled in the bedside cupboard and came up with a condom. 'I'll tear, you unroll.'

'Or maybe not,' she said, tugging me towards her. 'Why wait a minute more?'

chapter 15

'We're going to have a baby.'

'Man, that was fast!'

'I know! It's so exciting!'

'Is it a boy or a girl?'

'Don't know yet. A girl, I hope. I've had enough of boys.'

I heard this through the crack in the bedroom door. Eavesdropping is a sneaky business but it's every parent's duty, especially on big occasions like your daughter's tenth birthday. I strained to overhear what sensational disclosures Gloria was making to Lisa's daughter Jasmine, Camille's daughter Chantelle and the rest of her girl gang. The voices mixed and merged in a hot, hormonal hubbub.

'When my mum had me they had to pull me out with giant tweezers!'

'How can you get a whole baby out through *there*?'

Oh my, things had changed. The first birthday party I'd arranged all on my own had been Gloria's ninth. In some ways that was just business as usual: invitations lovingly written by the birthday girl herself, sausages on sticks, balloons on the front door, and then the stream of little girls bearing little-girl gifts that would be lost, broken or binned within a week. They even played pass the parcel, although they no longer dressed up as fairies or groomed menageries of pastel-coloured ponies.

The kids were not a problem on that day a year ago. It was their parents who worried me. Not Lisa and Camille who both knew me pretty well – my only vague concern with them was that they might be plotting the removal of my trousers. With some of the others, though, my manner accommodated a lurking paranoia.

'Hello! Hello! I'm Joe! As you can see, the girls are having a good time!'

I'd also had to demonstrate my credentials to those of the visiting mothers – it was mostly mothers – whose daughters had been invited to Gloria's *first* ninth birthday party, the one organised by Dilys the preceding weekend. There'd been an outing to a theme park, pony rides, pizza and, tucked into the party bags, the deeds to prime slices of Florida real estate (I wouldn't rule it out). Still, let Dilys do posh and pricey. I could do big and cheap. I was more anxious to establish my standing as my former partner's equal as a parent.

'You see them on alternate weekends, do you, er, Joe?'

'Alternate weeks, actually.'

'Oh. Who looks after them for you?'

'I do. Didn't their mother say?'

Some things you really needed to get straight. Gloria was learning the same thing.

'That was a brilliant party, Daddy.'

'As brilliant as Mummy's?'

'Just as brilliant.'

'Maybe a little bit more brilliant in some small but decisive way?'

She fixed me with those brown eyes, replicas of ones that had fixed me just as firmly in another life. 'Daddy! I said it was *just as* brilliant. OK?'

This was the start of Gloria becoming more cool and funky. Six months or so later I'd taken her, Jasmine and Chantelle swimming. Absentmindedly, following my usual custom, I'd briefly locked myself and my young charges into the family changing room. Jasmine and Chantelle had begun to giggle.

'Daddy,' Gloria had said, 'we don't want to see your bum.'

'You won't be seeing it either,' I shot back, thinking fast. 'Not unless you've bought a ticket in advance.'

Giggle, giggle, giggle.

Bye, bye, bye.

I shuffled off to a cubicle of my own. It was a milestone episode. For gradually, over the following months Gloria embarked on the earliest stages of what I slowly realised was adolescent withdrawal. For the first time I noticed her protecting her privacy against the innocent incursions of her brothers.

'Billy! Jed! I'm getting dressed in here. This is my bedroom. Go away!'

I'd felt it becoming understood between us that certain intimacies had to become things of the past. She leaned against me less often on the old settee. She'd long ago stopped invading my bath. And when antiseptic cream was called for, she dabbed it on herself.

And now Gloria had got to double figures. Her friends traipsed through the front door in their belly tops and flares and headed straight up to her bedroom. Angela and I had given her a portable CD and tape player, and soon the 'groovy chicks' and 'party girls' – that's what it said on their T-shirts – were earnestly gyrating to Blue and Destiny's Child and gabbing indistinguishably in a *sotto voce* frenzy.

'My mum and dad gave me this book about babies when I was five. There was all these cartoons of naked women and men. My friend told me they're *sexing* one another!'

'My mum says it's called bonking!'

'Bonking!'

'Your dad bonked your mum!'

This was a dad-free zone; a boy-free zone too. That didn't bother Jed, who retreated with his sticker books and construction toys, but it disoriented Billy who felt the siren call of pink plastic slingbacks and hairslides with glitter stars. He too, though, was excluded. Only one male person was granted direct exposure to the girl-power frenzy. He strode straight into the fray, sparkling wine in one hand, cup cake in the other – 'Hi, Barbie Girls! I'm Ken!' – but even he didn't last long. The music got suddenly louder, everybody screamed, and Kenny emerged five minutes later with orange fingernails, a feather boa round his neck and a lipstick cupid's bow slapped on one cheek.

'Help,' he announced flatly, eyelids laconically a-flutter.

'What do you look like?' I snickered, rising from my furtive crouch outside the door.

He surveyed his face in the half-landing mirror. 'Like the world's most dangerous queer.'

'Be yourself, I always say.'

'What I say is you've got one wild child there.'

'Blame the parents,' I advised him.

Physically, it's plain that the distaff input dominates Gloria's DNA. Those aren't *my* looks for sure, and her fast-forming figure is, as I've already said, her mother's in miniature. I think, though, I may lay claim to shaping the best bits of her personality: her wit, her determination, her intellectual verve – all those qualities I'd like people to associate with me. What a bitter thing it is that my one-time closest supporter in my single-parent struggle now uses those very same winning characteristics to fill me with misery.

It began around the time Angela stepped from the bathroom holding that slim wand of white plastic, displaying that thin blue line. My wife's pregnancy and my daughter's puberty: these were parallel earthquakes.

'She's fascinated,' Angela said. 'She wants to know *everything*.'

'About what?'

'Sperm. Eggs. Deodorants. Tampons. Bras.'

'I suppose girls do at that age.'

'Yes, but she's so precocious. She's like a teenager already. She's growing up so fast.'

We were sitting in a waiting room that brushed up fading memories of mine: meadow-green vinyl silk and limpid Renoir rowers on the walls; low tables cluttered with vending-machine beakers and leaflets about antenatal classes. To Angela it was a key port on a voyage of discovery, but I had passed this way three times before.

'What do you remember?' Angela asked.

I said, 'I remember that a woman wearing a sweatshirt with an NHS corporate logo will come into this room and call your name – in about two hours from now.'

I was wrong: she arrived in five minutes.

'Are you Angela? Angela Slade?'

'I am.'

'Come on through. I'm Sinead.'

We stepped into the consulting room. Angela and Sinead sat down opposite each other. I knew my place in these proceedings – I sat nicely in the corner and stayed calm.

'So this is your first pregnancy, Angela?'

'Yes.'

'And how are you feeling so far?'

'All right. A bit excited. A bit scared.'

'Any bleeding?'

'No.'

'Any pain?'

'No. Just throwing up all morning, which *is* a pain.'

'And a good, healthy sign,' said Sinead.

I gave Angela an I-told-you-so expression.

'Right,' said Sinead, 'let's do the scan. If you could lie on the couch . . . pull everything down so I can see your tummy.'

Sinead drew a floral curtain, concealing herself and Angela from my view. I had a huge surge of nostalgia. Far from my childbearing days being over I was back in the consultation room again, half seasoned participant, half useless spectator, and delighted to discover that the arcane protocol surrounding female modesty had not changed. Once his expectant partner has *finished* lowering her knickers, the father-to-be is at perfect liberty to see what is revealed. He is not, though, permitted to witness the actual dropping of the drawers. That might be a bit sexy, and we can't be having sex involved in reproduction, can we now?

'You can come in if you like,' called Sinead.

I was already on my feet. There was a squelching noise and Angela went: 'Ooooch!'

'Sorry,' said Sinead. 'It's a bit cold.'

The blue belly jelly: ultrasonic pudding served directly from the tube. Sinead moved the sensor through the goo and looked for a grainy outline on the screen.

Nothing doing. I looked at her, questioningly.

'You often can't see anything this early. I expect it's just the angle of the uterus. I'll do a quick internal to make sure.'

This was new territory for me. With a clingy *splat* Sinead pulled on a rubber glove then tugged a condom down a hand-held probe: 'If you could just bring your knees up . . .'

'Nice way to start the day,' said Angela, doggedly upbeat. Sinead explored in silence. Angela hung on to my hand. I decided I was definitely glad I was a man.

'Everything seems fine,' said Sinead. Angela re-buttoned the jeans she wouldn't be able to button for much longer.

'Are you disappointed?' I asked as we made our exit through the antiseptic corridors.

'About what?'

'That we couldn't see anything?'

'A little. Can you tell?'

Yes, I could tell.

'It'll be much better next time. We'll see its head, its back, its legs. Sometimes they're sucking their thumb. The machine can print the picture out if you want to take one home.'

There had been such pictures of Gloria, Jed and Billy in the womb. Did Dilys have those, or did I?

'Is it weird, being back?' Angela asked.

'Not weird. Better.'

'Why better?'

'Because this time I really, really want to be here.'

'But you wanted the boys, didn't you? You wanted Gloria too.'

'Yes, I did.' And this was true. Although I hadn't asked for Gloria, once I knew that she was brewing I was never going to scarper. 'The difference,' I went on, 'is that I really want you too.'

'Stop it. You'll make me cry.' Too late. I pulled a tissue from my pocket and handed it to her. We leaned into each other for support.

'Will the other children love it?' Angela asked.

'I'm sure they will.' Well, I was sure about Gloria and Billy. With Jed you couldn't be sure about anything at all.

'They aren't going to turn against me, are they?'

'No, they won't. They aren't like that. They really love you, especially Gloria. You said it yourself – she can't leave you alone.'

Angela's face was buried in my neck. Her shoulders shook again, this time with laughter. 'She's an *amazing* girl. Everything she's had to deal with. She's handled it so well.'

'She'll be as tall as her mother before long – although that isn't very tall.'

Angela stood up straight. There were still teardrops on her face. 'It spooks you, doesn't it, that she looks so much like Dilys?'

'Sort of, yes. Well, it's not really how she looks but how she looks at me sometimes. The way she carries herself too.' I shrugged. 'It's inevitable, isn't it?'

We walked on, taking our time. Hospitals may be sterile structures, but emotionally they seethe.

'She and Dilys might get closer as Gloria gets older,' Angela said. 'Will you find that hard?'

'I suppose so. But all those adolescent girl questions – she's bringing them to you.'

'She's probably asking them at Dilys's house too.'

'But she is *so* interested in you.'

'I *am* having a baby, I suppose. That must make me extra fascinating!'

'True. Very true.'

Angela pressed her point home gently. 'What I'm saying is, it won't be long before she really needs her mum. I'm wondering where that's going to leave you.'

I'd blown the dust out of my studio, sorted out my gear and was ready to do my worst for brother Charlie. Commission number one: *Mike Tyson, Hunted Man*. But before flinging myself into creative prostitution I decided to do something that was better for my soul. I asked Gloria to sit for me. To my slight surprise, she agreed. Although she was becoming far more conscious of herself, she had yet to become hopelessly self-conscious: a fine distinction, but good enough for me. Under my rickety lights, she arranged herself comfortably on a kitchen chair.

'Look over at the door,' I said.

She looked. I drew. We said nothing for a while. Then I asked her, 'Are you happy?'

'Yes.'

How easy did that 'yes' sound? How defensive? Hard to say.

'Do you like Angela?'

'Of course I do. I, like, *totally* love her.'

Not much room for misperception there. I sketched a little more: the shoulders straight, the feet tucked under, the hand clasping a bangled wrist.

'Do you think Mummy's happy?'

'I think so, yes.'

'I hope she is,' I said. 'Do you like Chris?'

'Yes.'

'Do Jed and Billy?'

'I think so.'

'Do you want to say anything more about all that?'

'Not really.'

'OK. One last question.' She said nothing. I pressed on. 'Are you glad we're going to have a baby?'

'Yes!'

'How does Mummy feel about it? Do you know?' I'd gone for a casual tone. It failed to convince.

'That's two questions.'

'Sorry. But Mummy knows about it, doesn't she?'

'Daddy, please . . .'

'I don't mind. It's not a secret.' Secrets, secrets, secrets. I held off trying to discover the one that intrigued me most. Why hadn't Dilys and Chris made a baby after being together for all this time? Was it for career reasons? Were they just biding their time? Or were the Pillock's tiny tadpoles struggling to get upstream?

Even if Gloria knew the reason, her mood was not receptive. To lift it I went over and made a small adjustment to her pose.

'Just keep looking at the door. We'll take a break in twenty minutes. You're all right there, are you?'

'Yes . . .' A note of weariness had crept in.

I stroked her hair a little further off her face. 'Is that all right?'

'Yes, that's all right.'

'Hold still now. You'll love it when it stops.'

chapter 16

'Daddy?' said Billy.

'Yes?'

'You know Chris?'

'Not in the Biblical sense, no.'

Billy, Neil Seal and Beautiful Lettuce were tucked up in their bed. They scrutinised me closely.

'Daddy?'

'Yes, Billy?'

'You know Chris?'

Resistance was futile. My puny Earthling powers were no match for the alien seedling. His Endless Repeater Truth Ray bored into my brain.

'Yes, Billy, I know Chris.'

'Daddy?'

'Yes?'

'You won't *believe* this.'

'No, I'm sure I won't.'

'Chris told us about the Rites of Spring.'

Gloria, Jed and Billy had returned that day from a

199

week in Sussex with Dilys and Chris, the first week of the Easter fortnight break. Details from Dilys had been sketchy – a landline phone number in case mobile reception was poor (*for emergencies only*, she'd written). I'd rung it immediately.

'*Hello, Quester's Lodge.*'

'*Hello. What are you, exactly?*'

'*Pardon?*'

'*What are you? A campsite? A hotel? A country club?*'

'*We're more of a sanctuary, really. We call it a spiritual retreat.*'

'*What does it cost to stay there?*'

'*We don't give those details over the phone. But I can send you a brochure if you give me your address. What's the company name?*'

'*Thank you! Bye!*'

I said to Billy, 'Tell me, then, what are the Rites of Spring?'

'About rabbits, bees and things.'

'Anything else?'

'And Daddy?'

'Yes?'

'I like Mary-Kate and Ashley. Isn't it they're not real?'

'Depends what you mean by reality,' I said. I wasn't in the mood for Deep Philosophy. Across the room, Jed was buried in a book about reptiles. I appealed to his seniority.

'Do you know about the Rites of Spring, Jed?'

'Uh-uh,' he said.

'Is that "uh-uh" meaning "no" or "uh-uh" meaning "yes"?'

'Yes.'

'So what did Chris tell you?'

He didn't look up from his book. 'About nature. Flowers. Birds. Trees. About new life. What Easter is really all about.'

I saw pagan rituals in ancient woodland. I saw Dilys reclining naked among bluebells, her modesty protected only by her waterfall of thick ebony hair. I saw Chris in a fluffy suit, shaking floppy ears, shaking a cotton tail, shaking heaven knows what else.

'Wow,' I said. 'Good old Chris. What else did he tell you?'

'That Easter isn't just about Easter eggs,' said Jed.

'True,' I conceded. 'It's about a lot of things – including Jesus, I believe.'

'Uh-uh.'

'But Easter eggs are important, aren't they?'

'Yes!' said Billy.

'Not really,' said Jed.

'Not really?' I said in fake amazement. 'Not *really*? Be careful what you say, boys. The Easter Bunny may be listening.'

The mythic rabbit was my trump card. She was central to what Angela and I had planned for Easter Sunday morning. It was *my* year to provide the orgy of confectionery and I would not stand idly by and see it undermined by some New Age fabrication in which crass consumerism did not feature at all. I'm a stickler for tradition.

Jed, though, took a different view. 'Easter Bunny,' he scoffed. 'Give me a break.'

I looked pleadingly at Geoff Giraffe. I gazed beseechingly at Germaine Bear. Neither rushed to my aid.

'Don't you want an Easter egg, then?'

'No, I don't want a stupid Easter egg.'

'How about a sensible one?'

'Very funny, Daddy. Ha ha.' He put out his bedside light and pulled his covers up over his head. I kissed Billy and left the room in turmoil. Where, I wondered, should I conceal Jed's chocolate Pikachu? Behind a radiator, maybe?

We heard nothing from Dilys until a short letter arrived detailing Pillock Central's summer holiday plans.

Dear Joe,

We will be taking our summer holiday in Kenya this year, leaving on 21 July. We will be staying on a wildlife reserve. I will provide you with details of our accommodation shortly.

Yours sincerely, Dilys.

Terrible thing, envy.

Don't feel bad about me, Dilys, while you, the kids and Chris the Pillock are bigging it up in Africa. Don't get bitten by a mongoose. Don't get eaten by a lion . . .

I entertained these finer feelings while down in my studio, knocking out paintings for young Charlie: a misty rendering of a Formula One Ferrari; a sub-Athena pastiche of a drooling vampette sinking her bloodied fangs into a tumescent choc ice on a stick. 'You'll be happy when the cheques come through,' Charlie had assured me, tapping on the side of his nose. 'Yeah, yeah,' I'd snorted graciously. 'Happy and forever free of credibility.'

And yet for all their aggravations these were fruitful times. I loved my life. I loved my wife. I loved my three children and the prospect of a fourth. My Pillock envy faded as Gloria, Jed and Billy became quite enthusiastic about the no frills holiday package provided for their summer vacation by Daddy's Home. They came back from Africa tanned and tired. They didn't say too much about it and I left it that way. I busked it for a few days while they acclimatised and Angela was still working, taking them to play schemes, farming them out to friends or just messing around with them at home. Then we packed up the ailing Astra and headed off to Angela's parents' house, a welcoming semi on the outskirts of Derby within easy striking distance of the Peaks.

Ralph and Blanche were in residence for the first two nights then headed off to Scotland for their own holiday. Left to our own devices, we explored the surrounding country. We went to a theme park to celebrate Jed's seventh birthday. We wandered in the sunshine. We roamed. Sometimes I took off with the boys to do dangerous things in parks leaving Gloria and Angela to spend girl time alone. It was during one of those times that my daughter made a staggering disclosure. Being a really wicked stepmother Angela wasted no time passing it on.

'Chris is going off to a Manly Men convention.'

'What the fuck is that when it's at home?'

Angela told me all she knew. It would be happening in a forest near San Francisco at the beginning of November over a long weekend. There would be outdoor activities. There would be campfires and tents. It would be deep and spiritual.

I asked, 'Is Dilys going with him?'

'No. Women aren't allowed.'

'Is he taking the boys?'

'No. He's going on his own.'

That was a relief.

'A Manly Men convention. So that's a bunch of blokes all huddled together in Ernest Hemingway T-shirts miles away from home. Sounds a bit unnatural. What will it do for Chris?'

'Apparently,' said Angela, 'it will improve his bush-craft.'

'His *bushcraft*? I thought you just said women aren't allowed.'

Angela threw a cushion at me. We joked and speculated rudely but it all seemed a lot less funny when I woke worrying about it before dawn. I eased out of Angela's arms, checked that Gloria, Jed and Billy were still sleeping and shuffled silently downstairs. I switched on the computer in Ralph and Blanche's study, called up Internet Explorer and searched for 'Manly Men'.

I was rewarded with a long list of gay porn sites. I took a peek at one or two and was interested to discover that in the information age entire careers can be constructed from half a yard of salami and a scowl. I scanned the contorted faces of the writhing hunks. Not a beard between them; not Chris's kind of men at all. I returned to the inventory of the dick worship industry and scrolled down until I found an entry that you couldn't fly a flag from. 'The Brotherhood of Manly Men,' it said, 'announcing Annual Hog Roast Weekend.' I opened up the site. Beneath a 'Manly Men' logo fashioned from strips of bark, a graphic gradually formed. I waited, nervously.

First, two hats appeared: a furry racoon-pelt effort and a white stetson with fur trim. Then, beneath the hats, the heads and facial hair of two middle-aged white men, the first one (large moustache) grinning like a kid who'd found two Muppet figurines in his morning cereal instead of the usual one, the second (small beard) glaring with the joyless fervour of an avenging crusader. Their shirts were square dance tablecloths, their shorts were Army surplus tents, their knees were the colour of bleached maggots. I could form no impression of their calves, ankles or feet, for these were obscured by about a ton of bacon-rashers-in-progress, also known as a big dead pig. Captions disclosed that the men's names were Cash and River. The pig and I did not get introduced.

'Join Us?' asked an icon at the bottom. I clicked.

A picture of a lake formed, overlain with a list of options arranged upon an image of a leaping fish: *brotherly values*; *calendar*; *spiritual sages*; *hog weekend*.

Where should this nightmare begin?

I tried *brotherly values*. Click.

The Brotherhood of Manly Men is dedicated to the recovery and nourishment of True Manhood. The timeless manly virtues have been eroded in our age, sacrificed on the altars of vanity and consumerism. As a consequence, sons do not respect fathers, women have lost respect for men, and many a man no longer respects even himself. Through the Brotherhood, men may rediscover what their forefathers knew, through the struggle with nature, through poetry and music, through the stories that they tell. By seeking the lost spirit and embracing one another, men may yet transcend the false and trivial and get back into their balls . . .

Balls, I mused, being the operative word. I cut to *hog weekend*.

Hog Weekend – workshops, activities, events. *Friday: Arrival followed by nightfall Drumchant Welcome. Beating a hello to the Brotherhood of Braves!*

Gulp.

Saturday: Hog Feast Day. Morning, hunt for herbs and berries. Lunch, mobile window (one hour for those business calls that just won't wait). Afternoon, raft fishing parties and fire-kindling. Evening, poetry and song, roasting and feasting.

Gulp again.

Sunday: Day of Manly Spirits. Morning, dew bath, mud massage, the art of tree homage led by Brother River.

Mantalk Special – Visitor from England Christopher Pinnock shares with us his understanding of the bond between the Earth Father and the boy.

Funny how the threatened mind protects itself. I read these words, yet somehow resisted taking them in. Instead I kept on skipping round the Manly Men site, noting that on the Sunday night Hog Weekenders would be entertained by a man dressed as a sheep called Shaman Phoenix. In *spiritual sages* I discovered that he is usually a realtor called Henry from Wyoming. I also checked to see if Christopher Pinnock was included in this list but found he was not there.

The bond between the Earth Father and the boy . . .

Something was stirring at Pillock Central; something I wasn't sure I liked at all.

Early September. Only two months to go. In Billy, the combination of Angela's spreading belly and his own fifth birthday triggered an unrelenting interest in the early development of the human child.

'Daddy?'

'Yes?'

'What will the new baby eat?'

We were shopping for toys for newborns: fabric butterflies, musical apples, teething rings that juggle plates. Just me and Billy – his treat.

'It won't eat at the beginning. New babies only drink.'

'What will it drink?'

'Angela's milk.'

'Where is Angela's milk?'

'In Angela's bosom.'

'Where is Angela's bosom?'

I looked quickly around. There were seven other people in the lift. 'I'll tell you in a minute.'

'Why, Daddy? Why?'

'Just wait, Billy! Just wait!'

Selfridge's toy department was on the third floor. It felt like the three-hundredth by the time I'd hustled Billy through the sliding doors. I squatted and spoke softly in my pest progeny's ear.

'Angela's bosom means her breasts. You know, those round bits on her chest?' So what was I meant to do? Make melons with my hands? Tug the front of my jumper into a pair of pointy peaks? Thankfully Billy smiled in joyful recognition. He'd always been strongly drawn to those parts of Angela. From her earliest nights beside him she'd been impressed by his ability to find them in his sleep. 'The puppy dog and you have quite a lot in common,' she'd remarked.

I struggled on. 'Well, Billy, her breasts are where Angela will keep the baby's drinks.' I'd hoped to close the subject there. But Billy wasn't finished.

'Did I drink Angela's drinks?'

'No. You drank Mummy's drinks. We didn't know Angela then.'

Billy thought this over. 'Will the new baby drink Mummy's drinks?'

'No.'

You could almost hear the Alien Cognition Unit clanking. 'And Daddy?'

'Yes?'

'You know Chris?'

'In a manner of speaking.'

'Will he be the baby's daddy?'

Holy shit . . .

'If he is it'll be proof Satan exists.'

'Pardon, Daddy?'

'Sorry, Billy. No: the answer's "no".'

'Why?'

'Because I'll be the baby's daddy.'

'Isn't Chris my daddy, then?'

'No, Billy. He's not.'

His eyes held my eyes. My eyes held his.

'Why not?' Billy asked. 'Why isn't Chris my daddy? *You're* my daddy, aren't you?'

'Yes.'

'So why isn't Chris my daddy too?'

'Jesus, Billy. Because he's not, OK?' I died a bit inside when I said that. I kept on dying for days.

Billy put a finger to his chin to help him think. 'But Daddy . . .'

Surely, I told myself, the mother ship would soon return. After all, it came back for ET.

'Billy?' I interrupted.

'Yes, Daddy?'

'Would you like to be a baby?'

'Yes, ga-ga.'

'Would the baby like a drink?'

'Yes, ga-ga. A drink of Coke, ga-ga.'

'Anything for my baby. Anything at all.'

October ushered in the final countdown: my talk turned to cots and midwives, my thoughts turned to vomit epaulettes. I went to a football match with Kenny, dragging Jed along for the ride. The new season was proceeding in the great Crystal Palace tradition: long periods of mediocrity enlivened by crises and false dawns. Jed packed a little lunchbox for half-time. For him, cutting the sandwiches to fit the box precisely was the best part of the day. He wasn't big on football, but I felt it was important for his social education that he saw real live fanatics working themselves into a frenzy at close range. Such a creature was near us throughout the first half.

'Wanker referee! Wanker!'

I tapped him on his shoulder. 'Mind the language, will you, mate? There's a little kid down here.'

He turned to me with feeling. 'Why is it you can't stand to see me happy?' Kenny loved it at Selhurst Park. It gratified his taste for comic pathos. 'Yellow card, bollocks! You bollocks, referee!'

The half-time whistle blew. Kenny collapsed into his seat, a steaming heap of umbrage. Jed had fallen asleep.

'Kenny,' I said, 'would you like a Bakewell tart?'

He looked at Jed's lunchbox hopefully. 'He's got a Bakewell tart in there?'

'Yes. But first I have a question.'

'Shoot.'

'Have you heard of the Brotherhood of Manly Men?'

'You're joking,' he said.

'I would never joke about a thing like that.'

Kenny frowned. He said, 'Are they the ones that strip each other naked, grope each other blindfold, sit in a circle jerking off and insist that they're not gay?'

'It doesn't say so on their website.'

'You surprise me. Why do you ask?'

'There's some event near San Francisco. The Pillock's going to it.'

Kenny looked concerned. 'How about the Tracy brothers?'

'Who?'

'The *Thunderbird* puppets. Will they be there? *They're* all gay, you know – Scott, Virgil, little Gordon. Their dad is in despair.'

'They're not all gay,' I countered. 'Alan's always got the lovely Tintin on his arm.'

'A fag hag,' Kenny snorted. 'Anyone can tell. It's a dog's life for those boys stuck out there on Tracy Island. They're oceans away from an Abercrombie and Fitch and there's no disco for miles. Imagine being John – up

211

there in that satellite twenty-four hours a day with nothing for company but a box of mansize tissues and a pocket solitaire . . .'

'Listen, Kenny,' I said. 'He's billed to give a talk at this Manly Men brotherhood convention about Earth Fathers and spiritual bonding between men and boys – or something. The daft bastard seems to thinks he's everybody's daddy, including my two boys'.'

Kenny finally caught on that I was not messing around.

'When I get home I'll check this website and ask Rothwell to look too. He may know more about it. He's spent a bit of time in San Francisco.'

'Thanks, Kenny. You're a pal.'

'And so are you, Joe. Even though I think you're lying about the Bakewell tart.'

chapter 17

Here are some things that I don't do:

I don't do: Miracle of Birth.

I don't do: Breathe, Darling, Breathe, Let's Push Together Now.

I don't do: Guys, That Was, Like, The Most *Amazing* Experience of my Life.

Here are some things that I do do:

I do: Please Let This Be Over.

I do: That Baby's Going To Die.

I do: That Woman's Going To Die.

I do: I Am Going To Pass Out And Then *I* Am Going To Die.

Angela was good about it, though. 'Don't worry,' she said. 'You're not George Clooney.'

I said, 'Don't you mean George Clooney isn't me?' We were in bed, anticipating. Her due date was upon us and we were prepared.

'Cosimo?' offered Angela. 'Crichton? Crispin? Curt?'

'Horatia?' I countered. 'Hortense? Huldah? Hyacinth?'

We didn't even know the baby's sex. Its parents being decent folk, it kept its legs together during scans.

'Vanda?' she recited. 'Valetta? Vashti? Veronique?'

'Milton?' I droned sleepily. 'Merrill? Mungo? Merv?'

There were name books in our bedroom, by the toilet and in the car. There were lists of contender monikers magnetised to the fridge. We'd had help from everybody, including all the kids.

'Trogsoozle,' shouted Billy.

'Gerry,' said Jed. (Or 'Jerry'? We didn't ask.)

'I like Lucretia,' announced Gloria.

'Lucretia?' I said. 'Why not Cruella or Morticia?'

'Not funny, Dad,' said Gloria.

'Not funny, Joe,' Angela agreed as Gloria walked crossly from the room.

Not funny, I agree.

Later on, in bed, Angela sat next to me, bare-chested. Sheila Kitzinger was propped up on her bump. 'Did you know,' she said, 'that I am going to open up like a flower? Or that my breasts will engorge with milk? Not fill with milk – *engorge*.'

'As it happens, yes. I heard the boys discussing it the other day.'

They'd been perched on the settee, talking intently.

'The baby will drink its milk from Angela's nibbles,' Billy had explained.

'Nipples,' Jed had said. 'Not *nibbles*, idiot.'

'Daddy said they were nibbles.'

'Then Daddy's an idiot, too.'

I turned to her and said, 'We could try hurrying you up. Let me wipe a rosehip teabag round the lips of your vagina. My Great-Aunt Melba swore by it, you know.'

'It's a lovely idea, Joe, but we've only got PG Tips.'

'Or there's semen on the cervix. That often does the trick.'

'Don't even think about it.'

'Honestly, a midwife told me.'

'When?'

'Just after we'd had sex.'

She said, 'Joe, stop being silly. Be real. Be real for me.'

I made a mental note: *reality – keep in touch.*

The night passed without contractions. The following evening was Bonfire Night. We celebrated it at Carlo and Jill's.

'I feel enormous,' Angela groaned.

'You look beautiful,' I said. I stood behind her with my arms reaching around. At the far end of the garden, Carlo read by torchlight.

'Vesuvian Lava,' he announced.

'A relative of yours?' I asked.

Wearing a cashmere overcoat, a silk scarf and trilby, he bent to dig the firework into a tray of dirt, took a glowing safety spill from between his teeth and bent to light the fuse. 'Stand well back,' he growled. I counted up the children: Billy, Gloria, Emily, Paulo . . .

'Jed!' called Angela anxiously. 'Jed, don't go too close!'

He'd emerged suddenly into the lamplight from behind a rhododendron, out of Carlo's view. 'I'm all right,' he complained, his breath turning to vapour as he spoke.

'I think he's OK there,' I said. 'And Jill's got her eye on him.'

Carlo retreated and stood by his wife's side. The firework erupted in cascades of orange sparks. All the children cheered.

Angela tutted to herself: 'I'm being too anxious, aren't I?'

'Well, it's an anxious time.'

I was making a poor job of supporting her aching back. We could have stayed at home but it was nice to be asked round. I left Angela for a moment and stepped over to Jill.

'How are things in darkest Dulwich? Anything deep and meaningful going on up there?'

The Hog Weekend was upon us. I'd been thinking of Chris packing his bags. What would he need for such an adventure? Swiss Army knife? Solar-powered laptop? A spare scrotum or two?

'Deep and meaningful?' Jill replied. 'What makes you think so?'

'Oh, this and that. Tales of transatlantic travel. Rumours of strange rituals in the woods . . .'

'Stop pumping me for information, Joe.' Jill changed the subject sharply. 'I'm going to get a drink for your poor pregnant lady.' She called over to Angela. 'Tea? Mulled wine? Or will your bladder stand a beer?'

Not beer. By that stage poor Angela peed even if she sneezed. She accepted a small brandy and moved closer to the fire. Before re-joining her I tried a different line with Jill – a straighter one.

'Look, Jill, I realise I'm out of order, but I would like to know that Dilys is, you know, OK. About our baby, and everything.'

Jill frowned at me. I tried to appear sincere.

'Well,' she said, 'it's bound to make her feel a bit strange, isn't it?'

'Why?'

'Well, if I was in her position I expect I'd be giving some thought to what it all means: you having another kid and how that might affect the other children.' Her eyebrows made an 'obviously, Joe' expression.

'Or even make you wish that *you* were the one with the bun in the oven?' I probed some more.

There was a finality about Jill's heavy exhalation. 'Come on now, Joe. There are some things we ladies don't discuss with the weaker sex.'

'Aaaw. I can pair socks, you know.'

'So?'

'And I'm worried that my usual washing powder causes bobbling . . .'

'Sorry, Joe. You'll have to have it chopped off if you want to be a sister. Come on, let's join the others outside.'

It was cold in the garden, but dry. The quiet of the neighbourhood made a striking contrast with South Norwood and gave me a tinge of impatience and regret: why hadn't I done as well for my family as Carlo and Jill had done for theirs?

The fire burned brightly in an aluminium incinerator. Carlo reached into the box of fireworks again. 'Astral Sparks,' he boomed, striding once more towards the dirt tray, about three grand's-worth of coat-tail swishing in his wake. If the man inspected sewers he'd do it in Hugo Boss.

'Astral,' I said to Angela as the fountain of sparks flew. 'That's a nice name for a girl.'

'Do you want a go at this, Joe?' Carlo called over, holding the safety spill in a questioning way.

'I wouldn't want to spoil your fun. And anyway, I'm too mauve.'

As Astral Sparks subsided, Carlo pointed his torch downwards again. 'Stellar Flame,' he announced.

I spoke enquiringly to Angela again. 'What about Stella?'

'Don't make me laugh,' she begged. 'I'll wet myself, you know.'

'Or Ella,' I continued. 'Or Estelle – in honour of Esther. Or Esmond for a boy . . .'

The Stellar Flame burned brightly, the light casting a glow on to the faces of the children.

'It will all be all right, won't it?' Angela asked, squeezing my hands.

'It will. I'm sure it will.'

* * *

'Do you know the maternity suite?' the receptionist asked.

'No.'

'Yes.'

The first answer was Angela's, the second, mine. We'd have both laughed out loud, but for the danger of releasing waves of amniotic fluid all over the floor.

'Oh God, here comes another one. Ohhhh . . . !'

Crouching painfully, Angela held on to the desk. A hospital volunteer helped her into a wheelchair. For days we'd hung around waiting, and now we'd been caught on the hop. Whoever this kid was, it was desperate to make up for lost time. I hoped it wouldn't make a habit of stirring at the crack of dawn.

The volunteer took us up in a lift and along a corridor. I recalled the old landmarks: a payphone, a children's mural, the sign above the main swing doors – *Maternity Suite – please switch off your mobile phones*. A midwife came to meet us. 'OK, Angela. Your husband can help you change.'

It was a relief to be useful. I'd felt helpless confronted by Angela's pain. She handed me her jewellery and was racked by her next contraction as she climbed on to the bed. To my relief the midwife then took over. 'I'll ring the mums and dads,' I said and nipped back to the payphone. I felt a pang of heartache over Gloria, Jed and Billy. They were back at Mummy's Home. I couldn't call them there.

I rang my parents first. 'Hello, Dad. We're at the hospital. We're fine.'

Angela's parents' number was written on my hand. 'Hello, Blanche. Sorry it's early. This is it. It's her time.'

I calmed myself and walked back to the suite. Angela was surrounded by medics in blue scrubs. A tube protruded cruelly from the back of her hand and a wire trailed out of her vagina. At its other end an electrode was attached to the baby's head. Another monitor was strapped on to Angela's belly. I heard the sub-aquatic *buh-buh* of a foetal heart – a sequin that had grown into a jewel. I kicked myself for being absent while all this had been done.

'Angela. I'm sorry. I only had my back turned for a minute . . .'

She laughed bravely. I wanted to hold her, but I wasn't sure which parts were safe to touch. She answered weakly, 'It's all right. Everything's happening so fast.' A consultant then stepped forward. They are a varied bunch. This one was briskly condescending and gung ho.

'Hello, Mr Slade.'

'Mr Stone, actually. Hello.' I let him sniff some attitude: deferential with a hint of menace. *So, rugger bugger. That term 'medical negligence'. Does it ring a bell at all?*

Angela flinched a little as he felt for her cervix.

'Three centimetres, I'd say. Head's pushing down well. How frequent are the contractions?'

'Every eight minutes,' said the midwife.

'Good. I'll be back soon.'

He and then the others left the room. Angela gasped in agony, sucking hard on the gas and air. 'Joe,' she said, 'Joe.' She was emerging from her tunnel. 'I'm so happy that you're here.'

I kissed her forehead. I listened to the frantic pumping – *buh-buh, buh-buh, buh-buh* . . . 'I know. I feel useless, though.'

'You should have brought something to do.'

'I could have brought a camcorder like other blokes do.'

'I'm glad you didn't.'

'I could have brought my motorbike and stripped it down.'

'You haven't got a motorbike, you fool.'

'Aaah, that's what I've been telling you.'

'Stay close to me, won't you?'

'Later, you'll yell at me to get off you.'

'No, I won't!'

'Yes, you will. It's a recognised feature of labour.'

'You're the expert, I suppose.'

Every five minutes.

Every four minutes.

Every three minutes?

Every two?

'Get off me, Joe! Get off!'

'Told you so.'

'Get *off*.'

I got off.

Every one minute? No one was counting any more.

'Hold my hand, Joe! Hold my hand!'

Please Let This Be Over.

That Baby's Going To Die.

That Woman's Going To Die.

I Am Going To Pass Out And Then I Am Going To Die Too.

'Oh! Oh! Uhhhhhhhhh!'

'Keep pushing, darling.' That was the midwife, not me.

'Ah! Ah! Aaaaaagh!'

'Come on, sweetheart, one more time.' Wrong again. That was the student nurse.

'Oh-uh-oh! Uuuuuh-oh!'

I had my mouth right by her ear. 'Angela, I love you. I love you. I love you.'

A new life squeezed into the light.

'You have a daughter,' said the midwife.

'Please let me see her,' Angela cried.

'Hello, Estelle,' I said. 'I'm Daddy – and you're stuck with it, I'm afraid.'

chapter 18

As Billy would say, you won't *believe* this but . . .

There was still a little daylight left when I saw Dilys heading towards me – it was around 4.30 on a Friday afternoon. She was sitting high at the wheel of the latest Pillockracer, a shiny 4×4. Chosen by Chris, I thought unkindly – the vehicle of a technology freak in thrall to rustic longings.

I was pushing Estelle along the pavement in her deluxe new buggy. Angela was at home, catching up on sleep. I lifted the baby quickly from her berth and held her up to face the onrushing car. As it swept by I took hold of Estelle's hand and flapped it up and down in imitation of a wave. From behind the passenger windows three young faces turned our way. No smiles were flashed, no cheery hands were lifted in return as I held up their semi-sibling like a hopeful Valentine. Dilys swung the Pillockracer round the first corner she came to and was gone.

'Goodbye, Dilys,' I muttered. 'Don't get trapped in

223

a lift with a boa constrictor or anything.'

Something was wrong. I knew this in an oddly calm way. Dilys had broken off our last vestige of contact shortly after Estelle was born. She'd written to decline another pre-Christmas meeting. She'd assured me that it was 'nothing personal', but she was very busy and she was sure that I was too. She'd also requested that she and Chris had the children for the first half of the Christmas break, taking in Christmas morning, the same as the previous year. For the sake of peace Angela and I had consented, but had puzzled over whether they had got some special reason. Now the sight of me and Estelle at the roadside had got Dilys burning rubber. What was going on?

Adding to my disquiet was a creeping fear of Fate; a sudden lurking certainty that by the law of averages my bubble of happiness was due to burst. Estelle and Angela were both alive and hearty – this was far too much good fortune for a start. And then there was the pleasure Gloria, Jed and Billy had taken in the baby's arrival. During their Daddy's Home days they'd been pure sweetness. Billy had invited her to cuddle Beautiful Lettuce. Jed had instructed Billy on the correct way to hold her. ('Keep your arm under her head. She's not a *toy*.') Gloria had sat on the carpet with her back against the sofa, her foot jiggling the baby recliner, her shoulders in between my knees as I wove her tresses into a plait.

Tranquillity had ruled. I'd worked very little, but

popped down often to my studio sorting through old pieces, reflecting, taking stock. Since my teens I'd wondered if there was something vivid and original inside me. For the first time in many months I felt ready to resume the task of finding out. And now the three blank faces and Dilys cornering at unusual speed.

The school was a five-minute walk away. Estelle yawned contentedly – Estelle Slade Stone to give her her full title, though she would only use the 'Stone' half normally. That way she would know how much she belonged to her big sister and brothers. I tucked her in under her blanket – a few more minutes of trundling through rotting leaves and she would be asleep – swung the buggy round and cut back through a side street. Soon, the lights of the school were visible, already standing out starkly as December darkness fell. I shoved through the entrance gateway, Estelle now napping peacefully, and made my way into the foyer. From the open door of the head teacher's office I heard voices low in conversation. It was unusual for staff to be working so late on a Friday.

'Hello,' I called out, nosing Estelle's wheels before me. 'Brian, are you there?'

The voices dropped abruptly. I heard a chair scrape back. Head teacher Brian Hartley's face appeared round the door. 'Come in, Joseph, come in.'

I knew all the other faces too: Begonia Gento, Billy's teacher, Reception class; Deirdre Spicer, Jed's, Year 3; Colin Long, Gloria's, Year 6. Each of them eyed me, none spoke. I took my hands off the handles of the stationary buggy and stood tall.

'What's happened?' I asked.

Brian cleared his throat. He constructed his next sentence with trepidation. 'Dilys has just been to see us. She's put us in a difficult position, I'm afraid.'

part iii: losing it

chapter 19

Brian said, 'I was going to call you, Joseph. The meeting ended a few minutes ago.'

'Nice of Dilys to invite me along too.'

'Well, she said she'd be consulting you and . . . Joseph, this is extremely difficult. We're not comfortable with it either . . .'

I looked at the exercise books piled upon his desk. They were Gloria's, Jed's and Billy's. Rectangular white labels had been stuck over the places where the children's names had originally been written. New names now appeared in their places: Gloria Pinnock; Jed Pinnock; Billy Pinnock.

'Jesus fucking wept.'

I dropped to my haunches next to Estelle. So that's what Dilys had been up to.

'It seems,' said Brian nervously, 'that she has decided to adopt Christopher's surname for herself. And it also seems that she is entitled, legally that is . . .'

I finished the sentence for him: '. . . to give the children her new surname instead of mine.'

'It does appear that way,' Brian said.

I stood up straight again and scanned the other teachers' faces. 'So what do you all think?'

They glanced one to the other.

'She *is* their mother, I suppose,' Begonia ventured. She looked at me with sympathy and shrugged.

They were words I would rewind in my mind a thousand times.

'Have they suddenly got married then?' I asked.

'I assumed they had, although she didn't say so,' answered Brian.

'Dilys had the children with her, didn't she?'

'Well, yes. They were in the library during our meeting.'

So she'd decided not to let them witness the deed as it was done. What line might she have spun them? It was plain from their expressions glimpsed through the car window that they knew something momentous was happening. How momentous, though?

I said, 'Did you get any impression of where they were heading next?'

Brian's voice emerged from a few awkward *ums* and *ers*: 'Straight back home, was it? Perhaps to collect her, um, partner?'

He was asking the others if he ought to give that detail away. Sensing moral confusion, I pushed on. 'Did she say anything about them all going away?'

'Well,' said Brian, 'I think she was keen to be on the move. What with the rush hour and everything.'

I swivelled the buggy round and hurried with Estelle out of the office, through the entrance door and back across the playground. Halting outside the gate, I glanced to left and right before reaching for Angela's mobile. I could never find mine, and she'd popped hers into my pocket as I was leaving the house ('just in case I need you'). From memory, I punched in Dilys's number and felt my gut contract as the ringing tone began. It dawned on me I hadn't any idea what to say. Then came my ex's voice.

'*Hi! This is Dilys. Leave a message and . . .*'

A kind offer, but one I declined. I didn't want Dilys ringing back on Angela's phone, not on that or any other day. I punched in the Pillock Central landline number. Another tightening in the stomach, another ringing tone. My ex's voice again. This time I had something rehearsed:

'*Hello Dilys. Any chance of some prior warning next time you nail me to a cross?*' I never delivered that line.

'*Hello! I'm afraid we can't take your call at the moment. If you have a message for Chris, Dilys, Gloria, Jed or Billy . . .*'

I shunted Estelle back towards the High Street, her sleeping softly, me breathing hard. The car was parked in its rough bay on the access road that served the back gardens and works yards to the rear of our shop. Luckily, I had the keys. Soon, Estelle was in the baby seat and the buggy was in the boot. I hesitated for a moment,

Angela's mobile once more in my hand. I'd been out for over an hour, longer than intended. Should I call to let her know what I was about to do? What if she was still sleeping? I could see the kitchen window. No light showed, suggesting that she hadn't woken. Putting the mobile between my knees, I fired the ignition then checked that the sudden noise hadn't disturbed Estelle. It hadn't. I pulled away.

With the rush hour still roaring it took a full thirty minutes to crawl up from South Norwood and infiltrate the leafy enclave where Pillock Central lay. I idled past their gated driveway and pulled over. Estelle was waking now. She blinked at me as I heaved her from her seat. 'Oooh, Estelle,' I prattled, flopping her on to my shoulder like a big beanie toy. 'Let's go out into the scary, scary dark.' She'd started snuffling. I knew she'd need feeding soon. I swung the gate open and crunched down the gravel drive towards the porch, growing edgier with every step. I'd never been so close to Gloria, Jed and Billy's other lives before.

'Guess what, Estelle,' I said, 'a light will come on at any moment.' And so it did, defying the evening gloom as we advanced upon the house. I mumbled on. 'The thing is, baby girl, if you believe in magic, magic things happen to you.'

There was a little stone porch with a wide step forming an apron, and luxurious growths of ivy up each side. I slowed for a few seconds, looking for signs of life behind the curtains: none downstairs that I could see, and none upstairs either. I wondered for a second which upper-floor window might belong to which child. Then I stepped up to the door. A handsome holly wreath was fixed below a heavy knocker and in the corner hung a bell-pull.

I knocked. I rang. I kicked the door a few times to make sure. Nobody home. So then I leaned against the porch wall and used the mobile once more.

'Hello! Doctor's surgery.'

'I'd like to make an appointment for my daughter.'

'Certainly. What's her name?'

'Gloria. Gloria Stone.'

A short pause followed. 'And you're her father?'

'Unless someone's been telling lies.'

There was a giggle followed by another short pause. 'We don't seem to have a Gloria Stone on our computer.'

'Trust me, she exists. She's been a patient of yours since she was born: Gloria Stone, ten years old. Dark-brown eyes, dark-brown hair, perfectly divine.'

'I can't find her here.'

'OK. Try looking under "Pinnock".'

'Pinnock?'

'It's her mother's name.'

I heard the keyboard clickety-click. Then: 'Ah yes, here she is. Gloria Pinnock, Lobelia House . . .' The very place where I was standing. '. . . and you're Christopher?'

'That's me.' I cut the connection abruptly. Unreliable, these mobiles.

Estelle's snorts had turned to whimpers then to sobs.

I offered her the solace of an index finger knuckle. She suckled it greedily, but as fleeing heroes say in movies when they wedge chairs in front of doors, it wouldn't hold her for long. I turned back up the gravel path, walking fast, head down.

'Good evening,' said a voice. It was taut with a false politeness that shook me from my daze.

'Good evening,' I replied. 'Don't worry. I'm only *really* dangerous on Tuesdays.'

He wore a chunky sweater. Poking stiffly from the neck I saw the open collar of his shirt. Welcome to deepest Dulwich – your wild weekend starts here.

Sweater man tried again. 'Were you looking for Christopher, by any chance?'

'No. I was looking for my kids.' I was pushing through the gate now. Estelle was beginning to rev nicely. Sweater man backed off a bit – crying babies affect some chaps that way. 'Good thing, Neighbourhood Watch,' I barked in passing. Then Angela's mobile struck up the theme from the Lone Ranger – '*Hi ho, Sil-ver!*'

'Hello.'

'It's me. Where are you? You've been engaged.'

I slung Estelle under my coat to hide her cries. 'Don't worry, Angela. We're OK. I'm nearly home.'

Two minutes later I was driving in the dark, my head spinning and my baby screaming in the seat behind.

'I'm so sorry I scared you. I was stupid. I should have known.'

It was after 10 p.m. I sat squashed into a corner of the old settee cuddling my knees, my fingers drumming by the landline phone. Angela was in Jed's chair underneath my family painting, cradling Estelle. She said, 'Forget about it now. It was when I couldn't get through. I couldn't think who you'd be speaking to. I was afraid there'd been an accident or something. You start imagining things, don't you?'

'You do,' I said, 'you do.'

She hadn't been quite so forgiving a few hours before. She'd woken with a jolt. No daylight. No baby. No me. Then she'd seen the clock and fright had taken hold. By the time I'd got us home Estelle's face was purple and her screams were desperate rasps. I'd handed her to Angela, ashamed.

'I'm not going to be hysterical,' she said. 'I'm not going to scream and yell. But please, Joseph, please, don't ever disappear with her like that again.'

She hadn't said another word until the baby had calmed down. I'd seen an Angela I didn't know: angry and unnerved. For half an hour I kept my distance before padding into the bedroom where she held Estelle, finally quiet and still.

She asked me very coolly, 'What happened to you, Joe? Where did you go?'

I'd perched humbly by her blue toenails and replied, 'I've got a nasty feeling. It's about the kids.'

It was a different nasty feeling to others that I'd known. Different entirely from that sudden burst of terror three years or so ago when I was sitting by a park sandpit and realised Billy was gone, and suddenly was looking, looking, looking, from child, to child, to child, quietly, frantically, rising to my feet, staring wildly around. Which direction should I give chase in? Which fast-departing car had some sad and deadly loner bundled my boy into? If I threw myself on to his bonnet, would I be able to hold on? And then, of course, I saw him – Billy. He'd been there all along. I'd been looking for a pink T-shirt, forgetting that on that morning I had dressed him in a yellow one. He'd been half-hidden by a plastic toadstool. It was amazing how ten seconds could feel like a thousand years.

And this time? A dull ache of dread that I'd been living with for months was rising to a sickening throb. All those nagging anxieties about Gloria and Jed and what they found lacking in me were now jitterbugging madly in my head. My suspicions about the possible inadequacies of Chris were no longer a cause for smugness but a reason to contemplate the lengths to which unhappy people are sometimes prepared to go: we had a baby and they didn't; I was a father and Chris wasn't; the children carried my surname and that pissed Dilys off. She'd had a good look at her options and asserted her maternal privilege: to the lightly bearded Christopher, three instant little Pinnocks tied up with a bow. And that might only be the start.

Angela said, 'I'm sure they haven't stolen them. They wouldn't be that stupid. Or that cruel.'

'I should have sweetened up that neighbour,' I reflected. 'He might have known where they were going.'

We relocated to the living room where I tried Dilys's mobile again, this time leaving messages to call me urgently. Then I rang her mother.

'Hello, Beryl. Remember me? It's Joe.'

'Oh . . . it's you.'

'Either that or Noel Edmonds, I suppose.'

'Edmonds?'

'It was a joke, Beryl.' I sensed her filing the blade of her telephone manner. Good. At least that meant I had her full attention.

'How can I help you, Joseph?'

'I need to speak to Dilys urgently but she's not answering her mobile and she's not at home. It's about the children. Any idea where she might be?'

'Em . . . no.'

'Well, if she does happen to call you, or if you should feel a strong urge to call her, could you ask her to contact me *immediately* at home? Please tell her that it is a *very* serious matter.'

I then made an ill-mannered exit from the conversation, determined to leave Beryl frustrated and intrigued. That way, I calculated, she'd be sure to ring Dilys without delay, though what good that might do me was far from clear. I sternly told myself that Gloria, Jed and Billy were probably *not* cruising at 30,000 feet in the executive seats, proudly bracketed by Dilys and Chris, mother and pseudo-dad, just as I always knew that Estelle was probably not dead when Angela and I took turns to check she was still breathing.

'Joe?'

'Sorry, I was miles away.'

'You were muttering to yourself.'

'Sorry, sorry, sorry.'

'Here. You hold the baby for a while.' Angela came across to sit beside me and I took Estelle in my arms. That was when the phone rang.

I lifted the receiver. 'Hello?'

'It's me, Dilys.'

'Where are you?'

'I'm ringing from Ranch Pillock, Land of the Free! Chris and I have decided to invest part of his filthy great fortune here. We've brought the children with us, naturally. Our attorney says I should allow you to see them every time an elephant plays the violin. I've ruined your life, haven't I? Sorr-eee!'

'I'm in the country,' Dilys said.

'Which country?'

'*The* country. Sussex. For the weekend.'

Quester's Lodge again. Bark burns guaranteed.

'What are you playing at?'

A pause . . .

'I know it's a bit late, but your message said it was urgent.'

'That's not what I mean.'

'What *do* you mean?'

'You *know* what I mean. You *know* what this is about.'

Silence.

'You've changed the children's surnames. You've been into the school.'

'Oh. I was going to let you know about that . . .'

'When?'

'Honestly, I really was.'

'You've changed them at the doctor's surgery too.'

'Yes, Joe, I know. I—'

'They've got Warrior Willy listed as their father.'

'I don't think this aggression is appropriate.'

'What about their passports? Have you been messing with those?'

'Look, Joe, it's quite late and—'

'What else have you been up to?'

'—and I don't want to have this conversation now.'

'What are you playing at, Dilys?'

She hung up. I re-dialled.

'*The Vodafone you've called may be switched off. Please try again later.*'

chapter 20

'In one respect, Mr Stone, you don't exist.'

That sounded about right – I'd long ago concluded that I wasn't quite all there. It was, though, a surprise to learn that my incompleteness had been recognised in law.

The solicitor went on, 'There's been a long-standing imbalance in the legal status of unmarried fathers. Whereas married fathers have always enjoyed automatic rights in relation to their children, *un*married fathers have not. Conversely, the *mothers* of their children have had the same rights as married mothers – and, indeed, married fathers. The position will soon change substantially thanks to new legislation. However, it won't be retrospective so it won't make any difference to you.'

It was the Monday afternoon following that nightmare Friday. After an agonised weekend I'd checked first thing that morning that Gloria, Jed and Billy had shown up at school, then bashed the telephone begging every legal firm within a five-mile radius to swing me an emergency appointment. This fellow had a cancellation. He charged £220 an hour.

Tick, tick, tick . . .

'So where does that leave me, then?' I asked.

'Happily for you, even as things stand, almost all unmarried fathers can obtain those basic rights even if the mother doesn't like it. We might almost say that only psychopaths and sex pests are denied them, and in neither case do you appear to qualify . . .'

'Thanks.'

'. . . so I strongly suggest that your first move should be to ask your former partner – Ms or Mrs Pinnock, as she now wishes to be known – to agree to your acquiring what is called Parental Responsibility for Gloria, Gerard and William.'

'I have to ask her?'

'That's correct. Parental Responsibility is, in the first place, Mrs Pinnock's to agree to. We only go to court if she keeps saying no. And unless she's very badly advised which, by the sound of it, she won't be, she will realise that fighting you over this matter will be futile.'

I pondered this for a minute. It seemed absurd having to go to Dilys on bended knee. We'd shared the parenting pretty equally. And it was she, strictly speaking, who'd broken up the happy home by leaving.

'This imbalance,' I enquired. 'Is it fair?'

'That depends on your point of view,' he answered crisply. 'One supposes it made sense to privilege the unmarried mother because it is so often she who bears the main or exclusive responsibility for childcare after relationships fail, while the unmarried father frequently loses touch, although the reasons for that vary. On the other hand, plenty of divorced or separated married fathers lose touch too, while not every unmarried father is, as it were, just passing through.'

'Or just passed up, as in my case,' I cut in, glancing impecuniously at the clock.

'Quite.' Mr £220 per hour smiled tightly. Possibly detecting that I had money on my mind he added, 'I should, perhaps, point out that the Child Support Agency does not act solely on behalf of mothers seeking financial support from their estranged former partners. It will act for fathers too – if they decide that the father is the principal carer, though in your case that would be a difficult judgement to make. This may even be something for you to look into if, as you suggest, the Pinnock household enjoys a substantially higher income than that of you and your wife.'

'You mean the CSA might decide that Dilys has got to give me a percentage of her income?'

'It's possible, yes.'

Now there was a thought: me accepting a cheque from Dilys – effectively from Chris the Pillock – every month to help me care for my own children. I'd rather take in laundry.

'It's all aggravation isn't it, the CSA?' I asked, hoping to be encouraged to forget the whole idea.

'There's always aggravation in these matters, Mr Stone, and no guarantees of satisfaction.'

I glanced at the clock again. I'd been there nearly forty minutes. I wondered if Mr £220 an hour would accept one of my recent paintings as advance payment in kind. Perhaps one of my tasteful renderings of Anna Kournikova bending over? Or that one of the dominatrix straddling the bishop? Either would set the filing cabinets off nicely.

'OK,' I said. 'If I had Parental Responsibility, what difference would it make over the surnames?'

'None whatsoever, of itself. All it really means is that the courts recognise that you are the children's father and are entitled to take legal action regarding their care. If you decide you want to obtain an order saying that Gloria, Gerard and William must always use the surname Stone, then you have a much bigger battle on your hands. We may have to secure the services of a barrister.'

'What do barristers cost?'

'They vary. Anything from three hundred to over a thousand pounds an hour.'

'For what?'

'In the first place for an hour-long consultation. After that, you'll have to decide if you want to carry on.'

'Greedy bastards, aren't they?' I said sweetly.

Mr £220 an hour smiled properly this time. My dislike for him was fading. At least he was straightforward and, compared with a barrister, he was cheap. 'All I will say,

Mr Stone,' he replied drily, 'is that unless you are on
legal aid, litigation can become a very expensive business
– with, as I said, no guarantee at all of satisfaction at the
end. And there are other costs, of course.'

'What do you mean?'

'To you, to your wife and to your children, maybe
most of all. They may be visited at your home, inter-
viewed, and their situation assessed by people called
Children and Family Court Reporters. The same thing
would take place at their mother's home. With the best
will in the world, the process can be quite distressing.'

I thought of Daddy's Home squatting above A Poor
Man's Wealth: dog-eared, chaotic and getting a bit
cramped. I compared this with what I knew of Pillock
Central: bijou, clean and fragrant. Which of their two
homes did my three children prefer? Which of their
parents? Such questions terrified me when I asked
them of myself. The thought of them being put to the
children, however indirectly, terrified me even more. I
shuddered to imagine what the trio might come out
with.

Gloria: 'Daddy is very nice, but we're not really as good
friends as we used to be. I think a girl of my age needs to be
with her mother. And the trouble with Daddy is he sometimes
shouts.'

Jed: 'Daddy isn't very interested in things that really matter.
Things like nature and computers or, you know, interesting

gadgets. He's untidy and he makes silly jokes that no one else can understand. It's quite annoying.'

Billy: *'Daddy's very clever. He's got much gooder at putting on my mascara. He mended my Tinkerbell wings. He says I'm a beautiful princess. He says that one day I will be a proper queen.'*

Tick tick, tick . . .

'Mr Stone, I know you're mindful of the time. I can summarise my view pretty succinctly.'

I was downcast. 'Go ahead,' I said.

'Don't go to court over this business. Certainly not for the time being. You see, Mr Stone, the law tries pretty hard to take account of real life but there's only so much it can do. I advise you to secure Parental Responsibility. You can instigate that process on your own: write your former partner a conciliatory letter, enclose the necessary forms – I'll help you with those, it won't take long. The value of having PR is that it makes the playing field level and shows your children's mother that you are serious, which may have a restraining effect on her in future.'

'But?'

'But you being recognised as a father in family law doesn't magically stop other people behaving badly. Theoretically your ex could still do all sorts of things on a whim, including changing the children's school, giving permission for them to undergo major surgery or moving with them to the other end of the country or even abroad. All that having Parental Responsibility will really entitle you to do, Mr Stone, is to contest any such actions through the courts or try to prevent them if you discover they're afoot. And even then, as I have hinted, that may not do you any good.'

'Oh stop it,' I begged. 'You're filling my heart with joy.'

'Let me give you a theoretical example,' said Mr £220 an hour. 'Let's say Mr and Mrs Pinnock suddenly moved to Scotland, taking the children with them and destroying your present co-parenting arrangement at a stroke. What can you realistically ask a judge to do? He's unlikely to order them to move back to South London. That leaves you arguing about where the children should live. Clearly, they can no longer spend one week in Scotland, the next in South Norwood and so on, because it simply wouldn't be practical. So the judge will have to decide which home will be the children's normal place of residence, then go on to consider how much contact the non-resident parent should have. On the first point, he may well decide that the best place for the children to be most of the time is with Mrs Pinnock, even though they're being uprooted – Mother knows best, and all that.'

'And what contact might I get?' I enquired.

'Can't be sure. Maybe a visit from them one weekend a month, plus a share of the school holidays.' He made a moue and closed his eyes.

'Great,' I said.

'There's something else you should consider, Mr Stone, as you think about what to do over the surname dispute. Quite apart from the expense and the further escalation of tensions, if you advance on that front you can easily find the whole situation spiralling out of your control. Once hostilities get started Mrs Pinnock may decide to, as it were, give you a bloody nose by applying for an order that the children live mainly with her in Dulwich. Asked to appraise the full circumstances, a more conservative judge might easily decide that your entire parenting set-up – with the two homes and the alternating weeks – is not in the children's best interests. And, remember, it is the *court's* assessment of the children's interest that ultimately counts, rather than yours. Even if you got what you wanted over surnames – which you probably would – you might also end up being reduced to just another weekend dad. Not a pleasing prospect from your point of view, I would have thought.'

I sighed forlornly. My hour was up. 'So what else *can* I do?' I asked.

'We'll fill in the PR application forms and send them on to you, Mr Stone. We have all the details we need. Let me see your letter before you send it and we'll get that ball rolling. Secondly, I recommend a mediation service. There are two or three that we've found very good. You sit down in a quiet room with a trained, impartial person and try to work things out. It may not seem as satisfying as waging all-out war but many are pleasantly surprised by the results.'

'Thanks. I'll think it over,' I said, rising to go. 'Anything else you'd like to tell me before you send me my bill?'

'Hmmm. Have confidence in your children, Mr Stone. Given time and reasonable peace of mind they're often more adept than anybody else at sorting these things out.'

I considered all my options.

I dressed up as a moose.

A strange course of action, some may feel. But it was that or a gorilla and I can't peel a banana with my feet. And as the woman with the rent-a-costume company observed, a moose is very similar to a reindeer.

'How would a moose feel about you saying that?' I asked her.

'I wouldn't know,' she shrugged. 'I've never been one.'

I have. I was a moose for one whole hour during the school Christmas concert on the final day of term. I wasn't meant to be there. Right from the beginning of the two homes situation Dilys had insisted on separate attendance at such events. They had the Christmas run-up – again – which meant they also had the Christmas show. Indeed, I reflected, as I strode into the school hall, my Velcro fasteners chafing, my antlers clattering the lintel above the doors, it was *their* Christmas all over. By stealing the children's surnames they'd stolen our half of the festive season too. Pinched it, like the Grinch.

I should have seen it coming. They'd cornered the market in glamour presents even before Estelle was born. Way back in October I'd had an edgy conversation about festive things with Jed and Billy.

'What would you like Santa to bring you this year, boys?' I'd asked.

Jed had said nothing. That was partly because he'd started to stop believing in Santa and partly because he'd started to stop believing in me. Billy – surprise! – had been more forthcoming.

'I already know what Santa's bringing me! An Action Man, a Scalextric, a remote-controlled aeroplane . . .'

'How very butch of Santa,' I'd remarked. 'And Mummy? What's she buying you this year?'

'Oh, Chris is in charge of our presents,' Billy had blurted out brightly. 'He's getting us a Dreamcast.'

My fixed grin ground into place. 'Great. I love anything by Andrew Lloyd Webber.'

I took up a standing position at the rear of the hall – I didn't want to be conspicuous, now, did I? – and scanned the rows of parents ranged on plastic seats and benches round the stage. I was certain Chris and Dilys were somewhere in attendance, but my restricted view was made still worse by the woeful misalignment of my moose-head eyeholes. It required a major effort to see anyone at all, and left me near defenceless against a large amount of unwanted attention.

'Hello, Mr Reindeer!' said Brian Hartley, squeezing past.

'I'm not a reindeer, I'm a moose.' (I said it in my finest moose voice. He would never know that behind my bland exterior I was really Superman.)

'Hello, Rudolph,' said a little girl. 'Where's Santa?'

'Advertising Coca Cola – he's gone back to his roots.'

She tittered uncomprehendingly and backed quickly away as Mr Hartley reached the stage and got the concert underway. By this time I was scarcely breathing, and not just because my respiratory organs were trapped inside a synthetic fibre cocoon. I was anxious: Dilys and Chris were in the room and I was breaking all the rules of non-engagement. Three of my children were about to go on stage and I was madly nervous for them – plus, that morning, a letter had arrived.

Dear Mr Stone,

I represent Dilys Pinnock, formerly Dilys Day, the mother of your children Gloria, Gerard and William. She has asked me to confirm to you that she has made the decision to change the children's surnames from Stone, as had been the case heretofore, to her new surname.

If they'd tied the knot, I wondered, how had they managed to do it without Angela or me getting a sniff? And how strange to think of Dilys embracing the most conventional of all marital conventions – taking her husband's name. I could see how it made sense, though. It had given her the justification for turning the three Stone kids into Pinnocks.

I felt defeated. Her solicitor's letterhead looked even more expensive than my one's did.

As you may be aware, Mrs Pinnock is the sole possessor of Parental Responsibility for the children and it is therefore within her legal rights to decide that using her surname best serves the children's interests . . .

The letter went on to maintain that, to Dilys, it had seemed 'logical' for the children to use the surname now shared by two of their 'adult carers'. It closed with the assurance that Mrs Pinnock regretted any distress this might have caused me, but that 'in all the circumstances' she had done what she thought best.

Each of these little bombshells kept exploding in my head as I stood under my antlers, terrified that I might be unmasked. And how would this escapade play in a family courtroom?

'My client accepts that the moose-suit incident was a little, ah, disturbing, but would ask Your Honour to accept that he was in a highly distressed condition at the time.'

Was I going mad? I didn't feel I was, but I suppose mad people don't. Was I deceiving my wife? Yes. I hadn't mentioned the moose suit to Angela, only that I was intending to sneak into the show without Chris and Dilys knowing. She was at home with Estelle, anxiously awaiting my return. I'd kept the moose suit in the car and slipped into it furtively, hiding behind a wall.

There was another question too: was I letting the surname wound fester too much? Way back in the beginning I'd had no overwhelming urge for Gloria, Jed and Billy to be called Stone. They could have been called Day. They could have been called Snodgrass, Smith or Jones and I'd have loved them just the same. Looked at from that angle, their surname didn't matter. And yet it *really* mattered now. Dilys's intervention felt like a brutal desecration, an attack on the relationships I treasured with the children and had fought so hard to maintain. Also it felt like a threat: *I am the mother, the propagator superior as set down in nature's master plan; I am the wife of the man with the money; I am the parent guv'nor and I do what I like*.

Sweat began trickling behind my moose forehead, down through my moose neck and towards my moose gusset. I started worrying that I wouldn't get back my deposit. Over on the stage the junior choir walked on and there was Gloria at last, standing radiantly in the front row. She sent a glance in my direction – as had everybody else – than raised her hand in greeting in another: to Chris and Dilys, for sure. I gazed proudly at Gloria as she and the other songbirds sang out 'Silent Night' and the traditional nativity play began. Hands clapped, cameras flashed. And, lo, there was Jed holding a piece of printed card under his nose:

'*And suddenly the shepherds saw a great light in the sky, And they were sore afraid . . .*'

A group of fearful shepherds collapsed gingerly to the ground. Then came another voice. Much louder. Billy's.

'*DON'T BE SCARED! I'VE GOT GOOD NEWS! IT'S ABOUT A LIT-AWL BABY IN A COWSHED!*'

A ripple of delighted laughter spread across the hall. Billy smiled beatifically, his angel robe and foil winglets glistening, a plastic harp tucked under one arm.

I had to get away. It was all too much. I sidled out of the hall and strode quickly from the school back towards the car and home. The catcalls of bystanders were of no importance. I had a moose suit to change out of, after all. Try wearing one yourself some time. Try out being the man I had become: a mad dad in a moose suit with his moose head in his hands.

chapter 21

I looked down from the window as Gloria emerged from the front door. I watched her walking down the street, eager now to go to Sindy's Salon on her own. Boy adolescents turned their heads as she walked past. They saw big brown eyes and a young woman's curves already emerging strongly from the outline of a girl. I saw those things too, and felt again the wrench of separation. It was a Friday afternoon not long after Christmas and she'd returned from Mummy's Home like a guided missile carrying a personal payload.

'Hey, Gloria.'

'Yes, Dad?'

'It's good to have you home.'

'I've got two homes, you know.'

'Oh come on, you know what I mean.'

'Yes, I do know what you mean, and it's not nice.'

That would teach me to be pleased to have her back under my roof. It would teach me too that living in two homes had worked fine for her so far, but now the child was feeling torn apart. And I suppose I can't deny I did a little of the tearing.

'Gloria, I know you don't want to talk about it, and I don't want to force you to, but . . .'

'But what?'

I'd followed her to her bedroom and made her sit beside me, cross-legged on the floor. Soft toys and mounds of clothes obscured the bed and chair. Posters of dolphins and pop stars filled the walls. All of them were grinning. Neither of us were.

'I only want you to understand why I think what Mum has done is out of order.'

'But Mum doesn't think that. She thinks it's for the best.'

'Has she told you *why* it's for the best?'

'No, but . . .'

I heard the anguish in her voice, saw the same thing in her face. She kept half turning away. I took her hand.

'I'm sorry, Gloria. I'm so sorry. I'm not asking you to take sides, but I want you to see the way it looks from *my* side. I don't know what made Dilys do it. And, don't you see, I'm scared of what she might be planning next.'

'She isn't planning *anything*.'

'Isn't she? How do you know?'

'She just *isn't*.'

'Gloria, she's in the wrong.'

'You mustn't say that. She's my *mum*.'

'That doesn't mean she's always right.'

'I know, I know, I know. *Please* don't make me talk about it any more.'

I knew that Gloria would back away from me one day. I wasn't fool enough to think she'd forever be the little girl who used to fall asleep beside me as *Changing Rooms* volunteers pretended to be happy that their lounge had turned maroon, or while the *Ground Force* team stood beaming as innocent householders looked on in disbelief at perfectly good grass suddenly over-run by decking. But I had never foreseen her drift to independence being so dark and charged. I'd imagined slipping quietly into the middle distance, confident that once Gloria had survived her adolescence our father-daughter closeness would return again. Instead, my gnawing nervousness about the schemes of Dilys and Chris cast a constant pall of doubt. In tiny little tiffs I heard great rumbles of foreboding. I scrutinised each minor tremor for signs of earthquakes to come.

'Gloria! If you're in the bath much longer you'll dissolve.'

'Excuse *me*! I've only just got in.'

'You've been in there half an hour!'

'That's not very long.'

'It's three times as long as I take.'

'But that's *natural* for you. You're not a *female*, are you!'

I didn't mind the emphasis on personal hygiene. It was the memories it triggered that unnerved me: Dilys in the wine bar flicking back her hair; Dilys going all

Barbara Cartland when she talked about Chris. What new affectations might she pass on to our daughter next?

'What are you getting at Mummy's?' I asked, as her eleventh birthday approached.

'A mobile phone.'

'*Very* nice,' I said.

'They think I'm mature enough to have one,' she went on.

'Because you can walk and talk at the same time?'

'No,' pouted Gloria. 'Because they want to treat me as an adult.'

'So why the flouncing round like you're some silly little girl?'

Stomp! Stomp! Stomp! Stomp! SLAM!

I made a mental note: next time she goes back to Dulwich remove her bedroom door. But limiting the damage would take more than DIY. I'm sure I could have handled her hormonal transitions, far ahead of schedule though they were. It was the character adjustments I found hard. Our shared past had ensured that Gloria had always been much more than just her daddy's little princess. Yes, there had been sugar and spice and other sweet stuff that was nice, but there were slugs and snails and puppy dogs' tails too. Suddenly she was ceasing to be her father's daughter and turning into someone else's child, someone who was married to a Manly Man and rapidly becoming . . . Well, what? Angela and I spent many hours speculating. Was Dilys now a Girly Girl? A Wifey Wife? A Mother Who Knows Best?

'Dad?'

'Yes, Gloria?'

'Isn't it Kenny's gay?'

'All day and every day. The man's a pro.'

'When did you find out?'

'It sort of dawned on me when we were eighteen. Before that he'd been just another of us weirdoes.'

'Oh well, at least *one* of you's changed.'

I had been pleased she'd asked the question – the times when I felt useful to her were becoming scarce – and I knew her pay-off line was just a joke, almost the sort of joke I used to have with her. So why did it disturb me?

More sticky moments were to come.

'Look, Angela, I've had my ears pierced. Mum took me. Aren't they cool?' She rushed off to admire her reflection. Angela and I swapped loser faces – why hadn't *we* thought of that first?

Then Gloria decided that she didn't like the portrait I'd done of her when she was ten.

'I look so *stupid* with that bangle. I look so *stupid* on that chair.'

'I'll give it to Uncle Bradley for his restaurant then,' I said, all passive aggression as I removed it from its place of honour on the half-landing.

'As long as *I* don't have to see it.'

'You won't say that when it's hanging in the National.'

258

'Yeah, *right.*'

I blew a raspberry at her. 'Sabrina, The Teenage Witch. She's a nice girl,' I said.

Everything was changing except for all the things I wanted changed. Winter gave way to spring but there was no response from Dilys to my conciliatory letter or my legal forms. Meanwhile, the impact from the surname *putsch* spread wider. I couldn't keep it from my parents because I couldn't depend on Billy not to talk. They accepted the news calmly, but their dismay was plain. 'It's not for me I'm upset, Joe, it's for the kids,' my father said. 'It doesn't do to mess with youngsters' minds.' My mum's line was the same. 'I can't believe a mother would do such a selfish thing. But then I suppose Dilys has been selfish before.'

She meant by leaving me, of course. But I had never thought of that as selfishness. I'd lost interest in Dilys, remember? And she had lost interest in me. When she'd gone I'd danced and sung and sat in the space where the kitchen table used to be, inspecting myself fruitlessly for signs of misery. And that was why the surname change puzzled as well as enraged me. What was her motivation? Conventionality? Destructiveness? Spite? I tried to match these motivations with the Dilys I once knew. None of them really struck me as her style.

A different set of chemistries started formulating in the Daddy's Home emotional lab. For Gloria, Angela was becoming the key element: her new confidante and confessor. For me Angela became a double agent: my intermediary, my information lifeline.

I'd sit with her in bed as baby Estelle slept and be lost in gratitude as she related her public relations work on my behalf ('I know he's sharp sometimes, Gloria, but he's not the only one, you know'). I'd sit rapt as she described Gloria going through the motions of resisting ('Doesn't he know how *horrible* he can be?') before strategically retreating ('I suppose we are a bit alike – maybe that's the problem') and slowly, grudgingly, but recognisably emerging as a version of the Gloria I used to know ('He's quite a special dad, really. He's kind and makes me laugh').

And then I'd marvel at her skill in teasing out those small tales and details from which we tried to figure out the state of play at Pillock Central. Imagine the subtleties required: Angela wanting Gloria to tell her everything but mindful of the perils of directly asking; Angela knowing that Gloria would disclose as long as it was not acknowledged that she was disclosing; Angela understanding that Gloria was pretending not to know that Angela would take away her wisps of information and pass them on.

'I've found out about the wedding!'

This was one of Gloria's earliest revelations, extracted from her by Angela one weekday morning. Unable to speak freely in the crowded flat, she'd rung me on her mobile during her bus journey to work.

'Tell me more,' I begged.

'It looks as if they did it as soon as Chris got back from the Manly Men convention. It was an alternative wedding – at that place they stayed at before.'

'Quester's Lodge? In Sussex?'

'Right.' Angela listened to the penny dropping.

'Ah!' I said, my row of cherries lighting up. 'That's where she was ringing from that night!'

'Correct.'

'Is it legal?'

'I don't think so. Maybe they don't want to be official.'

'Why didn't the kids say anything?'

'I think it was all supposed to be a secret.'

Gloria, though, had been quite forthcoming. There had been beards and flowing robes; there were tom-tom drums and poems; there was firelight in the night; and there was a goat. A sacred billy-goat, maybe? A big unholy *ram*?

'Weird,' I said. 'Too weird!'

And maybe a little scary. After Rothwell had done his promised Manly Men research, I went round to Thicket Road for the lowdown. Kenny sat and listened, picking at profiteroles.

'With most of these groups we're mainly talking straight suburban guys,' Rothwell said. 'Middle-of-the-road Americans who worry that their desk jobs have turned them cissy. There's a touch of the old frontier romance about it, and for a lot of them it's really just a new way of being with the guys at weekends and eating all the steak they like without their wives nagging them about cholesterol.'

'But what about the tree-hugging?' I'd asked. 'What about the drums and dressing up?'

'Some of them go in for all that hokum more than others. There are a lot of different ones and more than one called Manly Men. I seem to recall that there was one in Washington state that had tool belt competitions and ate a lot of Spam. But the one your friend the, er, Pillock – charming old English word – has got into seems a lot more keen on all that questing-for-the-essence stuff. They'll probably have links with England. But I'm sure they're pretty harmless.'

'I'll relax then, shall I?' I asked.

'Relax by all means,' Kenny purred like Ernst Stavro Blofeld fondling a fancy cat. 'But they do get down on all fours and pretend to be coyotes. They bark and sniff each other's arses. I don't want that to worry you, though, Joe . . .'

Oh, how we laughed. Except that my laughter sounded a bit hollow.

When Gloria reached eleven she, Angela, Estelle and I went on a clothes-buying excursion in Croydon. We left Jed and Billy with my parents. Jed would have been bored rigid, while with Billy there was the constant risk of over-stimulation. That made me the token male, a role I often savoured. I usually found the world of girly shopping perversely liberating – that Sindy's Salon thrill of trespassing in the feminine domain. But the chemistry was different on that day. Gloria's growing up had become the object of clandestine inter-household competition. Little things gave me away: my smirk of satisfaction when Gloria asked if she could wear *our* trainers back to Dulwich rather than theirs; the way I leapt and punched the air because the open evening of her future secondary school had fallen on a day when she would be with Angela and me.

It was a Saturday morning. We were browsing in a boutique. I noticed Gloria and Angela fall into a huddle, then separate. Casually, Angela picked her way over to me, Estelle sleeping in the sling. I was about to find myself at a major paternal crossroad. 'Guess what?' Angela said. 'Your daughter wants a bra.'

Brassières. I had some knowledge of the subject, but it was rather specialised. How to unfasten them with one hand in a confined space. How to playfully tug them off a shoulder with my teeth. How to remove them, basically. I'd also worked out some ground rules about buying them – but only where sexual partners were concerned. You got her size, you memorised it – you didn't want the fragrant sales assistants giggling at you squinting at some crumpled bit of paper, did you now? When appraising the merchandise, you didn't wear a mac or fidget and especially not both at the same time. And you never bought *any* item of ladies' underwear during the run-up to Christmas; *never* became one of those guys queuing for the check-out with something flimsy and unwearable dangling hotly from his fist and an invisible thought bubble above his head that said, 'OK, OK, I'm desperate. But at least this way I get it once a year.'

It was clear I wasn't fitted for the task.

'Can you deal with this, Angela?' I muttered.

'I think I ought to, really.'

Gloria stood a short distance away, flicking through the clothing rails, wondering which shell of impending womanhood she wanted to inhabit. To me all the clothes appeared ridiculously small. Even Angela with her 'narrow sort of build' as Clip-Joint Len had called it would have struggled to squeeze into most of them. I imagined the shop interior hung with satirical pop art slogans picked out in flashing neon.

Only eat lettuce!

Never leave the gym!

Be thin, be miserable . . . and then you die!

The underwear department beckoned.

'I'm sorry, Joe,' said Angela. 'I think you'd better disappear.'

Estelle's toes were dangling, sockless, from the sling. I bent to kiss each one. I nodded towards the changing rooms. 'When you've bought it, let's lock ourselves into that cubicle and do it against the wall.'

'Oh yes. And what about the baby?'

'Gloria can take her to McDonald's.'

'*What* a thing to say.'

'Oh come on,' I bleated feebly, hanging out my tongue. 'I'll only take a minute.'

'Not *that* long, surely,' Angela replied.

'OK,' I said at last, lifting out Estelle. 'I'll take Girl Junior for a walk.'

I found a seat outside and flopped there, my infant crooked passively in my arm. A troupe of teenage girls went striding loudly by, their trousers hanging off their hipbones, their phalanx of belly buttons swivelling. They lived in a different world to me. I thought of Gloria and felt I was redundant as her father – the first time I had thought so in my life.

chapter 22

'What would make you happy, Jed?'

Stick to the easy questions. Like, how big is the outside of the Universe? Or, if everyone stopped sleeping, where would all the nightmares go?

'I'd like my room to be more tidy,' Jed replied. He eyed Billy's bed area with distaste. It was covered in discarded frocks and socks.

'Well,' I said defensively, 'Geoff Giraffe and Germaine Bear haven't complained.'

Jed ignored this quip. 'It's really *crusty* in this house,' he went on, turning up his nose.

'You're only seven,' I replied, trying to hide how much I hurt. 'You're not supposed to notice dirt.'

'I'm eight soon, though.'

'Not before I'm thirty-six.'

He shrugged as if to say, 'It's not a competition.'

I was sure I sensed low-level background grappling. The cause? Domestic cleanliness. The weapons? Mops and brooms. The prize? Superior parental virtue in the eyes of young Gerard-but-call-him-Jed-for-short-spelled-with-a-'J'-and-don't-mention-the-surname-it's-a-sore-point. Signals had been bouncing off the Gloria satellite that Dilys was spending much more time at home. She was sponging down work surfaces and fighting hidden grime. She was nurturing and nesting. She was being Natural Woman, Mother Superior. Was it merely a coincidence that Jed had become even more of a paradox? So fragile at times, yet so unbreakable? So sensitive and yet so *hard*? I wasn't the only one to notice. His teacher had buttonholed me after school.

'He's not joining in with things?' she'd said. 'Like, he won't sit on the mat with all the others? He walks off to a corner of the classroom?'

Miss Spicer was all upspeak and *can do*. She'd been born and raised in Tooting, but like everyone else in England under the age of twenty-five she might have just arrived from Ramsay Street.

'He isn't disruptive or anything? He doesn't shout and rave? He reads or draws?' Even her assertions tailed up into questions. 'He's *very* bright?' she'd continued. 'He's *really* interested in animals? And the computer? He's very adept with that? And still excellent at maths? And that's even though he's an August-born boy? They're often a bit behind as they're the youngest in the class? He is adorable? But it is worrying?'

My pleasure at her praise for Jed was sullied by the fact that he excelled at the wrong subjects. Why not art? Or even English? I was good at that too. Why all those

Christopher Pinnock sorts of things? Was he being groomed as Chris's heir? Would he one day inherit the sought-after title of All-Conquering Pillock Master, Supreme Champion of the Pillock Olympiad, Pillock *in excelsis Deo*. At least I could relate to his athletic powers. I would never forget his last sports day.

On your marks . . . get set . . . GO!

For most of the other kids it was a bit of fun. They'd fallen over, fooled around and tripped each other up. Jed, though, was total commitment, eyes fixed on the finish line. I must have seemed relaxed and friendly with my fellow parents. Behind my shades, though, I was Competitive Dad.

Go on, Jed! Burn them up, son! Skin 'em, lad!

(Yes, yes, I was pathetic. But would you like to see Jed's trophy? 'EGG AND SPOON RACE WINNER'. I've had it engraved, and everything.)

Miss Spicer then said, 'I don't want to raise this unnecessarily, but hasn't there been some concern about Jed before?'

Ah yes, the therapy. Precision Thing. It took me back.

'Daddy. We have to take my socks off.'

'Why, Jed, why? We've only just got them on.'

'Because you put the wrong one on first. You have to put on the one with the hole in first, BEFORE you put on the one without the hole.'

'It doesn't matter.'

'Yes, it DOES, Daddy! It DOES matter.'

'YOU'LL DRIVE ME MAD!'

I wondered if he was having a relapse, even though the symptoms were different this time: withdrawal rather than frustration, silence rather than insistence. Who could blame him after Dilys's surname stunt? Or her weird wedding. Had Miss Spicer mentioned Jed's behaviour to her yet?

'I'll be doing that next week?' she'd said.

I'd stuck the knife in then. 'This business with his surname – you try to carry on as usual for the children's sake. But he's not daft.'

Miss Spicer had looked a little helpless. To my relief the upspeak flagged. 'I'm not supposed to say this, but we all feel really terrible about what happened.'

Jed's untidy bedroom.

Jed's uncomfortable dad.

I returned to my original question. 'Come on, Jed. What would make you happy?'

'A kitten,' he replied.

Kittens? Joyful little things that chased cotton reels and got all tangled up in balls of wool? Sounded out of character to me.

'What can I *do* with him?' I'd asked Angela in despair. 'I wish he liked me more.'

'He loves you, Joe. He watches you. He watches what you're doing all the time.'

What *was* I doing, though? I was sinking into gloom. Another letter to Dilys had been ignored and I had been bickering with little brother Charlie.

'I need more lesbians, Joe,' he'd told me. 'In throbbing S&M action if you can.'

'Charlie! It's so tacky!'

'It sells, Joe. It sells.'

It had been selling, too – around a thousand pounds a time. It was a steady earner. Trouble was, it was doing my head in.

'It's pornography, Charlie, and you know it.'

'Not at those prices, it isn't. It's erotic art.'

'*I* know what erotic art is, and it doesn't look like that.' We were debating my most recent confection: *Whiplash Maiden Warriors from Hell*.

'Joe, what *is* your problem?' Charlie had complained. 'It doesn't degrade women. Those babes are *in control*.'

'Bollocks, in control!'

I suppose it beat decorating, but not by much. At least 'interior upgrading' qualified as honest graft rather than something I kept secret from my parents. And the paintings weren't only silly, they seemed to me symbolic: shabby artist, shabby dad. What sort of a bloke had I become?

Angela tried cheering me up. 'Why don't you and Jed do some things together, just the two of you? I think he'd love it.'

I wasn't so sure. Idealised father-son relationships had long made me suspicious. All that blood and bonding. Happily, neither Jed nor I are made that way. We're much better at getting on each other's nerves.

'Will you time me running, Daddy?'

'What, again?' We were in the Roaring Tunnel. Jed was keen to quantify his athletic performance. I was getting bored.

'I might do it even faster this time,' he pleaded.

'And I might lie to make you smile.'

'That would be silly.'

'I agree.'

'Why do it then?'

'Why not?'

Trust me to behave like a mean prat and Jed to turn a bit of fun into an endless stream of data. Even walking down the street became a scientific survey of some kind.

'That's a Daewoo ... that's a Vauxhall ... that's another Ford ...'

Chris knew about cars. I only knew about my own one and the Aston Martin Agent 007 used to murder foreigners in. And that's only because it featured in the *Bond Girls Classic Series* I was hacking out for Charlie. *Meet Plenty and Pussy. Vroom! Vroom!* I didn't think I'd be showing Jed those.

I had better luck with bedtime stories. Admittedly my motives for introducing him to Harry Potter were not completely pure. I was certain Chris the Pillock would be banging on to him about good old Bilbo Baggins any time at all and I wanted to get my wizardry in first. But so what? He was enthused, and I was too. What a shame success went to my head.

Gloria spilt gravy down her front. 'Ten points from Gryffindor!' I cried.

Billy used the toilet and forgot to pull the flush. 'Ten points from Gryffindor!'

But pretty soon it stopped raising a laugh.

Jed: 'Isn't that joke a bit old now, Daddy?'

Me: 'All right, Draco Malfoy, don't make me turn you into a ferret.'

The pitying look he gave me made me feel that I'd been hexed by my very own Dark Lord, the Manly Man from Dulwich, my equivalent of You Know Who.

I took Jed to the pet shop the first Friday I could. There were seven kittens to choose from. Jed watched them gambol in their glass showcase, a tumbling ruck of fluff and tiny paws. One was less boisterous than the others. It had a perfect jet-black coat.

'I want that one,' Jed said, pointing.

'Don't you want one that's more lively?'

'No. I want that sad one.'

He was absolutely firm. The woman who ran the pet shop fished out the chosen weakling and packed it in a carrying box. 'It's a female,' she said. 'You might want to have her spayed when she gets older. She'll need her jabs before that. Here's a leaflet all about it. I expect you know your local vet.'

She smiled nicely down at Jed. 'Don't look so worried, son. It might never happen.'

Jed and I discussed names on the journey home. I risked a wisecrack. 'How about anything that doesn't start with "G" or "J"?'

'Oh, I've already decided,' Jed replied. 'We'll call her Tiger.'

I was gloating inwardly. Hair-shedding, furniture-clawing, fur ball heaving creatures would never be allowed in the pristine Pinnock home. Welcome Tiger – Tiger Stone.

'She's *brilliant*, Daddy!' Jed cried.

Brilliant! Thank you, me! I'd finally done something right.

And she *was* brilliant too. She was playful, she was mischievous, she was cute. She was planted on her litter tray and did what was required. Best of all, she slept at night on Jed's bed – he made sure of that. From the start he moved decisively to establish himself as primary kitten-carer, saving her from the grabs of the now quick-crawling Estelle, making Billy back off when he caught him trying to fit her with the lace-and-ribbon bootees Beautiful Lettuce sometimes wore, intimidating Gloria with the breadth and scale of his kitten-raising expertise. He had a book about it. He had a wall chart. He was Tiger's mentor and protector, her surrogate dad.

'It's working!' I said to Angela. 'It can be done! He smiles!'

Throughout the next Mummy's Home week I did everything I could to maintain the momentum, checking Tiger for flea bites, supervising her diet, even moving into Jed's bed to maintain body warmth. I thrilled at the thought of Jed's return.

* * *

'Jed?'

'Uh?'

'Are you still happy?'

'Yeah.'

It was one of those answering yeahs that says the questioner's a fool to even ask.

'Happy now you've got Tiger, I mean.'

'Yeah.'

I'd gone up to his bedroom after tea. Tiger was sleeping on his pillow. Neither seemed keen to be disturbed.

'Sorry to distract you from your Lego.'

He was constructing a heliport on his bedroom floor – *his* side of the floor. Jed had lately insisted on the room being divided in half. A line of toy traffic cones marked the division between his territory and Billy's. On one side lay dressing-up chaos, on the other side lay order with a big 'O'. Jed policed the boundary with zeal. At the slightest incursion he'd summon me with outraged howls.

'What is it now, Jed?'

'It's Billy. He touched my stuff.'

'Billy?'

Billy was all innocence: 'I'm a puppy dog!'

'Not any more, you're not. Not now we've got a cat. Did you touch his stuff?'

'No.'

'He did! He touched my stuff!'

'All right, Jed. The world hasn't ended. Remember, lots of children on the planet don't even have any stuff to touch.'

'Good.'

'Jed. That's pretty nasty.'

'Good, GOOD, GOOD!'

What he really needed was a line of guys with guns and light-blue helmets. Or a fully-submersible mobile bedsit equipped for lengthy periods of ocean-floor survival and a sign hung on the front saying *Keep Out*. When you've sired a sociopath it can be hard to make wise judgements. I know a balance must be struck between sternness and understanding, but where is the bloody fulcrum meant to go? I felt my little pond of optimism draining. I couldn't tiptoe around him any more.

'Are you happy living in two homes, Jed?'

He shrugged. 'Yeah.'

'I wish you hadn't turned this into two rooms.'

'I'm going to have my own room.'

I'd heard that before but it still jarred me. 'When?'

'I don't know. Soon.'

Was there a spare room at Pillock Central even now being prepared for him to move into? Was I about to be outgunned again? How far should I push him? I dithered. He didn't look up from the Lego. Remember, Joe, I told myself. Keep it breezy. Keep it light. I'd have tickled him except he wasn't ticklish. I'd have thrown him in the air with a big Daddy Bear guffaw, but he'd only have complained about the noise.

'I used to play Lego,' I said. 'Exactly where you're playing it now.'

'No, you didn't,' he replied. But in his frown I saw a tiny chink of light.

'Yes, I did. This used to be my bedroom when I was your age. I shared it with Uncle Charlie. You know he's my little brother, don't you?'

'Oh yeah, I remember. And Uncle Bradley is your big brother.'

'That's right. He had the room that Gloria's in now. And my mum and dad had the room Angela and I sleep in. You know who they are, don't you?'

I got scared of this conversation as soon as I began to like it. It was good because it chimed with Jed's favourite intellectual process: filing facts in mental boxes, getting the details straight. It was bad because of where it might be heading.

'Granny and Grandad Stone are your mummy and daddy, and Granny Day is Mummy's mum . . .' said Jed. 'But who are Ralph and Blanche?'

'Um. Pardon?' Now I was feigning deafness. Had it really come to this? I scoured my frontal lobes for an emergency diversion. 'Anyway,' I said, 'let's have a good look at this Lego.'

Jed persisted. 'Who are Ralph and Blanche?'

'They're Angela's mummy and daddy.'

'I know *that*. What I *mean* is: are *they* my granny and my grandad too?'

It was one thing to be panicked. To be exposed as ignorant was even worse.

'To be honest with you, Jed, I don't really know. I

276

don't think so. I don't think they can be because Angela's not your mother. So you don't have a blood tie to Ralph and Blanche. Do you know what I mean by that? They are not the parents of either of your two parents.'

'Mmm.'

'They love you like real grandparents, though,' I went on, anxious not to downgrade the senior Slades. 'Ever since they met you they've treated you the same as they treat Stephen's children – Angela's brother's two. Remember them?'

I was snowstorming, hoping the blizzard would bury Jed's next question. He out-chilled me, though. He was glacial.

'What about Granny and Grandad Pinnock?'

Miss Spicer was quite right. He *is* very bright. Logic tests, he loves them. He'll be an architect or an engineer. Or a computer nerd – like Chris. Would I be proud of him? Ask me some other time.

'To be like real grandparents, Chris's parents have to *behave* like real grandparents. Have you met them, then?'

He ignored that and pressed on. 'The same way Angela *behaves* like a real mummy. The same way we *behave* like Estelle's a real sister, although she's *really* only a half-sister?'

Only a half-sister? This wasn't sparring any more. He was moving me around the ring, measuring me for the knockout blow. I mustered a defensive jab.

'Well, yes, except that Angela *is* a real mummy. She's

277

the *real* mummy of Estelle. She's *like* a real mummy to you.'

Whomp! He switched on the black lights.

'A bit like Chris. He's *like* a daddy to me and Gloria and Billy.'

'No, he's not,' I snapped. 'He's not.'

'Mummy says he is.'

'Mummy *would* say that, wouldn't she?'

'What do you mean?'

'Because Chris hasn't got any children of his own and Mummy wants to make him feel better. That's why. *That's* why she gave you his surname without bothering to ask me, even though I didn't want her to and even though it's made me very sad.'

I was shouting. I saw his face begin to crumple.

'For pity's sake, Jed!' I begged.

Oh Daddy.

Oh Daddy.

Oh Daddy Joseph Stone. You won't ever forget the slow-motion of those silent tears erupting. You didn't even have a tissue in your pocket, like proper dads do.

chapter 23

Let's keep this whole thing in perspective. There were days when I *didn't* think Dilys was on a quest to detach our children from me and put Chris the Pillock in my place. Such special days, they were. There was the one when Babe the sheep pig arced across the moon munching a big bag of pork scratchings. There was the one when John Lennon came back from the dead and ended Third World hunger with a song. And what about when Fred Flintstone dropped by to install a water feature in our garden?

And then there were the bad days, when I managed to convince myself that things were getting better and then somebody said something.

For instance . . .

We were squashed into the front room eating fish and chips, all seven of us together – seven including Tiger. From my end of the settee I looked across at Angela in the Other Armchair. She looked back at me. We exchanged same-wavelength glances and provisional smiles. Gloria sat next to me being too cool to let it show how thrilled she was that Estelle was dozing on her knee. Tiger slept next to Jed who sat next to Billy cross-legged on the carpet, absorbed by the TV. What was going on in *EastEnders*? Phil had shot Lil had shot Gill had shot Will. Lena had kissed Sheena who played the concertina. The entire cast was miserable. The closing credits rolled.

'Daddy!' said Billy, turning theatrically towards me. 'We've *got* to watch *Who Wants To Be A Millionaire*!'

'What do you think, Jed?' I asked.

'Yeah, fine,' he nodded, not looking round.

'And what about you girlies?'

I looked at Gloria. Gloria looked at Angela. Angela replied, 'As long as we can squeal and giggle, we girlies don't mind.'

'That's right,' added Gloria. 'All we girlies want to do is sit and be impressed by you clever boys.'

Angela fixed me with warning eyes. I didn't pay much attention. I'd smelled a rat. I set a trap.

'I don't like that *Millionaire* show myself,' I said. 'Only dopes and nerds are into quizzes.'

Step forward, Billy boy. 'But it's *brilliant*, Daddy! Chris is really good at it! He knows all the answers straight away!'

'Does he? I'm impressed.'

'We watched it every night last week. Mummy says that Chris would win it easy!'

'I'm sure he would,' I chuckled. 'OK. Change the channel.'

Jed made the switch. I cleared my head for war.

The first contestant on the show was Ronnie Stout, a window cleaner from Wrexham. He breezed through his first five questions, though not as breezily as me. 'You're brilliant, Daddy,' Billy announced. I let out a smug patrician chuckle. Ho, ho, that's my boy!

On to the harder stuff. Invited to select which part of London has the same name as Bill Clinton's daughter, Ronnie got the audience to help. 'I'll go with Chelsea, then,' he said. Correct! £2,000! Then he guessed that Miles Davis played the trumpet. £4,000! But doubling that figure meant tackling this tester: which group of islands is ruled by Portugal? The Maldives? The Seychelles? The Canaries? The Azores? I wasn't completely certain. Ronnie wasn't either. He said, 'I'll phone me dad.'

I was struck by the way he said it, a way that advertised his loyalty, a way that told the world that his dad was the one he'd turn to in a crisis such as this, even if his dad was not the best man for the job. Then Billy said, 'If I was on that programme, I'd phone Chris! He knows everything.'

There was a noise from the chip papers. There was a noise from the TV. And yet a graveyard silence seemed to fill the room. Gloria looked at me sideways. Angela's lips pursed. Jed stared at the screen. On to the line came Ronnie's father. He thought he could help his son.

'The Azores, I reckon.' He didn't sound quite sure. Ronnie agonised.

'Does your dad love you?' presenter Chris Tarrant enquired.

'I think he does,' Ronnie smiled. He had a big decision looming. Love showed him the way. 'He hasn't let me down before so I'll stick with his advice now.'

The Azores was the right answer. Ronnie went 'half-and-half' over a teaser about different sorts of cabbage, but decided he'd quit while he was ahead. He pocketed his cheque for £8,000. I slunk out to the kitchen and sat under the table for a while. Emotionally disabled by a game show. Could things have really got that bad?

And the correct answer is . . .

It was Billy. He couldn't help it.

'I'm nearly ready, Daddy! I'm putting Neil and Lettuce in their pram.'

We were going to the off-licence for sweets, a journey of about eleven feet.

'Oh, Billy. Why can't you just put them in my bag?'

'But Daddy, they don't like it in your bag.'

I hated it when Neil and Lettuce travelled in their pram. I had to lug it down the long stairs, get it through the shop door, apologise to all the people who tripped over it . . .

'Billy,' I said. 'They *love* it in my bag. They can look after the money, and when we get there they can choose their favourite sweets.'

'Daddy . . .' He was nearer six than five now. His repertoire of intonations had improved.

'Yes, Billy?' I replied.

'They don't eat.'

'Well, they can talk to one another.'

'Daddy . . .'

I had my head over the basket. I sensed the guillotine about to fall. 'Yes, Billy?'

'They don't talk.'

They don't eat. They don't talk. Were their lives worth living? I decided not to ask.

Once, at a children's party, a mother had approached me. 'Are you with that little girl?' she'd asked.

'Yes.' Billy was in full drag of course. Sometimes it was more trouble to explain.

'What a fantastic little girl she is.'

'Oh?'

'She's coping so *wonderfully*. She's so *incredibly* brave.'

I'd investigated later. Billy had approached the mother and informed her with doe eyes, 'My mummy and my daddy have both died-ed.'

'Have they, my darling? Have they really?'

'Yes. They've died-ed and gone to Heaven.'

What made him so different from his brother? Billy was the kind of child who told you all about the fruit gums that were dancing in his head.

'Fruit gums?'

'Yes, Daddy. Fruit gums. The fruit gums are dancing, Daddy! They are dancing in my head!'

With Billy I could look forward to rainbows all the way.

'Daddy?'

'Yes?'

'What's your name?'

'Joe.'

'How do you spell it?'

'J. O. E.'

'That's not how you spell "it"! Hee hee hee!'

How long could his bliss last? Maybe not for too much longer. He'd put up a long resistance but conformity was tightening its claws. At a girl friend's tea party he'd come to the attention of her bigger brother.

'Billy? That's not a girl's name,' he'd announced.

'That's right. He's a boy.'

The brother had computed this indecent revelation. Then he'd nudged his nasty mate. 'Poof!' he'd said under his breath.

'Pirate clothes are good,' Billy had said thoughtfully on the way home.

It hurt to see him disillusioned, though part of me was relieved. After the summer he'd be moving up to Year 1 from Reception. He'd be the oldest in his class, turning six within a week of starting. He'd also be the most precocious. Yet in some ways he was utterly naïve. True, he'd learned at three that frocking up in formal settings could make a chap the centre of the wrong sort of attention, so he toned it down accordingly for school (just the three necklaces, maybe; joggers and tops in floral pastels; positively no heels). But soon he would be entering a bigger rougher world, sharing a bigger playground with bigger, rougher children. I didn't want him hunted down by gender vigilantes and punched till he resembled strawberry jam. Had I prepared him for survival?

'Daddy?'

'Yes, Billy?'

'Do you know what?'

'What?'

'Chris does tai-chi.'

'So? I do lie-ying-down.'

'And Chris taught me some judo.'

'Is there *anything* Chris can't do?'

'I can throw you on the floor, Daddy!'

Thud!

'Ouch!'

'Told you so!'

One day in Billy's classroom, while sifting through some of his work, I saw he'd made a family tree. Tiny pencilled faces denoted Gloria, Jed, Estelle and Billy himself in a neat row. Above them he'd depicted a woman with long dark hair and a lightly-bearded male.

'Where am I on this?' I asked him gently.

'I did it when I was at Mummy's Home.'

'So?'

'You're, sort of, not my daddy when I'm there.'

'Yes, I am! I'm always your daddy! I'm your daddy wherever you are!'

He produced an I-goofed face.

'And what about Estelle?' I pressed. 'She isn't Mummy's and Chris's baby, is she?'

'Ummm. No. But she is always my sister.'

Yes and no. No and yes. But genealogy was not the point. What got me was the feeling I was being erased. I got out the family photos from the pre-Angela era and cornered the kids with them. Gloria and Jed indulged me. Billy was amazed.

'Did Mummy used to live here?'

'Yes, Billy. She did.'

'You're not *serious*!'

'As serious as your life.'

'Did Chris live here as well?'

'No. He lived in a jungle idyll many worlds from here learning the ancient secrets of the lost Microsoft tribe and how to crochet his own lentils from recycled underwear.'

'Did he, Daddy?'

'Yes, indeed. He'll tell you all about it if you ask.'

'Daddy?'

'Yes, Billy?'

'Can we have Playstation 2?'

'Not until you're older.'

'But Chris got one for Mummy's Home.'

'Did he? Does he let you play with it at all?'

'Daddy?'

'Yes?'

'You haven't really got a job, have you?'

'Yes I have.'

'It's only *painting* . . .'

* * *

'Estelle,' I said, 'it's Father's Day.' I dropped her on the bed and started tickling. Tickling and then tickling some more. 'Come on now, out with it!' I demanded, digging my fingertips into her tiddly little ribs. 'Are you a ticklish little girl?'

She squealed and tried to catch my hands. What was that she tried to say? Mamamamama! Dadaddaada! Eight months after leaving the maternity suite there was so much Estelle could do: This Little Piggy; Pat-a-Cake Pat-a-Cake Baker's Man; Round and Round the Garden, Like a Teddy Bear. But nothing beat the thrill of Tickling Terror.

'I must warn you, Miss Stone, that resistance is futile. I repeat: are you a ticklish little girl?' I tickled and tickled and tickled: terrible, merciless tickling.

Tickling Terror was a Stone family tradition. It had never worked for Jed, but Gloria had loved it and Billy still did. Come to Daddy, little children! He only wants to torture you!

I paused for a moment, listening. There was a clinking on the stairs and the sound of careful footsteps coming nearer. Enter Gloria, Jed and Billy bearing homemade Father's Day cards, a mug of tea and breakfast on a tray. Angela supervised from the rear.

'*Eeek!*' I screamed. '*It's Mr Toothy!*' I dived under the duvet to escape.

'Be Afraid of Mr Toothy,' said Billy in a deep, deep voice. He was dressed like the Virgin Mary and holding Mr Toothy by the tail. 'Be Very Afraid.'

Mr Toothy was a bath toy, a water-squirting plastic shark. He sometimes launched surprise attacks at dawn.

'But it's Father's Day,' went up my muffled quail. 'Shouldn't Mr Toothy be at home with Mrs Toothy and the tiny Toothy brood?'

'All right, then,' Billy relented. 'But before he goes home for his breakfast Mr Toothy wants to talk.'

'Speak, O Mr Toothy,' I intoned.

'Mr Toothy says I'm going to have a bigger family,' Billy said.

'Oh, does he?' I said with sudden interest. 'What else does Mr Toothy say?'

'Mr Toothy says I'm going to live in a big house!'

'Oh yeah? In your dreams.'

'A palace that costs a million pounds! With Mummy and Chris! Far, far from here!'

I came out from under the duvet. 'And what happens after that?' I asked, not quite so jolly now. 'Will I ever see you again? Tell me, what does Mr Toothy say?'

But Mr Toothy was already on his way back to the bathroom. He'd done his work, the beast.

'A palace, eh?' I said to Gloria and Jed. 'That costs a million pounds? That's far, far away?'

They stood there and said nothing.

'Sounds lovely,' I smiled, choking a little on my toast.

chapter 24

'HelloCountryWaysestateagentsDwayneherehowcan-
Ihelp?'

'Sorry. Could you repeat that? I had a heavy night.'

'Hello. Country Ways estate agents. Dwayne here.
How can I help?'

'Thanks, Dwayne. You're a mate.'

'My pleasure, sir.'

'I'm interested in a house that's on your books. It's in
Haydown. A charming village, I believe.'

I was on an undercover mission. What I said about a
heavy night was fiction. I'd only had one glass of whisky
and it had lasted a long time – until about four in the
morning when my head at last stopped spinning and I
dropped off on the settee. Once awake I'd scoured the Net
for posh estate agents. There it was, pride of the Country
Ways website. Huge and handsome. Many acres of land. A
snip at £950,000. Not quite a million, Billy, but on its way.

'Tell me, Dwayne,' I continued, 'has there been much
interest?'

'Quite a lot, sir, yes.'

'Not that much, then?'

'Well, as I say, sir, quite a lot . . .'

'But no firm offer so far?'

'Not so far, sir. But we expect to move this property quite soon.'

He might not have been lying. I knew Mr and Mrs Pinnock had been round there for a look with the three children. You don't do that unless you're eager. Gloria had divulged the key details to Angela. 'It's very big and posh,' she'd said. 'A bit old-fashioned, though.'

'All right then, Dwayne,' I said. 'I'll give it the once over.'

We agreed to meet at two that afternoon.

Angela and I had made a plan. While Gloria, Jed and Billy were at Mummy's Home she would visit her parents with Estelle leaving me to give the living room a serious makeover – replace the mucky mauve with gorgeous gold.

'Seven days is plenty,' I'd assured Angela as I'd seen her and Estelle on to the train.

On Saturday I rested.

On Sunday I lazed around.

On Monday I piled the armchairs on top of the settee. Then I lay on the carpet and looked at them. What were Dilys and Chris up to? Would they *really* move to the country without a by your leave?

On Tuesday I pulled up the carpet and threw it into a skip. I felt a little better for it.

On Wednesday I thought about the kids. I wanted to be with them. I wanted to tell them everything was going to be OK. Angela phoned from Derby. I told her the decorating was going absolutely fine.

And on Thursday... That's when I rang Dwayne. Haydown wasn't as distant as the far-flung places to which the Pinnocks relocated in my gloomiest reveries, but it was still another country in its way: sylvan, smart, sickeningly far out of my financial range. If my children were going to live there I believed it was my duty to give it the once-over. I did not expect to have another chance.

I parked the Astra on the road and walked up the winding gravel drive. Dwayne was waiting at the other end, leaning on his metallic lilac Laguna. Given that I was old enough – just – to be his father, it was absurd I was so keen to create a good impression by concealing my tatty old banger. But then I was pretending to be someone else.

'Mr Dali?' He held out his hand. 'Very good to meet you, sir.'

'Good to meet you too, Dwayne,' I replied. 'And good of you to drive a car that goes so very nicely with my suit.'

Dwayne was speechless for a moment. Perhaps he was intimidated by my wedding get-up, which was enjoying its first outing for some time. I raised my shades to let him know that I was joking. 'We aim to please, sir,' said Dwayne, recovering his urban poise.

'Shall we go into the house? The owners are in. They're very nice people. I think they quite enjoy these little visits.'

I stood back to appreciate the front elevation, all ancient timbers and fine gables. In the forecourt area there was room for several cars. Handsome shrubs bloomed lustily and crickets chirruped in the ornamental hedges.

The front door was old and heavy. It began to open before Dwayne's finger reached the bell. Behind it was revealed a grey-haired man of medium portliness aged about seventy. He had the complexion of a fine spring radish and a bright, carefree manner, suggesting that his mortgage had been paid off long ago. 'Hello again, Dwayne. Bring the gentleman through!'

Dwayne did as he was told and I was suddenly transported back in time. It was fussy, it was floral and the smell of Pledge hung heavy in the air. Oblivious to the mockery of IKEA commercials, this was the proud and stubborn habitat of Chintz-Man and his wife Chintz-Woman. She hovered eagerly at Chintz-Man's side clutching a stack of coasters. They inspected me as if I was some exotic new arrival in the human zoo.

'So you're in showbusiness Mr, Ah?' asked Chintz-Man tentatively.

'It's Mr Dali. And yes, I am in showbiz.' I'd got a bit carried away chatting Dwayne up on the phone.

'How marvellous!' exclaimed Chintz-Woman. 'What branch?'

'Ballroom dancing,' I chimed. 'I specialise in the jive, as did my father and my mother before me . . .' That last part at least was true. '. . . I've just been to a rehearsal for a new show in the West End. Hence the outlandish gear.'

'It certainly is *extremely* gay,' said Chintz-Man. His wife giggled. 'Oh dear. We're not supposed to say that these days, are we?'

'Don't mind me, darling,' I said. 'Why don't you just whisk me straight upstairs?'

'It's a family home, of course,' said Chintz-Man. 'Ideal for children. Ours are long gone now.'

Chintz-Woman asked, 'Do you have children, Mr Dali?'

'What do *you* think?' I flirted.

'Oh, I couldn't possibly tell!'

'I've got four of them,' I told her.

'Four! Busy fellow, then,' Chintz-Man chuckled, glad to have discovered it was safe to invite me into his bedroom after all.

'Ho ho!' I obliged. 'Never a minute's rest!'

Chintz-Man bustled towards the stained wood stairway. Dwayne said, 'If you people would excuse me, I need to nip out to my car.'

'Polite young fellow,' Chintz-Man whispered. 'It's surprising how many of the coloured people are, once you get to know them.'

'Oh yes, indeed.' I moved him quickly on. 'It is *five* bedrooms, is it? That's not just estate agent talk?'

Chintz-Man reassured me, talking me through each bedroom as I mentally assigned one to three

293

absent members of my family. It was a beautiful house for any children to grow up in. Downstairs, the tour continued: two reception rooms, a study, a spacious stone-tiled kitchen, a toilet, a utility room and a garden that was more like the grounds of a stately home. Who else might have lived here? What might their stories be?

Dwayne had rejoined us by then. 'We can assist you with financing if you require it, Mr Dali.'

I'd quickly come to admire my Country Ways chaperon: his professional commitment, his polished etiquette, his sartorial style. Carlo would have loved him.

'No you can't, Dwayne,' I said. 'Not unless your company robs banks.'

Laughter all round. 'Have you had many people looking?' I asked Chintz-Woman.

Chintz-Man answered for her. 'A few, a few,' he said, though not with much conviction.

'How many is a few, Dwayne?' I enquired.

'We had a family in here just last week.'

'Oh yes,' butted in Chintz-Man. 'Shortish fellow with a beard and a rather attractive wife.'

For my benefit, Chintz-Woman rolled her eyes.

'They brought their three children with them,' Chintz-Man went on. 'Very polite children, weren't they, dear?'

A tide of pride washed through me as Chintz-Woman concurred. 'Oh yes, very polite. A girl in her teens, the image of her mother. A rather quiet boy and his younger brother. He was a bit of a character.'

'Oh really?' I remarked. 'I love those sorts of children. Tell me more.'

'Oh well,' enthused Chintz-Woman, warming to her task, 'he told me all about how he is *really* Cinderella and was only *pretending* to be a boy.'

'How charming,' I chuckled. 'Sounds just like one of my own. And tell me, has this family made an offer?'

'Not yet,' Chintz-Man conceded. 'Although Dwayne is very hopeful. I must say this does seem to be exactly what they need. The chap told me he hoped he'd be adding to his family very soon.'

I woke up the next morning thinking, Get off, lazy cat. You're like a dead weight on my legs. I gave a gentle shove with my feet and heard a thud as Tiger hit the floor.

'Sorry, Tiger,' I said. I hadn't meant to push her off the edge. 'Good job you kitties always fall on your feet.' I sat up groggily, rowing myself forward to peer over the far end of the bed. Tiger lay rigid on the carpet. She had indeed been a dead weight – stone dead.

'UH!' I blurted out. I didn't need to touch her to see that it was over and had been for some hours. Dead cat comedy has an illustrious history. But I didn't think my eldest son would laugh.

'Oh Jed!' I wailed. 'Oh Jed!'

It was 8.07 a.m. I pulled a worn-out fleece from Jed's bottom drawer and gingerly wrapped it round the cat's stiffened form. What now? Go out to the garden and quickly dig a hole? Wait in misery for the family to come home? Wasn't this how you trained children to deal with the fate that we all faced?

'Jed, Jed. Don't be too upset. Think of it as a kind of preparation.'

'For what?'

'For when I'm dead.'

'Don't be stupid. You're not a cat.'

'No, I'm your dad, but . . .'

'I'd rather have a cat.'

'Do you really mean that?'

No, I couldn't handle that. Cradling her tenderly I slipped Tiger inside my old Nike hold-all and zipped her up. Twenty minutes later I pushed my way into the vet's and went up to the receptionist, who smiled.

'Hello. I'm Joseph Stone,' I said. 'I've brought my little cat to see you. Unfortunately, she's dead.'

Her eyes swept the premises as if searching for hidden cameras. Might Jeremy Beadle be revealing himself soon? But no. She quickly saw that she was dealing with a gentleman in distress.

'But Mr Stone,' she said, 'if your cat is dead, why is she here?'

'I don't know, I just . . .'

A Pekinese was staring at me. Frantic to seem insouciant, I slung the hold-all over my shoulder. Tiger's redundant body bumped against the sides.

'I don't know, I just . . .'

'I understand. It's so distressing, isn't it? Here, now. Have a tissue.'

I blew my nose. 'I can't believe this happened. He was so happy and now this . . .'

The receptionist looked at me strangely. Had the dead kitten changed sex? Of course, she couldn't know that I was now talking about Jed. She spoke to me again. 'We can take a look at the, er, kitten, if you'd like, to try and find the cause of death. Is that what you were hoping?'

'Yes. No. It's all right. I'm sorry, I shouldn't be here. I'm holding up the Pekinese. I'll go away.'

My corpse and I departed. What should I do next?

'Back again, then?' The woman in the pet shop recognised me. I could have cut up rough. *You sold my son a dud. A kit with ticker trouble. It pegged out on my legs. You say you don't believe it? Look at this.*

But I didn't. Meekly, I said, 'Yes. But now I need another one. You see, the shy lad's got a brother . . .'

'Should have seen that coming!' the woman laughed.

There was only one black kitten in the tumbling ball of fluff inside the glass-fronted pen. It was a bit bigger than Tiger, but not much, otherwise it was her doppel-gänger.

'I'll take the black one, please,' I said. Another mewing feline infant. Another cardboard carrying box.

'There you go,' the woman said. 'I hope they won't get muddled up!'

'Don't even *think* about that happening,' I said bravely.

The woman laughed. I headed for the door.

'Don't forget to get it neutered,' she called after me. 'You know what these tom cats are like!'

I froze. But there was nothing I could do. With my dead girl kitten swinging from one hand and my live boy one from the other, I turned and ran for home.

chapter 25

The six of us assembled round the kitchen table for dinner. I cleared my throat and said: 'Sorry about the carpet, everyone. And the, ah, lack of decorating.'

'You haven't done *anything*,' Angela had said, almost in awe. 'You've been here nearly a week and you've done nothing at all – except throw out the carpet so Estelle will get splinters when she crawls across the floor.' She'd taken the baby off me without a word.

I chewed on my fish fingers in silence.

'Daddy?'

'Yes, Billy?'

'You know what?'

'What?'

'You know Andy?'

'Yeah.'

'Andy hasn't got a daddy.'

The Andy in question was the little boy in the *Toy Story* films, the owner of Woody and Buzz. Billy was right: so far as anyone can tell, Andy only has a mum.

She is not a major character, but at least it is clear that she exists. By contrast, Andy's co-progenitor is a mystery. Who is this unseen father? A hopeless workaholic who never gets home before dark? A shameless love rat, deservedly divorced? One of those internet sperm spivs whom broody women pick from websites to provide vials of alpha male semen for a fee?

'You're right, Billy,' I began. 'Andy doesn't seem to have a daddy. I wonder why that is?'

'The mother dumped him, I expect,' said Gloria. 'He probably couldn't deal with commitment.'

Jed said nothing. But he whispered something to Billy, and Billy instantly announced, 'He's probably just dead!'

I soldiered on. 'I suppose the people who made *Toy Story* thought if Andy was only going to have one parent it would have to be his mum. After all, lone dads are exceptional. You don't get very many.'

'Yes you do,' said Billy firmly.

'Oh really. Like who?'

'Like in *Pocahontas*. She's only got a daddy.'

'All right, then,' I countered, 'what about *Dumbo*? That's just him and Mrs Jumbo against a cruel, uncaring world. Not a dad in sight.'

Jed whispered to Billy again. 'What about Princess Jasmine in *Aladdin*?' Billy demanded. '*She's* only got a daddy!'

'And the Little Mermaid!' said Jed.

'She doesn't count,' I blustered. 'She's a vain, silly sea creature who wants to marry into a family of sea creature-eaters. She's a bimbo and a collaborator.'

'There's only a dad in *Beauty and the Beast*,' Gloria said. 'He's a bit mad!'

'There's only a dad in *The Swan Princess*,' said Billy.

'And in *A Goofy Movie*,' said Gloria.

A Goofy Movie: a story of the most embarrassing dad ever.

'Can't you think of a cartoon dad who's not a laughing stock?' I begged.

'How about *The Lion King*?' Angela suggested, having a little pity at long last. 'He's a really nice dad.'

'Yeah, Mufasa!' Billy enthused. 'Big an' bad out there in the jungle. Chris really likes him.'

My mind began to wander at that point. It wandered first down to the far end of the garden. 'Hi Tiger,' said my mind as it loitered at her graveside. 'Move over and I'll join you.' And then my mind drifted to Bambi. He had a mum *and* a dad. His mum was shot by hunters – everyone remembers that. But what of Bambi Senior, the distant patriarch who stomped round the forest giving gruff commands? I wondered if he'd had the right idea.

part iv: letting go

chapter 26

'Joe, wake up!'

I reached out a hand. Angela took it. I said, 'It's not tomorrow.'

'Yes it is,' she said. 'It's half past three.'

'Where's the baby?'

'She's here, she's fast asleep.'

'And where are you?' I still had my eyes shut. I kept them shut and pulled her closer to me.

'Joe,' she said. 'I don't want to alarm you, but . . .'

'But what?'

'I've been talking to Dilys.'

I sat bolt upright, blinking. My penis had been rock rigid. I felt it shrink down to an inch. 'You're joking,' I decided, peering up in shock.

'I'm not,' she said. 'I've been with her for two hours.'

'Where?'

'At her house.'

'But what about the Pillock?'

'He wasn't there. Away on business. Actually, he rang while I was there.'

It was too much to absorb. Primitive instincts took command. I remembered I was naked. I found I was in touch with my Neanderthal side.

'I'm still dreaming really, aren't I?'

'No. I think Dilys was quite pleased to see me. She was feeling lonely.'

'Lonely, you say?'

'Yes. In fact I think she often is.'

I rested my head on Angela's thigh. 'What happened?' I said.

'We talked. Actually, I talked mostly.'

'What about?'

'I talked about Estelle. And she ... I think she genuinely wanted to be friendly – to be open with me. Yet she seemed inhibited as if she was afraid of giving too much away.'

'You have to tell me *everything*,' I said.

'Well. They have a bell-pull in their porch,' she said.

'I've pulled it. I know.'

'Behind it there was Dilys.'

'And?'

'She *is* beautiful, isn't she? And Gloria will look *exactly* like her. She wasn't what I expected, though.'

'What did you expect?'

'A smouldering sexpot – Kylie's mouth, Pammy's chest, Madonna's attitude.'

'Why?'

'Because that's why you used to fancy her, isn't it?'

'No, it's not,' I said.

'You lie,' she replied. 'But I forgive you. Anyway, I was surprised she was so . . . mumsy.'

'Mumsy?'

Angela sucked her teeth in mild frustration. 'Oh, that's not really the word. It sounds too mean. I don't know. I suppose I thought she'd be a lot more . . . Feisty? Funky? Formidable, really. I expected to be more scared.'

'Weren't you?'

'A little, but not very. I phoned her first, which helped.'

'You *phoned* her?'

Angela laughed. 'Oh *yes*. After you'd dropped off.' She said it like it was nothing. 'She was half-expecting me, you see. Because Jill had sort of told me that Dilys had sort of told her that she'd quite like to meet me – and that it would be OK.'

'You evil women,' I said. 'I should have known.'

'Jill also let me know that Chris was going to be away for a few days.'

'When did she let you know?'

'While I was at my mum's. She called me on my mobile.'

I was lost in admiration. 'So you've been plotting this?'

'Oh, we're so devious, we females,' Angela said. 'She led me through the lovely hall into the lovely kitchen where she offered me a lovely glass of wine. And then she asked me all about the baby.'

'Oh,' I said, in mock surprise. 'Did she now?'

Dilys had asked about everything: the pregnancy, the birth, the afterbirth, the hospital, the medics, the jabs, about mastitis, pelvic exercises and post-natal vaginal lubrication. But she hadn't said a lot about herself. And she'd said nothing about me. 'That was bizarre,' Angela said. 'She hardly mentioned Gloria, Jed or Billy either. That was very odd, given that their shoes were in the hall and their art was all over the walls. It was as if she didn't dare admit that any of you existed. It was almost ghostly. Weird.'

'Did she hold Estelle?'

'Yes,' Angela said.

'Did you offer or did she ask?'

'I offered. I wasn't sure if I should have.'

'How did Dilys seem? When she was holding the baby?'

'It's hard to say. She seemed OK. She tucked her under a blanket on this elegant kitchen sofa and congratulated me on having such a good sleeper. It didn't seem to faze her, if you see what I mean. But the whole situation was unreal. And then the phone rang.'

'Hubby calling?'

'I'm sure it was, although she never said so. I felt a bit embarrassed and visited the toilet to escape.'

'Did you have a good look round?'

'Of course.'

'Any folic acid there?'

'No.'

'In the bedroom with the Viagra, I'll bet.'

'Anyway, when I got back he was still on the line. She didn't say a lot. She mostly listened. There seemed to be a lot of sort of buttering him up. You know: "I think you're right, honey, I think you're right".'

'Honey? She never called *me* "honey".'

'She finally put the phone down and apologised for ignoring me. I said that was OK but I was impatient by then so I asked her what she thought we ought to do about the surnames.'

'Did you? How did she take it?'

'Like everything else, really. Rather detached. I was very calm. I told her I was sad for Estelle's sake; that we'd given her both our surnames but that she was known only as Stone so that when she was older she'd have that connection with her big brothers and sister.'

'Did she say anything to that?'

'I don't think she'd thought about it in that way before. But like with everything else she seemed quite distant. She said, "It's all so difficult, isn't it?" and not much else. I didn't push it. Then I asked if it was true that they were moving house.'

'And?'

'She said they'd done a bit of looking. I mentioned the big place in . . . where was it, Haydown? – that we'd heard they'd looked round. She seemed a bit amused I knew about it. But she implied that moving to the country was only a fantasy. Maybe she was covering up, I couldn't tell. Disappointing, isn't it?' Angela shrugged. 'She seemed a bit lost and listless like an old-fashioned housewife waiting for her husband to come home. I can picture her fussing over him. You know: putting his dinner on the table and ironing his socks like a proper wife.'

'That *would* be a novelty,' I said.

'I wonder,' Angela continued, 'if Dilys has decided to surrender. You know – to become a surrendered wife.'

'What's a surrendered wife?'

'The invention of some American writer woman. She did a self-help book saying that the way for a wife to keep her marriage on track was to give in to her husband.'

'Give in to him how?'

'Basically, you spend a lot of time telling him that he's right. Even if he isn't.'

'Very liberating.'

'She says it's all about giving a man respect. Honouring his natural masculine desire to take command.'

I looked at her beseechingly. I said, 'Undo your dressing gown.'

She allowed it to fall open at the front. With my knuckle I brushed the inside of her thigh.

'Surrender now,' I commanded her, reaching inside.

'Ooh I give in,' she said. We lay down next to one another on the bed.

'I have been useless,' I said.

'I forgive you. You probably needed a rest.'

That was when I confessed. 'You know the house in Haydown? I went and had a look at it.'

'You *didn't*!'

I let it all out, there and then: the crazy trip as Mr Dali; the madcap Tiger escapade; the paralysing worry and guilt that had rendered me too weak to lift a paint-brush while everybody else had been away. Angela listened in amazement. She laughed a bit. I said, 'The thing I hate the most is being useless. I swore the day Dilys left that I would never be like that. And now I've let you and the children down.'

Angela lay close beside me. 'Put your finger in me,' she said.

'But it's so happy up my nose,' I said, surprised.

'Put your finger in me *now*.'

I put my finger in her.

'Now put in two.'

I put in two.

'Look after me,' she said.

I looked after her mouth. I looked after her earlobes, neck and nose. I looked after her belly and her breasts. I looked after the nibbles that I still shared with Estelle. And then I gently turned her over.

'How does that feel for you, angel?'

'Heavenly. Just heavenly. So deep . . .'

Deep. I was doing deep. And breathless, suddenly.

'Not yet,' she said. 'Not yet.'

Like a gentleman, I took my mind elsewhere. A bucketful of maggots. A cowpat on a plate. The nasty knobbly knees of Uncle Ned.

Where were we now? Oh yes.

I sat back on my heels. She wheeled around and faced me. Knee to knee. Eye to eye. Cheek to cheek.

'Don't touch me,' I panted. 'We'll have to sponge the walls.'

She didn't touch me yet. She only spoke. 'Put your hands behind your back.'

I put my hands behind my back.

'I want to look at you,' she said. Her palms cradled my face.

I asked, 'We love each other, don't we?'

'Always will,' she said.

chapter 27

'Oh my *God*!' she said, wide awake suddenly.

'Sweetheart, take this.'

'*Oh my God!*'

'Put it under you. Wrap it round.' It was a claret-coloured beach towel. I said, 'I've got what you need here in this bag.'

Gloria looked horrified. 'I can't put one of those things in out *here*!' She'd been slumbering in a yellow one-piece costume, a floppy hat and purple plastic shades. I leant closer to help her feel more concealed.

'I know you can't,' I said, 'but you don't have to. Nobody's noticed. Cover yourself up and we'll slip out through the hedge. The ladies' toilet block's just over there.'

We'd been in Devon for a week, building a few sandcastles, dodging a few showers, changing a few hundred smelly nappies in the tent. Being a long way from South Norwood had improved the atmosphere. Estelle was adorable, Billy and Jed were entertained.

Angela was anticipating her impending return to work with as much fortitude as she could muster – at least Estelle would be in Esther's loving care. The only tension in the air was courtesy of Gloria – and, I suppose, courtesy of my antipathy towards the adolescent boys with fluff on their top lips eyeing Gloria from a distance, trying to work out if she was old enough to kiss. At times it was like being in some natural history series.

'The young males begin to circle. They sense that the young female is mature. But the young female is uncertain. She remains close to the herd. The bull male becomes aggressive. "Back off, spotty," he seems to say. "She's much too young for you . . ."'

It was as Gloria's policeman that I'd gone to the pool that day. Unlike Jed and Billy she didn't care for rock pools or crazy golf, and since Angela had insisted that she, together with Estelle, should do boy duty that day, it fell to me to lounge alongside my blossoming daughter and by my presence repel teenage would-be boarders.

I was not over-protective: if there had been a boy worth kissing and she'd been drawn towards his lips I'd have slipped quietly away. But for all her precocious pubescence she'd expressed few nascent sexual interests beyond the smooth-skinned boy bands on her bedroom walls and I sensed she found the rituals of her spotty stalkers wearing. I sympathised and hoped she knew it, though I realised my solidarity should be kept to myself.

'Which way is it?' she panicked, staring around.

'This way,' I said, taking her elbow and leading her around the scruffy privet. She clutched the bath towel to her midriff, flip-flops flapping. The toilet block was starkly concrete and a violent shade of green but it had showers. 'Here you are,' I said, pulling a carrier from the hold-all and pressing it into her hand. It contained clean clothing and a sanitary pad. She took it and scuttled forth.

I love Gloria. I *always* love Gloria, even when she drives me up the wall. And when she emerged all clean and dressed and happy, I loved her more easily than I had done for a while.

'Do you always hang round outside ladies' toilets?' she enquired, walking towards me, the claret towel now tucked under her arm.

I was loafing in a neutral manner a suitably non-weirdo distance from the entrance.

'Are you all right?' I asked, ignoring her remark.

'Yes. Thank you.'

'That's OK. I'm like a Boy Scout. Be Prepared.' It was anxious dad blather. But when I offered her an arm, she accepted. We walked together, slowly, her head bumping against my shoulder now and then.

'We could go back to the tent and read,' I said. 'What do you think?'

'I'd rather play table tennis.'

'Are you sure?'

She knew what I was thinking. She said, 'Haven't you seen those adverts?'

I cottoned on. 'Oh, all those women windsurfing with confidence, you mean?' We reached the recreation area. 'You serve,' I said.

She crouched expertly and sent the ball skimming towards me. I knocked it into the net. Before I tossed it back to her I said, 'I've got a question for you, Gloria.'

'Is it about Mum and Chris?'

'Sorry. Afraid it is.'

'That's all right,' she said. She loosed off another lightning serve. 'Are you going to ask me if they're going to have a baby?'

'Blimey, am I that see-through?'

'Yes.'

'So are they?'

Gloria caught the ball and put her bat down on it to stop it rolling. She shook the neck and shoulders of her T-shirt to let a little air get underneath.

'I don't know, Dad.'

'Has Mum talked to you about it?'

'Yes.'

'Is it fair to ask you what she said?'

'No.'

'Sorry.'

'It's OK.' She took up her bat again and this time sent over a gentle lob. I shovelled the ball back and risked another step into the minefield.

'Is Mum very upset?'

'Yes.'

'Do you think it will be all right?'

'We don't know yet.'

'I don't hate Mum, you know. She doesn't think that, does she?'

'She knows you're very cross.'

'About the surnames?'

'Yes.'

'I think she and I ought to talk about those things. Try and sort everything out. How would you feel about that?'

Gloria spun a backhand past me, bringing the rally to an end. She rolled her head from side to side, meaning, 'Well, maybe'. And then she said, 'For secondary school I'm going to have my name back.'

I caught the ball and held it. '*What?*'

'I'm going to be Gloria Stone again. I asked and they said yes, now it would be OK. And Pinnock is a silly name,' she laughed.

'No it isn't!' I replied insincerely.

'Yes, it is,' Gloria giggled. 'It sounds like "pillock"!'

'You're not supposed to know rude words.'

'I told Chris that.'

'That his name sounded like "pillock"?'

'Yes!'

'Did you? And how did he react?'

'He didn't mind. He said that's what he was sometimes called at school.'

I was curious now. She'd never really said a lot about him. 'What sort of school did he go to?'

'A posh one, I think. A boarding school.'

'And is he really, really rich?'

'Ooooh!' Gloria said. 'You're not *threatened* by him, are you, Dad?'

'Yes.'

'Ha! You can't be *threatened* by Chris!'

'Why not? He's got more money than I have. He's an IT wizard and a thrusting entrepreneur. I'm just a struggling artist.'

'Chris isn't *threatening*. He never stops *worrying*.'

'About what?'

'Dunno. Secret things that children aren't to know. Can't artists be rich then?'

'Only some of them,' I said.

'Why did you become one?'

'I was good at it. I liked it. I was naive enough to believe that I could make a living at it.'

'Don't you, then?'

'Sort of, now and then.'

'I've seen those ones you do for Uncle Charlie.'

'Oh dear, have you?'

'Yes. Well, they're a lot more interesting than that one you did of me that Uncle Bradley and Malika have got now.'

'Nonsense,' I said. 'It graces their restaurant. It's the sort of work I want to do: honest and soulful and pure.'

'Oh *stop*,' she said. 'You're *embarrassing*.'

'Good. Is Chris embarrassing too?'

'Questions, questions!'

'So?'

'He is sometimes, I suppose.'

'Like when?'

'Like when he wants us to pose for photographs. All nice and neat like a *proper* family, is what he says.'

'Does that happen often?'

'Lately it has, yes. And at the Christmas concert.' Her brown eyes rolled like heavy marbles. 'He stood up in front of everyone, videoing that nativity stuff. He said he liked Christmas traditions and was going to send a copy to some relatives of his to show them what a perfect family he was part of.'

'Sounds rather sweet,' I said. Such virtue. 'Did he video the moose?'

'The moose?'

'I mean the reindeer. The person who went in costume as a reindeer.'

Gloria gave a surprised laugh. 'Oh yes, I remember. No one ever found out who it was. Who told you about it?'

'I had inside information.'

That night I sat under the awning with a torch.

Dear Dilys,

It is getting on for three years since our relationship ended and I feel I must appeal to you one more time to try and find a way to settle our disagreements . . .

I wrote it with great care and it was nearly 2 a.m. before I finished. Then I ran to the campsite post box and slipped the letter through the slot before I could change my mind.

chapter 28

Veronica looked at us both. 'Now,' she began, 'we need to decide which issue we are going to talk through first.'

I've never felt quite so nervous as in that neutral-coloured room with the blinds closed against the dusk, Veronica the mediator speaking soothing words and Dilys Day herself sitting a few feet away.

'Any thoughts?' asked Veronica, lifting her brow in invitation to each of us in turn.

'I'd like to talk about my husband Chris,' Dilys said. 'I'd especially like to talk about Joe's attitude to him and the relationships that Chris has with the children.'

As these words emerged I kept my eyes on the floor rug's geometric pattern and tried to put the brake on a crazy carousel of mixed emotions. Dilys looked tired, I thought. I'd noticed, too, that she'd gained weight. Was that age creeping on? Sorrow stirred inside me, perhaps a recognition that time was passing for me too.

Veronica said, 'And what about you, Joseph?'

I said, 'I want to talk about the change of surnames and the damage it has done.'

There was silence before Dilys said, 'Maybe I ought to respond to that.'

I fixed my eyes back on the rug. She was looking at me now, I could tell that from the direction of her voice. I knew I should find the nerve to return her gaze and worked on it as Dilys went on talking. 'I realise, Joe,' she said, 'that you might find this difficult to understand. But I did have my reasons for taking that decision . . .'

At last I became able to lift my eyes to hers but the consequence was that I stopped hearing. Her hair was as long and luxurious as ever, but I was shocked by the way her face had changed. Was it just my memory deceiving me? I hadn't seen her for a while. But, no, something more dramatic had happened than the routine passage of two years. Her cheeks seemed to have swollen and her skin had a glassy look. The absence of make-up – none of the familiar lipstick – heightened the look of malady. My realisation that I was staring gave me absolution to look away again. Dilys was still speaking. I tried to tune back in to whatever she was saying.

'. . . it isn't something I can go into in detail. But I have got a suggestion to resolve the situation.'

I was disorientated now. The mediator spotted my discomfort. 'We've moved down this path quite quickly,' she said, intervening deftly. 'Are you all right about this, Joseph?'

'Uh, yes. Go on, ah . . .' I nodded to Dilys to continue. I found I couldn't say her name.

'We could go back to using Stone in everyday life, including at school. But could the name Pinnock be added? Perhaps for formal things, like passports? It is my name now, after all.'

A coffee-table lay between our matching easy chairs. On it stood a box of tissues, two glasses and a water jug. I wondered as I filled my glass how obvious it was that I was only doing it to play for time.

'I mean,' Dilys went on, 'sometimes it will be easier for us to call them Pinnock if we're booking into a hotel as a family or something. But for everyday use they can go back to being Stones.'

I tried to conceal my elation. Adding a semi-silent 'Pinnock' seemed quite a small concession. Dilys was backing down gracefully on the really import-ant issue – and we'd only been ten minutes in the room.

'You mean like with Estelle?' I turned to Veronica and explained. 'She has two surnames – Slade and Stone – but for practical purposes she'll only use mine – to help her feel fully linked with her half-siblings.'

'Is that what you mean, Dilys?' Veronica asked.

'Yes,' Dilys nodded. 'Exactly the same thing.'

I surveyed Dilys for a second. Why the change of heart? Was there a catch?

Dilys kept on talking. 'It would be nice for my new surname to be officially acknowledged and I think it's a good thing for them to carry both our surnames now that we're apart . . .'

'Listen, Dilys,' I broke in. 'What I don't understand is why you did it in the first place.'

It was Dilys now who found the rug interesting. She spoke again at last, still looking down. 'I know I shouldn't have done it . . . I *was* going to tell you, Joe, straight after Christmas. But I was in a hurry. I suppose I told myself you wouldn't mind too much after a while. And you did say at the time when Gloria was born that you wouldn't mind her being Gloria Day. You said it didn't really matter. We only went for Stone because we thought our parents would think it was funny not to stick with tradition.'

I said, 'Chris is not their father, Dilys.'

'But he does want to be *like* a father to them,' Dilys answered, as if stung. 'The same as Angela is *like* a mother.'

I'd been kebabed on my own skewer. If Angela was *like* a real mummy, why couldn't Chris be *like* a real daddy? If such was the relationship, how much did blood and labels really count?

'I'm sorry, Dilys,' I said. I hadn't planned to say it but I saw her eyes were red.

'It's all right,' she said. This time I poured us both some water from the jug.

'I'm wondering,' Veronica ventured, 'would it be helpful if we talk about Chris and try to understand his needs in all of this?'

'That's OK with me,' I said.

Dilys only nodded her assent. She took a sip of the water. I sensed her gathering herself for a long haul.

'Joe,' she said, 'can you cast your mind back to the night before I moved out? That Sunday evening after we'd been to see the dinosaurs in the park? We'd been packing and I went out late to get some bits and pieces from a shop. I don't know if you remember.'

'Uh huh,' I shrugged. The truth was I remembered it distinctly. It was thanks to that odd excursion that I'd been able to sneak out and bury the photo albums in the garden.

'Well,' Dilys continued, 'I went to a late-night chemist and bought a pregnancy testing kit. I was worried, you see. There'd been some spotting and I wasn't feeling right. Are you catching my drift?'

I was catching it all right – catching it so well I didn't trust myself to speak.

'Anyway,' went on Dilys. 'It would have been Chris's.'

It was a soap opera moment. A Catherine Cookson climax. In this unscripted melodrama it seemed to be my turn to speak. 'What happened?' I asked feebly.

'I miscarried at thirteen weeks. A few days after we met for the first time at the wine bar to sort out the arrangements for Gloria, Jed and Billy. In fact it was the day after we agreed things on the phone.'

'I remember. Not long before Christmas.' Their first Christmas at Dulwich. The first time the kids had seen Chris's house, as transformed by Dilys's dedicated nesting. I remembered her in that wine bar. She'd been blooming.

'Luckily, we hadn't told the kids,' Dilys went on. 'We hadn't told my mother either. So that was something.'

I imagined Dilys's brave face for Chris's busy camera, remembered spying on the house on Boxing morning before going home to paint. I'd felt so sorry for myself.

'That's all so sad,' I said. 'I had no idea.' I imagined, too, the grim aftermath. Angela had read about post-miscarriage procedure. 'They have to scrape the foetus out,' she'd told me bleakly. 'It's called dilatation and curettage – D and C.'

'We've been trying ever since,' Dilys went on, 'and failing. But you've worked that out, I expect.'

'Not really,' I lied, protecting Gloria, who had hinted at such.

'I'm the problem,' continued Dilys. Everything about her was cast down. Her hair fell across her features. 'I've stopped ovulating properly. It's like the menopause come early. That happens to women sometimes. No one really knows why.'

Bad timing, I thought. She and I had never had a problem with conception. Dilys seemed to read my mind. 'Looks like you had the best of me in that respect,' she said.

Sex and procreation: that's what Dilys and I had mostly been about. Three years on it seemed unreal. The woman in front of me didn't remind me of any of the Dilyses I'd known. She didn't remind me of Gloria either. She had become another person, someone whose life force seemed completely spent. She sat up straight and looked down at herself, as if inviting my inspection. 'This is what you get with IVF,' she said. 'Fertility drugs. All puffed up and bloated. It's the hormones. And it's agony, you know. It's murder. And I don't think it's going to happen. It isn't going to work.' She shook her head. 'I'm exhausted with it now. I've had enough.'

There was a lull that I was not equipped to fill. I had only platitudes to offer: you're only my age, Dilys, you've still got lots of time. I kept them to myself. Veronica said, 'Dilys, if you need a rest . . .'

'It's all right,' Dilys said. 'We ought to get on with it. I haven't said anything about Chris yet.'

I saw my chance to step into the breach. 'Well, I suppose I've found it quite hard to accept him. You know, it isn't easy. I mean, we've never even *met*.'

'I don't *want* you to meet him, Joe,' said Dilys quickly.

'Why not?'

'Oh, come *on*,' she said suddenly. 'You'd only make fun of him. You and Carlo and Kenny. You three wise guys. Art-school types. You'd have a fine time taking the piss.'

I could hardly protest innocence. 'A techy twerp in bush shorts' was how I had described him to her face.

'Just put yourself in his place, Joe,' Dilys continued. She was looking straight at me now. 'Imagine having to hear the kids go on and on and on about how *wonderful* their dad is all the time, how he looked after them all on

327

his own, how brilliant his jokes are, how good his cooking is, how he lets them eat fish and chips on the settee. Especially the boys . . .'

I offered only a short splutter. I was reeling. Dilys ploughed on. '*Daddy* lets us eat chips in front of the telly! *Daddy* lets me be Tinkerbell! *Daddy* got me a kitten!'

'They're not like that often, surely,' I put in. 'They've learned how not to do that. They all try so hard to be fair.'

'All right, all right,' said Dilys. 'Yes, you're right. But when those things *do* come out, they *hurt*! And when Chris isn't hearing that stuff,' she went on, 'he's putting up with me: missing them when they're at your place, shuttling me in and out of clinics. All Chris wants . . .' She slowed herself. 'All Chris wants is to make a decent job of being some sort of a decent father – a father *figure* to our children with whom he just happens to share his home, his wife and his life.'

Jolted by her passion I felt humility invade.

'I shouldn't tell you this,' Dilys continued, blazing, 'but Chris has never had a proper family life. His father died when he was five and his mother died three years later. He spent most of his childhood at some stupid boarding school. He didn't have brothers or sisters or relatives he was close to. Yes, he's always had a bit of money. But compared with you or me he hasn't had much of a life. And I'm sorry about your surname, Joe. It was an awful thing for you. And I'm sorry I can't give you a proper explanation. At least we can put it right now – Gloria's using Stone again already. And, please, just think of one thing if it helps you to forgive me. The way things have turned out for Chris, our kids are the only ones he's got.'

chapter 29

'We'll put the boys in the back row,' I said, 'Angela and Estelle in the middle and Gloria can sit up front with me. It's so much better than the sad old Astra.'

'What if Jed and Billy squabble?' my mum asked.

'I'll have to yell at them,' I said. 'Just like I'm going to yell at you if you keep moving.'

'Sorry boss,' said Mum, darting her feet back to their original positions.

'No patience these women, have they, Joe?' said my dad. His head was buried in *The Encyclopaedia of Decorative Styles* exactly as it had been for the previous three hours. He'd only moved to turn the pages and make appreciative remarks. 'Some of these cabinets, Lana, you won't believe the detail . . .'

Three days ago was when this happened: on Friday afternoon at five past three. A Mummy's Home week was about to start and yet I felt no fear. Not since the first night I slept with Angela could I remember my life seeming more set fair. During the few weeks that had passed since mediation the dead weights on my shoulders had been lifted. Dilys had granted me Parental Responsibility. We'd agreed to wait till after Christmas for the boys' surnames to go back to being Stone. Dilys had said the buffer of a school holiday would make the reversion smoother. I agreed, and that felt good. The addition of 'Pinnock' as an official extra surname would happen in due course. The deal had been confirmed after I'd OK'd it with Angela.

'Go for it,' she'd said. 'Accept.'

'No ifs or buts?'

'You and I lose nothing that matters. We gain what we need most – peace of mind.'

'Don't you mind your surname being left out? Gloria, Jed and Billy will have everyone else's.'

'Come off it, Joe. I've bought your daughter her first bra, I've had Billy rooting through my wardrobe and I've had Jed's cat sleeping on my head. Do I seem left out to you?'

It was in this buoyant mood that we'd bought our nearly-new car – a Toyota Picnic. It was a genuine six-seater; it started on cold mornings; it was red. How could we afford it? It all began when Bradley telephoned.

'Hello, Joseph. Listen. A customer would like to buy your painting – the one of Gloria.'

'No!'

'I told her ten thousand.'

'*What?*'

'Is that OK?'

331

'Ten thousand quid? Has she stopped laughing yet?'

'No, no, Joseph . . .' Bradley had put on his patient voice – foolish artistic brother, please keep up. 'She's quite happy to pay it. She's standing by it with her chequebook at this minute. I called to clear it with you. Is ten grand enough?'

I'd let out a mighty howl of triumph. '*How-oooooooool!*'

'Joseph! Do you mind? You almost punctured my eardrum.'

'Ten thousand! Where did you pick that number from?'

'Don't you charge five thousand for those portraits of people in their homes?'

'Yeah, but . . .'

'I just pitched a little higher. She didn't flinch.'

Bradley. The sober Bradley. What a salesman! What a coup! And not a penny in commission. Charlie would be sick with envy.

'Big brother,' I said with feeling. 'Now I realise why I've always loved you.'

'Hmmm,' Bradley replied, reliably unimpressed. 'You'd better churn another one out quickly. There's a gap in the décor now.'

I'd decided to fill the gap with Mum and Dad. For the first time in a while I'd invited them over without having to hide a heavy heart. We'd spent Bonfire Night at their place the night before – another year gone – I had good news to tell at last – the mediation outcome, the ten grand and the car – and as I'd posed them on the old settee I no longer felt diminished by the link it represented between my present and my past.

'Done well, this suite,' my dad said, slapping the sagging cushions and looking at the armchairs fondly.

'I'm not sure you should have that cat on it, though,' said Mum, beadily eyeing Tiger 2. He'd colonised Jed's armchair long ago.

'Forget the cat and look proud of your trophy, Mum,' I said.

The All-Streatham Jiving Champions Cup glimmered on a plinth beside her knee. The portrait was shaping well. I'd never painted Mum and Dad with quite such confidence before. I'd even re-opened the door and shutters of A Poor Man's Wealth. I'd put a sign up saying *Please Come In and Look*. Three people had. So, then they'd gone away. But it was a start.

'OK! Relax!' I said. They'd been sitting since midday and I wanted to run them home before the Friday rush hour took hold and have time when I got back to make myself look lovely. Esther was going to babysit so Angela and I could have an evening out. To the cinema, maybe? Or to Bradley's? But first I had to visit Jed and Billy's school.

'Make yourselves a cup of tea,' I shouted, bouncing down the long stairs. 'This won't take long.'

I'd decided to drop by just before home-time. 'Hi Cidra,' I said to the school secretary. 'Is it all right if I give this book to Billy? His mum's picking him up and he'll need it for the weekend.'

Cidra nodded me through, smiling. I was smiling too. So was the entire world. Billy's latest teacher was Miss Cooper. She looked up with interest as I entered the classroom. As usual on a Friday, all the kids were sitting on the mat having a story. I scanned their upturned faces. 'Where's Billy?' I asked.

Miss Cooper looked at me quizzically. 'He left at lunch-time,' she said. 'Dilys picked him up.'

'Oh. Was he poorly?' Funny, I thought. He'd been on top form that morning. Tried sneaking out in Angela's clip-on earrings.

'No, no,' hastened Miss Cooper. 'He was fine. Dilys picked his brother up as well. They're going somewhere special, aren't they, children?'

Several voices said, 'Yes.' I looked down at the mosaic of infant features, black and white and brown.

'They're going on an airy-plane tomorrow,' someone said.

'For a long, long time.'

'They're going to Disneyland!'

'They ain't *never* coming home!'

'Now, now, Shanelle,' said Miss Cooper. 'I don't think that last part's true.'

'I hope not, Shanelle,' I added, playing up to the game. 'And where is Disneyland? Does anybody know?'

'It's in America,' announced Shanelle with great

conviction. 'That's where Billy's going with his family. He *told* us so.'

This time I didn't respond. For me the game was losing its appeal. 'Is everything all right?' Miss Cooper asked.

'Oh yes,' I said. 'Don't worry. It's only me being forgetful. Sorry to interrupt.'

You know how manic thoughts sometimes escape out of your mouth? It happened to me several times during the next few hours.

'I'm nuts,' I said. 'I'm nuts.'

That was the first time it happened, walking back from the school. Of course they weren't flying off to Disneyland. Of course they were coming home. But I said it again later, in the car.

'I'm nuts,' I said. 'I'm nuts.'

'Are you, Joseph?' said my mum. 'Why's that?'

'For not bringing you home earlier,' I answered, smartly. It was only 3.40 but Portland Road was clogged. Come off it, I told myself, Billy is a past master of invention. On the other hand, why *had* Dilys taken him and Jed out of school at lunch-time? There had to be some special reason.

At my parents' house I borrowed their telephone. (I'd left my mobile behind, as usual.) I rang Dulwich and got the answerphone. I didn't leave a message – relations with that household weren't quite ready for such familiarity yet. I called Dilys's mobile. The voicemail service kicked in. Was she ignoring me? I left a message this time – otherwise she might have called back Mum and Dad. 'Dilys. It's Joe. Please ring me at home.' Short and to the point.

'Are you all right, Joe?' called my dad.

'Fine, Dad, fine.'

I was beginning to flap. Where had those children gone? I rang Gloria's school and asked to speak to her tutor but he had left already – it was, after all, a Friday afternoon. I thought of calling Angela, but what would I say to her?

'Hello, darling wife. Darling husband here. Not for the first time I've an irrational suspicion that Dilys and Chris are abducting Gloria, Jed and Billy. I know it makes no sense but there it is. Just thought you'd like to know.'

I called Esther instead. 'Hello, Esther. How's the babe? Good. Look, I'm out at the moment and running a bit late. Could you let yourself in when you come round? Shan't be too long, I hope.'

I left my parents in a hurry. 'I'm nuts,' I said. 'I'm nuts.'

I chased back up Portland Road, through South Norwood and Crystal Palace, giving thanks that the traffic wasn't nearly so bad the other way.

'I'm nuts,' I repeated as I drove into Dulwich Village and eased through the gathering gloom towards Pillock Central. Only then did I wonder what I might do now I'd got there. If they were in I would feel stupid. And if they weren't, what then?

Their driveway was a hundred yards ahead. Suddenly, the Pillockracer nosed out into the road. 'Oh shit,' I said and pulled into the kerb, praying that the distance and failing light would conceal me; praying that whoever was driving would turn the other way. If they didn't, my only hope was that I was concealed in the Picnic, an unfamiliar car. The old Astra would have betrayed me instantly.

I peeped over the dashboard. Phew. The Pillockracer was receding. It was 4.20 p.m. I remembered what Mr £220 an hour had said.

'You being recognised as a father in family law doesn't magically stop other people behaving badly. Theoretically your ex could still do all sorts of things on a whim, including moving with them to the other end of the country or even abroad.'

'I'm nuts,' I said. 'I'm nuts.'

Then I put my foot down and gave chase.

chapter 30

Tap-tap! Tap-tap! Tap-tap!

It was right next to my ear. Quiet at first, then louder. I woke but I pretended to sleep on. I wasn't totally bewildered. My frozen bones confirmed that I had indeed spent the night in the red S-reg Picnic in a country lane. Through a slit between my eyelids I worked out that the sun had yet to rise. Now all I had to do was decide how to respond to my unscheduled wake-up call.

Tap-tap! Tap-tap! Tap-tap!

I ruled out Woody Woodpecker. I might be hearing Loony Tunes but this was no cartoon.

Tap-tap! Tap-tap! Tap-tap!

A roving rural policeman, maybe? That would be OK. I wasn't breaking any laws and had a cast-iron explanation for my unusual behaviour.

Me: 'It's perfectly straightforward, officer. Somewhere at the top end of that long and winding drive sleeps the Last of the Mohicans with his comely Minehaha and the three little injuns she and I made together in our former lives. I'm here to intercept them in some way I've yet to think of should they attempt to leave the country. I'm sure you understand.'

Roving Rural Policeman: 'I understand perfectly, sir. Now just relax and get back to your kip. I must away and strip search Squirrel Nutkin.'

I moved my head a little. Through a bead screen of condensation I made out the sleeve of a waxed jacket. Oh no, I shuddered. Bound to be some toff landowner with a gun. I saw fingers move towards me once again.

Tap-tap! Tap-tap! Tap-tap!

Could such a tap be friendly? It didn't sound especially hostile and there'd been no attempt to try the Picnic's door. Knowing I could hide no longer I rubbed clear a section of the clouded side window. A man's face looked in. It said, 'Greetings! I come in peace!'

I wound the window down. He looked every bit as worried as I must have looked crazed. I took in the green Barbour, a floppy canvas hat and a tasselled fabric bag that dangled from his neck. I took in the facial hair. I said without expression, 'You'd better get in.'

He came in out of the mist. 'You're Chris,' I said.

'And you're Joseph.'

He held out his right hand. I reached over to accept it and found his grip was fierce. I suspected that the fierceness was rather over-practised, though I suppose you shouldn't judge on a first date. Or have intercourse. I ruled that out as well.

Chris then took off his hat. His hair was dark and curly and the same length as his beard, making him look as if he was sprouting a balaclava helmet made of wire wool. I noted the emerging 'V' of a widow's peak. Added to my height advantage – he can't have been a lot taller than Dilys – this gave me confidence that I could cope with any physical encounter. True, I was feeling pretty stupid and in severe need of a leak but I was further fortified by the same recklessness that had seized me in the Palace of Chintz. Being an outraged crackpot had its uses. I said, 'OK Chris, tell me this: are you about to fly off with my kids?'

I watched as his eyes widened. He leaned back in the passenger seat, his hat and tasselled bag clutched tightly in his lap. Underneath his moustache his lips made the shape of horror. 'No, Joseph!' he burst out. 'Absolutely not! Is that why you're here? Do you really think Dilys and I would do that?'

'Well . . .' I began slowly. Suddenly, the truth was that I didn't. The force of his shocked denial was instantly deflating. I was revealed as a fruitcake, a yoyo, a buffoon.

'*I* am flying to the States this morning,' Chris resumed, leaping into the vacuum I had left. 'On business. But only me. The others are staying here for the weekend – at Quester's Lodge.'

I believed him. It was awful. I mustered my resources for an ungracious retreat. 'So *you're* going. But they're not?'

'That's right. Not any of them. Not yet.'

340

'What do you mean, not yet?'

'I mean, Dilys might join me later. It depends.'

'Depends on what?'

'Oh, boy.' He puffed a bit and shook his woolly bonce. 'I can't really explain. But if the kids go there at all it won't be before Christmas. And not *for ever*, Joseph. I could *never* do a thing like that!'

'Excuse me,' I said blankly, opening the driver's door and half-tumbling to the ground. Wet ground. Muddy too.

'Joseph?' cried Chris. 'Are you all right?'

'Don't follow me,' I barked, getting to my feet and wiping ooze from my coat. 'And don't disappear either. I'll be back.'

I staggered a dozen yards and pointed Percy at the hedge. In the nippy morning air, steam seemed to engulf me as if I was about to go on stage with Spinal Tap. Relieved, I shook off, zipped up and checked my watch. It was 6.15. I heard the approach of a milk float and waved down the startled driver, my good faith indicated by the rattle of my loose change.

'Bottle of semi-skimmed please,' I said, smiling as if I'd lurked in dirt tracks hijacking passing milkmen all my life. Then I thought of my new companion. 'Better make it two.'

As the milk float buzzed away I tottered back towards the Picnic, a chilled bottle in each hand, considering the next thing I might say.

'*Hi Chris, old buddy! You call an ambulance, I'll*

plead insanity and let's pretend this whole thing never happened.'

Or.

'So you're Christopher Pinnock! What an amazing coincidence! Wait till I tell my twin brother Joseph!'

'Good thinking!' he proclaimed as I opened the driver's door. During my brief absence he'd been busy. From his bag he'd produced two earthenware mugs and a gadget that he'd plugged into the socket of the cigarette lighter. He was deep in concentration. Having a gizmo to attend to seemed to calm him down.

'Excellent device this,' he informed me. He pulled out a plastic water bottle and filled both the mugs from it. Then he stuck the gadget into the one nearest me. 'If you wouldn't mind turning your key round to ignition for a tick.'

As I obliged he reached into his jacket pocket and produced two English Breakfast tea bags. The gadget was a miniature water heater. Out in the wilds of Sussex Chris was brewing up a morning cuppa. This bushcraft business clearly had its uses. I cleared my throat. 'So, ah, Chris. How did you know I was here?'

He twiddled the mini-heater in the mug. 'I detected your Picnic in my rearview mirror on the journey down – on the motorway just after Junction Nine. I wasn't certain it was you, but I suspected.'

I felt disappointed, as if I'd just been told that my tailing technique wasn't up to scratch for MI5. It had been a hellish journey: a tortured crawl through Purley and Coulsdon a dozen cars or so behind the Pillockracer, tracking its chunky tail lights through the dark. By 5.30 my sweating armpits were joined by a stress pain in my side. I'd known Esther and Estelle would be at home and that Angela would be joining them any time. I'd shuddered at the thought of their exchanges.

'*Did he say what he was doing, Esther?*'

'*No. Just sounded harassed.*'

'*He's left his mobile here as usual. I hope everything's all right.*'

I'd known I had no mobile phone and would lose sight of my quarry if I stopped to use a payphone. I'd known it might be madness to keep going. I'd known it might be madness to turn back. Disabled by indecision I'd just kept on going: filtered onto the M23 and followed at a distance towards the Gatwick exit, prepared to peel off behind them as they approached the count-off signs; capsized into confusion when they'd kept straight on. Had they missed the turn-off? How far were they going?

Chris said, 'I knew you'd bought a Picnic because Jed told me about it – the colour, the seating plan, the dashboard details, you know how he is.' He snuffled edgily, as if to have such knowledge of the foibles of my son might be overstepping the intimacy mark. 'Anyway, it was you, wasn't it, who followed us off the motorway at Junction Ten?'

I nodded. I'd followed for another half an hour, down narrow roads and little country lanes until the Pillockracer disappeared up a concealed driveway marked with a handsome handpainted sign. *Quester's Lodge*, it said. *Country Club and Retreat*. And hanging underneath: *Public fireworks display tonight*.

'Well,' Chris continued, 'I admit I was a little para-noid. After the fireworks were over I checked the car park. You weren't there, of course.'

No. By then I'd settled in a convenient field gateway for the night. Before that I'd scoffed a sandwich from the silent pub in the nearest village. And before that I'd rung Angela from an old-fashioned call box. She'd answered before I'd heard it ring.

'Joe?'

'You won't *believe* this, but . . .'

She told me I must be crazy. I told her it was true. She told me that when she'd got in, there'd been a phone message from Dilys, left before Esther and Estelle had got there. 'It didn't say much, only "returning your call". Why don't you ring her now?'

'Because if they're planning to make their flit tomor-row morning she isn't going to say, and if they're not she'll think I've gone insane – and the deal about surnames might be off.'

'Why don't *I* phone her?'

'On what grounds? If she's up to something she'll smell a rat.'

'So you're going to stay down there and try catching them red-handed?'

But I was in for a penny. I'd already decided that I'd stay in for a pound. 'I just can't leave here, Angela,' I'd whimpered. 'I can't leave until I know they're coming home.'

The water in the first mug was steaming nicely. Chris said, 'I was concerned enough to wake up early. I had a hunch that I might find you out here somewhere. And when I did I thought I'd better say hello.' He transferred the mini-heater to the second mug, fished the teabag from the first, added milk and handed me my char. I took a sip and said, 'And now you must be thinking I'm a nutter.'

'Not at all,' Chris said.

'Do me a favour,' I retorted.

'No, no,' he insisted. 'I absolutely don't.'

'What *do* you think?' I asked him, as my bravado crawled into a hole. I dreaded what he was going to tell Dilys and the kids.

'What I think,' said Chris slowly, closing his eyes for emphasis, 'is that you are a concerned father who cannot bear the thought of being parted from his children. And fathers in that situation sometimes do barmy things.'

He was staring at me now. Was this his Scary Bear? Then he spoke again. 'Joseph, there are some things that you don't know. I think now is the time you should be told.'

chapter 31

I was ready for banality by then – a bit of chat about his business trip, some small talk of refinancing options going forward. Chris, though, had seized the moment. He was a man in desert boots who followed Little Brookham Wanderers. He was at one with himself in this muddy Sussex lane.

'We can be real together, can't we, Joseph?' he intoned. 'You know – talk together man to man. Get naked, as it were.'

'As it were,' I said.

He said, 'I'm going to show you something very precious.' From his bag he pulled a leather wallet. Into it he slid two scissored fingers and eased out a battered photograph. He handed it to me. 'That's Michael,' said Chris.

The picture told a story.

'Was he born with that?' I asked. I meant Michael's tangle of dark curls.

'Some of it,' Chris replied.

'How old is he in this? Six months?'

'Eight, eight and a half months. I never saw him walk.'

I framed my next question with care. 'Can he walk now?' What I meant was, Is he still alive?

'Oh yes,' Chris said softly. 'He can walk.'

'What else can he do?'

'He can drive a car. He shaves. He can leave school in the summer, and he wants to. I'm going to try and talk him out of that.'

I handed back the photo. 'Some business trip,' I said.

The Manly Man weakly acknowledged his earlier fib. 'I've been sending him money and I've told him I can support him through college. But he's very independent. He likes to do things for himself.'

As Chris spoke, his hand brought something else out of his bag: another photograph, this one larger. A boy youth looked out of it, smiling defensively. Limp Bizkit T-shirt. Big corkscrew mop. I asked, 'How old is he now then? Sixteen?'

'That's right,' said Chris. 'Same age as I was when I made him.'

He said it with no trace of outlaw pride. 'I didn't have you down as a teen tearaway,' I said.

'I wasn't,' Chris replied. 'Which may explain what happened between me and Michael's mother.'

He fell silent at that moment. My permission seemed to be required. 'The beginning,' I said quietly, 'is no bad place to start.'

Chris drained his mug. 'In the beginning,' he said, 'there was Melanie.'

* * *

Chris and Melanie.

Melanie and Chris.

Names from a forgotten sun strip with a wintry tale to tell.

'She was twenty-five,' said Chris. 'To me she was a woman of the world. I was a teenage virgin. Not the first she'd taken a shine to, but the first to make her pregnant.'

He outlined his situation at that time: how he'd left boarding school early and wasn't close to the aunt and uncle who'd been his guardians after his parents died; how he'd roughed it in East Grinstead with some mild-mannered layabouts he knew. He'd got a job in an electrical repair shop. There was a pub round the corner that turned a blind eye to his age. That was where Melanie found him.

'We talked about a termination,' Chris explained, 'but she was against it. I was surprised by that – I suppose I'd assumed that because she was promiscuous she wouldn't think twice about having an abortion. Instead, she suggested marriage. I agreed.'

'Just like that?' I said. I felt like I was turning the pages of a book, one in which eventually I too might appear.

Chris pinched his bottom lip. 'I thought it would be doing the right thing by the child. I had to get my guardians' permission. And I believed in marriage. I still do.'

Michael's first home was Melanie's rented maisonette. 'After he was born we played at being man and wife. At first it was OK, but then we argued. She was obsessed about the baby. She didn't want me near him. And *I* wanted to be as near him as I could. He was the best thing that had happened to me.'

Then came the call from Kansas. Melanie had relatives there who invited her to visit. 'We agreed I wouldn't go,' said Chris. 'She thought some time apart might do us good. Michael was nine months old when the two of them flew out. I haven't seen him since.'

His speech had become crisp, almost forensic. I had the impression he'd told this story many times, most often to himself.

'You're going to see him again soon, though,' I said, trying to break the spell.

'Yes,' Chris said. 'In San Francisco. Later today.' The way he said it made it sound a thousand years away, as if he didn't dare to let himself believe it.

'Didn't you try to find them at the time?'

'I rang Kansas, of course, but Melanie and Michael had gone. Her relatives were mad people; all her family were, as far as I can tell. I dread to think what she went through as a child. All *I* knew at the time was that I was seventeen and my son had been taken away. I had no one to turn to. And if I'd known what to do I doubt if I'd have done it. I let myself glaze over. I couldn't cope.'

Chris took a breather there. His fluster was all gone, as were his Manly Mannerisms. He had become a different person to the one I had constructed in my imagination after Dilys had taken the stereo, the kitchen table and, of course, the ancestral Babygros, garments for which she'd had plans I'd not suspected at the time – plans that never made it to fruition.

'At eighteen,' Chris resumed, 'I inherited my parents' money. They had been quite well off – big house in the country, financial investments, all that stuff. The house had already been sold. Funnily enough I looked round it the other day. Did Dilys mention it? It's in a village called Haydown, very close to Little Brookham, where my mother and father are buried. It was put back on the market recently. All of us went.'

How can I describe the impact of this disclosure? It was as if someone had walked over Mr Dali's grave.

'Didn't you want to buy it?' I asked woodenly.

'Not really,' Chris said. 'There was a part of me that did. But, you know, it's the road to madness – trying to recapture a past you can hardly remember. Being there didn't trigger lots of happy memories. Just stirred up a few ghosts. And anyway, it wouldn't have been practical, would it? The kids would be too far from you.'

'Well yes,' I agreed blandly. 'Not practical at all.'

'I didn't tell them I'd lived there when I was little,' Chris went on. 'Dilys and I just said that some day we might move somewhere bigger and that it was a bit of fun to imagine living in a big, big palace far away. Really I was fantasising about babies, or having Michael to stay. I don't say too much to them about my parents. I mean, they know they're dead, but it's a closed subject really.

The idea of losing parents at their age quite upsets them. It's bound to, I suppose.'

I thought of Billy then. '*My mummy and my daddy have both died-ed.*'

I thought of Jed too. '*What about Granny and Grandad Pinnock?*'

'Anyway,' Chris resumed, 'when I got my parents' money I bought the house in Dulwich and became one of those bug-eyed computer wizards. First I worked for other people, then for myself. I was quite successful. The problem was, I didn't have a life. That's when I found the Movement.'

'The Movement?'

'The Men's Movement – especially the Brotherhood of Manly Men. They saved me, basically. Through them I made contact with my essence as a man.' He looked at me apologetically. 'I know that stuff isn't your bag.'

I felt a little guilty. Was my cynicism so apparent?

'Whatever,' he continued, 'it was through the Movement that I found Dilys. We met at a talk by Mascal Danzon.'

'Who?' I asked. Dilys had never mentioned him. Or maybe I just hadn't listened.

'Mascal Danzon, the American masculinist? Expert on male psychology? Groundbreaking work on how to bring up boys? Amazing man, Mascal. Amazing man.' Chris seemed briefly overcome. I pictured him at the feet of an Old Testament fire-breather whose every chest hair could kickbox a kangaroo. 'Anyway, we got talking and we clicked.'

'How long ago was this?' I asked. I was doing a subtraction in my head. Billy is now six.

'Oh, more than six years ago,' he said.

'That long?'

'Well, yes.' He looked a bit embarrassed. 'It wasn't sexual at first though,' he added quickly. 'For a long time it was purely spiritual. Of course, I was *attracted* to her,' he went on hastily, as if needing to apologise for not shagging my then partner at first sight. 'She's a very attractive woman, the sort of woman men are *evolved* to want to mate with . . .'

He meant long hair, hips and tits.

'. . . it's wired into our psychology. But I'm a short guy with no muscles. I couldn't see myself as part of Dilys's mating strategy.'

'She had one of those, did she?'

'It's Darwin,' said Chris. He wore a look of resignation. 'She already had a fitter specimen – you.'

'Oh, come on,' I said.

'No, seriously, Joseph. I had to ask myself, why would such a woman want to reproduce with me?'

I was glad this was a rhetorical question. It spared me the complications of a sceptical reply. When I'd first met Dilys I'd wanted to have sex with her, but not to reproduce. We'd only reproduced when we'd got less interested in screwing. And how would Chris explain my all-consuming longing for Angela, my narrow-hipped, flat-chested, short-haired wife?

'You're far too modest, Chris,' I answered simply. 'What happened next?'

'We began meeting for lunch occasionally. We talked. We discussed concepts and theories. She was interested in my ideas on men.'

'Any men in particular?' I fished.

'She said that you were marvellous with the kids. She said once that it was better if she didn't get home till late, because it caused too much disruption. Anyway, one afternoon she visited my house to borrow some books and . . . I suppose she seduced me. Which didn't take much doing. I hadn't made love to a woman for a very long time.'

His eyes welled up with sorrow. I found myself hoping Dilys had shown him a good time. He said, 'Joseph, I ought to tell you that I'm sorry. For splitting up your family, you know . . .'

'It wasn't like that,' I broke in.

'I know she came across as ruthless,' Chris rushed on, 'but she did try to be generous – over the equity in the house and the old car. You see, she knew you might struggle financially and didn't want the children to think that you were, you know, the poor relation. That's one reason why we haven't let Jed have his own bedroom yet. We know that you don't have the space to do the same. "When you're older," we keep telling him. I don't know if he believes us. With Jed it's difficult to tell.'

'He doesn't do so badly,' I said. 'He's got a kitten.'

'We'd get him a kitten too,' said Chris, 'except I've got this allergy.'

He looked crushed. I switched the subject back to his triumph with Dilys. 'She didn't take much of the furniture, either,' I said. 'Just a couple of things. Odd choices, really.'

'They were things I needed,' Chris said sadly.

'A kitchen table?'

'I didn't have one. I ate my meals off my lap.'

'A stereo?'

'There was no music in my house.'

'You sad old bachelor,' I said. 'Except you weren't.'

'No,' said Chris, 'I wasn't. Although like a lot of sad bachelors I was good at getting women pregnant by mistake.' He slapped his forehead in self-reproach.

'What happened?' I asked.

He mumbled into his beard. 'Late withdrawal . . .'

'Weren't you using contraception?' I asked.

'No,' groaned Chris. 'We figured we were safe. Her periods were irregular already. At the time, though, she put it down to a hangover from breastfeeding Billy, which hadn't stopped all that long before.'

He was right. Billy is a bosom man. He'd still fancied the odd suckle when he was well into his third year.

'I suppose we told ourselves that if there was any, ah, misjudgement, we'd be OK. Ironic, isn't it, after all we've been through since?'

I nodded sympathetically.

'Anyway,' said Chris, 'it was my fault that she left you.'

'No, it wasn't,' I said.

'Yes, it was,' insisted Chris. 'I begged her not to get rid of it, even though she'd thought she should. That's when I told her about Melanie and Michael – I'd never mentioned them before. She took pity on me, I think. She knew she wouldn't be able to pass the baby off to you as yours, and even if she had I'd have wanted desperately to be its dad. I really only left her with one option.'

'It's just as well she loved you then,' I said.

'Do you really think she did?'

'Do me a favour. She was love sickness on legs.'

'It was after the miscarriage that I realised I just *had* to look for Michael, if only to discover whether he was still alive. You see, I suddenly understood why being pregnant is called "expecting". You know: that's what it's all about. Something's going to happen, something utterly amazing. And when it doesn't happen, when your expectation is dashed, it sort of . . . leaves an empty space. I know what *I* was expecting when Dilys was pregnant. I was expecting the baby to be Michael. That's ridiculous, I know it is. But that was how it felt. I thought he was coming back – and then he wasn't.'

That was when his hands went to his face, like mine did when Jed nearly got run over, or when I thought Billy had been stolen from the sandpit. He talked through his fingers for a while.

'It took well over a year to track Melanie down. I found her some time after you and Angela got married.

It cost me a small fortune: private detectives, missing person agencies and so on. Michael was still with her. Just about.'

'Just about?'

'He's run off a few times. Got into a bit of trouble. I can't blame his mother, really. She's just . . . just not really equipped for parenting.'

'So much for the feminine essence,' I remarked.

'Of course, she was shocked to hear from me at first,' continued Chris. 'She'd made a good job of forgetting. And I expect she was scared. But she answered my letter and soon we were exchanging e-mails. I assured her that bygones were bygones and all I wanted was to get in contact with my son – to let him know I was alive and would be happy to meet him if he wanted to meet me. I told her I didn't want lawyers involved. She said that was fine in principle, but she wasn't going to tell Michael that I'd been in touch until she'd found out what sort of man I had grown into – remember, I'd only been a boy when she left me. That was when I realised what I was dealing with. Bloody hell.'

It was his first swear word. He had my full attention.

'The thing is, she'd found God. So my work, my financial position, the place I lived, they were all fine. It was my family situation that disturbed her.'

'In what way?'

'Well, it bothered her that I was living with Dilys.'

'Why?'

'Because it meant I was committing adultery.'

'Eh?'

'Because I was still married to her – to Melanie.'

'Blimey . . .'

Chris fingered his face. 'And then there was a problem about the children . . .' He shifted in his seat. I twisted round to face him.

'What sort of problem, Chris?'

'I didn't tell the truth.' It was like when he'd handed me the snapshot from his wallet. He'd offered me a clue. I guessed the rest.

'Oh Chris,' I said. 'You pillock. You told her they were yours.'

At the outset it had been a lie that told itself. Melanie had assumed on hearing of their existence that Gloria, Jed and Billy were little Pinnocks. Chris had opted not to put her right. His runaway wife was having a big enough problem dealing with the misperception that he'd had children outside wedlock. To then be informed that Dilys had, in fact, had those three children by a different man to whom she'd not been married and who she had then dumped, and with whom those children still lived half the time would have had Melanie's version of the Guy Upstairs hurling thunderbolts. Chris's hopes of meeting Michael would have been dashed, he was convinced, at the very least until Michael became an adult at eighteen.

'I couldn't wait that long,' Chris explained meekly. 'So I let Melanie go on believing that Gloria, Jed and Billy were mine. It didn't become a problem until finally

I met her again. That was last December. Estelle would have been roughly six weeks old.'

There had been weeks of anxiety beforehand. A date had previously been fixed for the day after the Manly Men convention, where Chris had delivered his Earth-Man-and-Boy talk which had, of course, been all about the agony of not knowing Michael. Melanie, though, had pulled out of the appointment. She'd given Chris no reason.

'I can't describe the misery when I got back to Dulwich. I was no nearer seeing Michael, Dilys was still not pregnant after trying for two years and Angela was about to have a baby.'

They'd tried to insulate themselves. That's why Dilys had avoided a pre-Christmas parlay at the non-romantic wine bar – she'd have been wounded by my glow of happiness. It was also why she'd requested having the children with her in the run-up to Christmas for the second successive year. The thought of them not being there to open the last windows on their advent calendar had been too much to bear. There was no escape, though, from Estelle. Gloria and Jed had kept a diplomatic silence. Billy, though, had talked of nothing else.

'The school term had nearly ended,' Chris resumed, 'when suddenly Melanie got in touch again. She asked me if I could go straight over. She is not a very stable individual, I'm afraid.'

He'd gone, though. Of course he had. And while Angela and I were at home cooing at Estelle, he'd been sitting in a tatty diner with Melanie and her pastor.

'She said she had decided to agree to a divorce, but only when she had proof that what I'd said about my family life was true. She said her church knew how to check up on these things, and please could I provide copies of the children's birth certificates and give her the name and telephone number of their school and everything.'

I gazed out of the window of the Picnic and placed myself in Chris's situation at that time: edging closer to Michael but with the help of a huge lie; having to sustain that lie to Michael's erratic mother who had the full force of fundamentalism on her side; sitting in that diner fiddling with my pecan pie and thinking, how the fuck do I get out of this?

I turned to him and said, 'So, did you wait until they'd gone before you made the call to Dilys or did you do it from the men's room while they were still there?'

'From the men's room, whispering,' he replied.

Dilys had moved quickly. She'd called the doctor and, of course, the school. In less than an hour she had become Mrs Pinnock, and our children were becoming Pinnocks too. Before visiting Brian Hartley she'd telephoned Quester's Lodge and swung a last-minute booking. The trouble with telling kids that their surnames are changing because Mummy's getting married is that you have to provide them with a wedding. There was an outhouse at the Lodge where alternative ceremonies were held. Conveniently, a goat lived on the site. A brother Manly Man from Horsham who'd read everything by Jung said he'd be happy to preside.

Chris returned to Gatwick the following morning but not before Beryl Day had called her daughter. 'She said you'd rung impersonating Noel Edmonds. Dilys was concerned and so she called you straight away. That was when she found out that you knew what she'd been doing at the school.'

He sat and chewed his nails then for a long second or two, while I mused on the virtue of forgiveness.

'You were going to fill us in about that, right?'

'Right.'

'So why didn't you?'

Now Chris was the worried hedgehog. Now I was the juggernaut, bearing down. 'You were so angry. We took cover behind our solicitor and hoped that Melanie would be satisfied about me quickly. The crazy lengths we went to. Forging birth certificates. Taking a video of the school nativity play and sending it to her. That was a weird evening; no one could take their eyes off this crazy character in a reindeer suit.'

'It was a moose,' I muttered under my breath.

'Anyway,' Chris went on, 'we hoped everything would be sorted out before New Year. I was confident that once I was in direct contact with Michael we could start dropping the pretence about the kids. I knew he'd been asking Melanie about me for years. I *knew* once we were communicating we'd never stop again. The problem was Melanie, of course. Every week she'd change her mind or demand something different. The whole crazy saga just dragged on and on . . .'

The divorce wasn't completed until the summer. After that, Chris and Dilys beat the door of the register office down. Once they'd faxed their marriage certificate across to Melanie she at last gave the big news to Michael. He'd sent Chris his first e-mail message around the time of Gloria's poolside episode in deepest Devon. Chris glowed at the recollection. 'It began, "Hi Dad, been a long time".'

I suppose that was the moment when I stepped away from rage: sitting there in the red Picnic next to a fellow father who had felt the pain of loss and separation a hundred times more acutely than me. Chris filled in the last few details: how two people had been aware of both sides of the story all along – 'Jill knew everything in minute detail. Carlo too. It's been a tricky time for them'; how Melanie had never actually rung the doctor's surgery or the children's school – 'They wouldn't have told her anything anyway, I suppose'.

I listened, then I asked him, 'Looking back, Chris, how rational and reasonable has your behaviour been?'

'Not very,' he replied. 'But frightened people get backed into corners, don't they? Especially when children are involved. Like I said just now, I don't think you're a nutter. But tell me, Joseph Stone, how rational and reasonable is it that you're sitting here now?'

*   *   *

It was after seven o'clock. Loved ones would be waking soon.

'Presumably,' I said, 'you're going to tell Dilys about this.'

'I think I'm going to have to. It's a big secret to keep.'

'What about the kids?'

'They don't need to know.'

That was a relief. I had another small concern about them, though.

'What if Dilys flies out to join you? You said she might or she might not. You said "It depends".'

'Oh, for the seeding ritual,' Chris said.

'The *what*?'

'If she comes out in the next few days, it won't be to see Michael, I don't think.'

I could tell he was holding back. I could also tell that he was dying to explain.

'Be real with me, Chris,' I said.

'Some of the brothers, well . . . It's very common these days for guys to have problems producing children.'

'But I thought Dilys was the problem.'

'That's what she told you. But it isn't only her.'

It was the stress, he explained, that was the problem. All the worry over Michael, all his concern for Dilys, all his concern about being a stepdad too. It could sap a fellow's ardour, he explained. It could reduce output and quality as well.

'One teaspoon of my semen contains only 100 million sperm. And seventy per cent of those have got two heads.'

'I'm really glad you shared that with me, Chris.'

'Well, I've enlisted the help of some of the senior brothers: a chap called Cash, another called River, a fellow called Shaman Phoenix from Wyoming, maybe one or two more.'

'Interesting names,' I said. I kept my prior knowledge of the website to myself.

'Their fertility,' said Chris, 'is very high . . .'

'So?'

'So on the day of the planting, we gather at River's cabin and decant the seed together.'

'You decant *together*?' And I'd thought Kenny was joking. I was surprised by a faint stirring in my groin.

'There's a fertility bowl,' Chris said. 'Native American. Very old. But completely sterile, of course.'

'And easier to target than a test tube, I suppose.'

'Much easier,' confirmed Chris, 'which is enormously important. It will be pretty dark in there.'

'I'll bet it will,' I said.

Symbolically, the milk float was returning. I heard its sewing-machine engine and made out its puny sidelights through the thinning miasma of the dawn. A feeble sun was coming up. 'So,' I said to Chris, 'what will Dilys be doing while you gentlemen . . . unload?'

'She'll be waiting in the next room. I'll join her with the bowl, we'll blend the seed together and then sow it.'

'All of it?'

'As much of it as we can.'

'So,' I said, 'if it works you'll never know for certain who the father is. Unless, of course, it has your hair. You'll know for certain then.'

'Maybe not even then. Old Cash is pretty curly under his hat.'

'Will it matter that you won't know?'

'I can't predict that, Joseph. But at least I'll know that I was part of the process. It won't have been cold and anonymous like a sperm bank. I will have made a spiritual investment. I will have been *involved*.'

'There's no argument with that,' I said. 'No argument at all.' I'd meant to be reassuring. Chris, though, seemed perturbed.

'You won't, er, *tell* anyone about the seeding ritual, will you?'

'Of course I won't,' I lied.

'You see, it really is our last resort. And I'll be honest with you, Joseph,' he confided. 'I think it's a bit weird.'

It was time for us to go. Chris had a family to say goodbye to and then a plane to catch. I looked across at him again. His chin was on his chest. His eyes were fixed on an empty space six inches in front of the dashboard.

'Are you frightened?' I asked him.

'Terrified,' he said.

I had some tissues in my pocket – proper dads always do. I passed him a handful and he blew his nose. 'Chris,' I asked him gently, 'have you got a mobile on you? I think I should call home.'

chapter 32

Did I hear the doorbell? I was miles away.

'I'll go, Dad!'

I close my eyes as Gloria runs down from her room and heads for the long stairs. Let her think I've nodded off – that way she might leave me alone. A chemical smell trails behind her. What has she been messing with up there?

'Remember!' I yell weakly in her wake. 'The kitchen is out of bounds!' So much for relaxation.

Gloria's almost at the door now. If it's who we both think it is I'd better get this story up to speed.

The call came at five this morning.

'Hi, Joseph! We have an egg!'

'Pardon?'

'We have an egg! We have an egg! Dilys has an egg!'

'Hello Chris,' I said. 'I'm already getting dressed.'

Before I left him at Quester's Lodge Chris and I had made an agreement: he would tell Dilys about our unscheduled pow-wow in the Picnic and then he would suggest that if she ovulated later in the weekend she should let me take the children off her hands. Now it was action stations.

'There's one seat on a flight at seven thirty-five,' Chris said, his excitement carrying clear across the pond.

'Tell her I'll meet her at the airport,' I replied. 'I'll phone her on the way down. How is Michael, by the way?'

'Michael is amazing.'

I hung up, threw on some clothes and was about to leave the bedroom when Angela spoke from under the duvet. 'Don't forget your mobile this time, Brains.'

I climbed into the Picnic and sailed off through South London in the half-light of the dawn. I called Dilys who told me that she and the kids had left the Lodge and were halfway to the airport already. Then Chris checked in.

'What has Dilys told the children?' I asked. 'What's her excuse for rushing off like this?'

'She's told them that she's going to see Michael. She's told them all about him! You see, it's all going so well! In time I'll be able to tell him the truth about the children. He'll understand why I had to lie.'

'But what about Melanie?'

'Michael says she needs a lot of taking care of. I'm going to see how I can help. We'll deal with the problem of the truth about the Stone kids come the time.'

'You've got a busy schedule,' I shouted through the static. 'What happens when Dilys arrives?'

'I'll collect her at the airport. We can be at River's cabin in an hour. Then we can proceed with the decanting.'

'Good luck with that, brother,' I said. 'And while you're doing it, try not to laugh.'

I made it to Gatwick by six forty. I pulled into the drop-off zone and sprinted for the departure lounge entrance. Dilys and the children were standing by the queuing channel looking anxiously around.

'Daddy!' Billy said, spotting me first.

'That's me, Billy,' I said, panting. I accepted his embrace, then realised Gloria and Jed were hesitating. They weren't sure of the protocol. More than three years had passed since the five of us had last been all together. 'Children,' I said, looking at their mother's fretful face. 'Would you stay here for one minute? I need a quick word with your mum before she goes.'

'But Joe,' Dilys said, 'I've got to go now!'

I tugged her over to the Sock Shop, though hosiery was not much on my mind. I produced a cardboard envelope from inside my coat, the same size as the one Chris had passed to me in the car. 'This is for you,' I said to Dilys. 'It's the original. I've made a copy. I'll get the rest sorted out soon.'

She pulled out the photograph. It showed a family of five and a 1950s-style three-piece suite. 'I remember this one,' Dilys said. 'Your dad took it, didn't he?'

'He did.'

'The children look so *young*! You haven't changed at

all. I have, though. I'm older.' Strain showed in her face as she absorbed the image of the woman leaning against the back of the settee.

'You're still beautiful,' I said. 'And Chris agrees with me.'

She returned the photo to its envelope and slipped it into her bag. 'Thank you for that,' she said. She paused then added, 'You think you know everything now, don't you?'

'Not everything,' I replied. 'For instance, I don't know if Jed still recognises that "Joseph" is a name that starts with *juh*.'

'He does,' Dilys replied. 'He's pointed it out to Chris many times. Anything else you need to know?'

I hesitated briefly. Things were going so well. But I'd been so long wondering . . .

'Please don't be offended. But Billy is *my* boy, isn't he, Dilys?'

Her laugh was genuine, amazed. 'Who else's could he be? You're both so maddening. Any more questions?'

'No.'

'OK. Chris has one for you.'

'Chris does?'

'He wants to know if there's much of that ten grand left over now that you've bought the Picnic.' She said it with one eye on the departures info monitor.

'Pardon?' I replied.

'The ten grand you got for the portrait of Gloria that

368

was in Bradley's restaurant.' She looked quickly at her watch and beckoned Gloria over.

I said, 'What does Chris know about that?'

'He bought it,' she said. 'Well, one of his business friends bought it using his money.'

'*What?*'

'Of course, we can't hang the thing up because Gloria will see it,' continued Dilys indulgently. 'The reason I knew Bradley had it was because she kept on grumbling about it – how uncool she looked in it, how glad she was you'd given it away. Anyway, Chris's friend thought it was great. I think she might be putting a bit of work your way. Don't be afraid to overcharge. Big houses near Crystal Palace Park don't come cheap.'

I stood there, goldfish-mouthed.

'Shh!' hissed Dilys unnecessarily. 'Here she comes.'

Gloria stood expectantly between her mother and me.

'You know those things I gave to you this morning?' Dilys said.

'You mean the you-know-whats that you've been keeping in your purse?'

'That's right. Show them to your dad.'

Gloria was carrying a carpet-style shoulder bag, not unlike the one Angela owns. She pulled out a *J-17* diary and from between its pages produced three squares of shiny paper, each containing a grainy grey photographic image.

'Remember these?' Dilys smiled. Ultrasound scan printouts: the embryonic Gloria, Jed and Billy.

'You're not allowed to keep them for ever, by the way,' Dilys said sharply.

We walked back over to the boys. Dilys kissed each of the children and took her passport and her boarding card in hand.

'I know it's going to work this time,' I whispered.

She walked towards the barrier, almost smiling. I turned to the expectant children. 'Come on, you lot,' I said. 'I've got to get you all to school.'

What a day it's been. What a three years. Still, I shouldn't grumble. I really am a very lucky man.

'Is everything ready up there?' It's Angela's voice coming up from the foot of the long stairs.

'Of course everything's ready. I'm not one of those Hapless Chaps you hear so much about these days. I know how to make a birthday tea. Did you get the cake?'

'Yes, we got the cake. We got the cat from the vet as well.'

'Stone me!' I say to Gloria. 'What have you been doing with your hair?'

It is bleached blonde with green streaks – that explains the smell. She looks like the maddest tart in Trollop City. Her mother will go spare.

'It looks great, doesn't it, Joe?' calls Angela doubtfully. She's at the bottom of the stairs, her hands shadowing the progress of Estelle's padded rump as she ascends on all fours, panting happily.

'Absolutely fabulous,' I say untruthfully.

'Thanks, Dad.' Gloria puts her arms around my waist and reaches up to kiss me on the cheek. 'Mmmm!' she tells me fondly. 'You're such a *lovely* dad.'

Billy reaches the long stairs summit next. 'Daddy?'

'Yes, Billy?'

'Do you know what?'

'What?'

'Nothing! Heeheeheeheeheeheehee.'

'How's Tiger?' I ask Jed.

'She's fine,' Jed says. He lugs the carrying basket up one stair at a time.

'Here, Jed, let me help.' I jump down a few stairs and relieve him of the weight. I peep in anxiously at Tiger 2. 'So, Jed,' I say casually, 'do you think she'll be the same cat as she was before?'

'I expect so.' Jed is smiling. 'The vet says she'll be a bit drowsy for a day or two, like after you took her for her injections. He said that after she recovers she'll be exactly the same except maybe a bit calmer.'

'Hmm,' I muse under my breath. 'Sounds like the sort of op I need.'

'He was a nice vet, but forgetful,' Angela adds slyly from down below. 'He kept calling her "he". I don't know why.'

As if I hadn't explained it enough times on the phone. 'I know *you* can tell the difference! You're a vet! But *they* can't, you see. Cat genitals are not their field of expertise.'

Banned from the kitchen until it's time to eat, the

children disperse to their rooms, leaving Estelle, Angela and me on the settee.

'So, husband,' Angela says, 'have you recovered from your emotional exertions?'

'Not really, darling, no. I have no power of resistance. I'm yours to toy with, basically.'

Angela ignores this. Or pretends to. Instead she says, 'I'm so glad you've made friends with Chris. Maybe we can all be friends from now on. It would make things so much easier for the children.'

I agree with her. I mean, I don't think Chris and I will ever quite be kindred spirits, but I understand him so much better now. I'm certain that he's a good and generous fellow. I can even comprehend why he is so attracted to the Brotherhood of Manly Men. All that emoting and empathising. All that cuddling and confessing. They're like a great big bunch of girls.

'You should try it some time,' Angela teases. 'These men's issues are important. Why are you so flippant about them?'

'Men have to be flippant about men's issues,' I explain. 'No one takes you seriously otherwise.'

Tea-time approaches. I hope that jelly's set. Angela says, 'I wonder what Dilys is doing now?'

'She's got her feet up, I expect.'

'That isn't very funny.'

'It's a *bit* funny,' I say.

'And Chris?' Angela asks.

'Hanging out with Michael, probably.'

'And what about us?'

'We're going to light one birthday candle with Gloria, Jed and Billy and watch Estelle try to blow it out.'

'And what shall we do later?'

'Get cosy under Klimt.'

'You tear, I'll unroll?' she asks.

'Or maybe not,' I say, tugging her towards me. 'Why wait a minute more?'

You can buy any of these other **Review** titles from your bookshop or *direct from the publisher*.

FREE P&P AND UK DELIVERY
(Overseas and Ireland £3.50 per book)

Kissing in Manhattan	David Schickler	£6.99
Hallam Foe	Peter Jinks	£6.99
Itchycooblue	Des Dillon	£6.99
The Big Q	Des Dillon	£6.99
White Meat and Traffic Lights	Georgina Wroe	£6.99
America the Beautiful	Moon Unit Zappa	£6.99
In Cuba I was a German Shepherd	Ana Menéndez	£6.99
Mischief	Mark Bastable	£6.99
The Alchemist's Apprentice	Jeremy Dronfield	£6.99
Scar Vegas	Tom Paine	£6.99

TO ORDER SIMPLY CALL THIS NUMBER

01235 400 414

or visit our website: www.madaboutbooks.com

Prices and availability subject to change without notice.